# THE SINS OF THE CHILDREN

*An Alison Glasby Mystery*

## James Brownley

This first world edition published 2008
in Great Britain and the USA by
SEVERN HOUSE PUBLISHERS LTD of
9–15 High Street, Sutton, Surrey, England, SM1 1DF.

British Library Cataloguing in Publication Data

Brownley, James
    The sins of the children
    1. Women journalists - Great Britain - Fiction 2. Police
    corruption - Great Britain - Fiction 3. Detective and
    mystery stories
    I. Title
    823.9'2[F]


    ISBN-13: 978-0-7278-6664-6   (cased)
    ISBN-13: 978-1-84751-079-2   (trade paperback)

*All Severn House titles are printed on acid-free paper.*

Typeset by Palimpsest Book Production Ltd.,
Grangemouth, Stirlingshire, Scotland.
Printed and bound in Great Britain by
MPG Books Ltd., Bodmin, Cornwall.

# THE SINS OF THE CHILDREN

*The Alison Glasby Mystery Series by James Brownley
from Severn House*

PICTURE OF GUILT
THE SINS OF THE CHILDREN

# Acknowledgments

One of the greatest pleasures of writing is receiving feedback, criticism and suggestions from friends and others. I have again been blessed with the intelligence, care and thoughtfulness of those who volunteered themselves as reviewers on my and Ms Glasby's behalf.

It is a privilege for me to be able to use this opportunity to thank them all. I have named several below, and also would like to offer my sincere apologies to anyone whom I have accidentally omitted. Their input has shaped and improved my work, but any errors of fact, language or judgment are mine alone.

My gratitude and appreciation to James Attree, Gun Brodie, Michael Brodie, Mark Gethings, Stuart Hocking, Pat Nield, Phill Nield, Carol Price, Roger Rushton and Adel Uezbai.

As before I have benefited more than I deserve from the patience, wisdom and support of my agent Julian Friedmann, and my publishers Megan Roberts, whose care with my manuscript again put me to shame, and Edwin Buckhalter at Severn House.

I also want to acknowledge, on Michael Fisher's behalf, the quotations from John Donne at the start of Chapter Four and from the excellent 'Alison', which was written and performed by Elvis Costello, at the start of Chapter Eleven. The text at the start of Chapter Seven that Fisher received as spam was indeed just that; I'm afraid I have no way of knowing who originally created it.

If anyone would like the answer to the crossword clue before Chapter Nine, or indeed has any other comments or questions, an email addressed to long.hammer@hotmail.co.uk should reach me.

Finally, I would like to dedicate this book to my wonderful wife Neylya. She helped Mia with her recipe for Plov, Redgrave with his Russian conversation, and me with absolutely everything.

# One

## Ben Rosimore, Scottish Highlands, 1974

What had started off as a well-organized line of boys had long since spread out up the hillside. David Gold was one of the last, only Folkes and Russell, the two fatties, behind him. Dark hair was stuck down on his forehead with sweat and one knee was red from where he had slipped almost before they'd got going. He was beginning to feel sick, the sound of his own pulse hammering in his ears.

The track took a sharp left and mercifully flattened out, boulders giving way to a soft springiness which he thought must be peat. They had reached a plateau covered with heather and ferns. Gold tried to ignore the sight of an even steeper looking path up above him. He looked around instead.

There was a small lake ahead, on the far side of which the games teacher, Thicko Dickson, was sitting. A cluster of boys was gathered around him but they were too far away for Gold to see who they were. He wandered up to the edge of the lake, flexing his sore knee experimentally. It didn't hurt too much but it made him remember how everyone had laughed when he fell over. His shoulders were sore from the leather straps of the rucksack. It felt good when he took it off and put it down.

The pool was clear enough for the boy to see to the bottom. Reflected in it, clouds chased each other, sprinting across the sky. Some small brown fish came to the surface every now and again to swallow insects. Looking at the water reminded him that he was thirsty, but he knew that there wasn't much left in the metal bottle that hung from his belt, slapping against his jeans when he walked.

He wasn't sure if it was safe to drink from the pool but he thought that it must be OK to splash some water on his face. Gold bent down and as he did a glint from the edge of the pool caught his eye. He looked more closely. It was an old half-crown piece. They went out with decimalization, so it must have been there at least a couple of years. Unless someone had thrown it in more recently, for luck. Or maybe it had been there a lot longer, fifty years or a hundred, unseen by anyone until he came along.

Bending over further he tried to see the date on the coin. It would have been easy to reach down and pick it up without getting his feet wet, but he didn't want to. Breaking the water's surface would have spoilt the clouds which seemed more real the further he leant over them. He started singing to himself: '*Smoke on the water, fire in the sky . . .*'

A hand gripped his neck. 'Hooknose!' a voice bellowed in his ear. 'Hey, Yiddo!'

Gold's body tensed up; it was Gary Dickson, known to his fellow schoolboys as 'Sicko', Gold's tormentor in chief. Sicko, son of the games master, Thicko Dickson, with the same thick blond hair and square jaw as his father and the same bullying manner, too. Like all the other boys, Sicko had gone through a phase of building kits based on World War Two hardware. But he had moved from Spitfires and Hurricanes to making models of German half-tracks and dive-bombers, and then into collecting what he said was authentic Nazi regalia. Lately he had taken to wearing an SS swastika badge pinned to the underside of the lapel of his school blazer. He liked flashing it at the other boys, especially Gold.

'Hey, look, Jewboy's found some money! He's sniffed it out!' This was greeted by the usual laughter; some of the other boys must have arrived with Dickson. Gold was held bent almost double. His black-framed NHS glasses were starting to slip from behind his ears. He squirmed around trying to free himself but the hold on his neck was much too strong.

'Get off me, Sicko,' he squeaked, his face red from shame.

'Sicko?' Dickson roared backed at him. 'Who're you calling Sicko?' He kneed the smaller boy hard in the back of his thigh. Gold staggered forward, one plimsoll and the bottom of his jeans now in the clear cold water. 'It's Mr Dickson to you, Yiddo.'

'You're not Mr Dickson,' said Henry Dunne, one of the knot of boys behind him. 'Unless you're one of the masters now?' The others laughed again.

'Who asked you, Dung-ball Dunne?' said Dickson. He kept his grip up on the back of Gold's neck.

'I told you before not to call him Dung-ball,' said another voice. 'Dunne's name is Seddon. You've had your fun with Gold, *Sicko*, and now you can get off him.' Two hands closed over Dickson's shoulders. It was Richard Bedingfield, the only boy in the form who was as tall as Dickson and more or less as strong.

'What's it got to do with you, Bedbug?' asked Dickson, gruffly. 'Looking after one of your little bugger chums? Seddon will be all upset with you.' But this time the group of boys that had gathered to watch the fun stayed quiet, waiting to see what Bedingfield's next move would be.

'Sicko, we're half the way up a mountain.' The red-haired Bedingfield sounded calm but his hold on the other boy grew tighter. 'Your father' – at this, Dickson's shoulders tensed and he glared round – 'your dad told us to behave like adults. He said it's dangerous up here, didn't he?'

Dickson let the smaller boy loose with ill grace; then, changing his mind at the last moment, gave him a shove firm enough to push him into the water. Staggering, Gold momentarily went down on one knee as if genuflecting to Dickson's power. Bedingfield and the other boys stood and watched as he recovered his balance. Saying nothing, Gold trudged on miserably, keeping his eyes low.

Not until he was well past the sniggering group did he look up. Sitting a few metres away, perched on a large tussock, was a thin boy, with a beaky face and protruding eyes. He had an amused smile on his face but it wasn't clear whether this was directed at Gold or the others. Gold, at any rate, felt as hostile to him as to the rest of the world. 'Effing Fisher,' he muttered to himself disconsolately as he limped past, both feet soaking and his jeans sticking to his legs. The breeze was stronger now. He was starting to feel cold.

On the salary that Burstone School could afford, with more or less a full six-day week and evening duties as well, you couldn't really expect to get a much better games master than Alan Dickson.

Dickson was an ex-paratrooper with the physique and voice to match, so keeping the boys in order wasn't a problem.

He was short tempered, except with his favourites, and often surly even with his fellow masters, who avoided him whenever they could.

There was something less than pleasing about his looks, as Richard James, who had appointed him, remarked at the time to his wife. 'It's hard to say exactly what, except . . . his features don't quite match. The eyes are a little too small for the forehead; the nose is too broad for the cheekbones either side of it; and the mouth, well his lips aren't quite *right*, somehow.'

Burstone had never had much in the way of sporting success but for the first couple of years after Alan Dickson's arrival results had looked up a little, especially on the rugby field. More recently things had been worse than ever, though; the first XV had just completed a term with a one hundred per cent losing record. It wasn't the sort of thing that would help the governors' efforts to raise funds from parents for a badly needed new gym, and Mr James had been asked to make Dickson aware of this.

Of course if there was ever a need to replace him (or to ask him to look for another position, as James put it) there would then be the question of the scholarship place which had been awarded to Dickson's son, Gary. The rules on master's scholarships weren't entirely clear. No master had ever been asked to leave the school before, so long as anyone could remember.

So James had mentioned the issue – 'just in case, as it were, old chap.'

'Evil little dwarf,' Dickson had muttered in James's direction, as the man left the boys' changing room where he had sought Dickson out – which, by coincidence or not, was how the boys generally referred to the elderly headmaster. He had stamped out after James as if he was going to say more but stopped in the doorway, gazing moodily at the muddy playing field and the swimming pool with its broken tiles and rusting steps.

Not long after that conversation James had asked to see him again, this time in the headmaster's study. The interview granted to Dickson was brief but the message was clear enough: the governors would be very appreciative if Dickson would give up some days of his Easter holiday to take the fourth-form field trip up to Scotland. Alan Dickson's nick-name might have been Thicko, but he understood perfectly well what the governors' feelings towards him would be if he had chosen not to agree to this request. Which didn't come with any extra salary or time off in lieu, of course.

If it had been any less politely put you would have called it blackmail.

The day had started under a bright Highlands sky, a gentle breeze tugging at the heather and nothing more than the sound of a few sheep to compete with the excited chatter of the thirteen- and fourteen-year-old boys. Instead of enjoying all of this, Alan Dickson's thoughts had been on the unfairness of his own predicament. How the hell was he supposed to get a decent performance out of his first team, when he had to spend most of his time messing about with useless turds like . . .

Even Dickson realized that the problem was more than just Gold. But if you had to sum up everything that was wrong with his current situation, all you had to do was think of that smart-arsed little runt. Boys like him were a waste of space on the games field, worse than useless in the gym and yet somehow he was expected to turn them into young sportsmen. And now he was on a warning of losing his job and if he did, a fine lad like Gary might find himself kicked out of the school. You could just bet that it would be Gold's parents latching on to a reason not to cough up for the appeal. Everyone knew what their sort was like, when it came to parting them from their money.

So it was not surprising that Thicko Dickson's mood had been blacker than usual that morning, and those of the boys who were usually inclined to a bit of silliness were keeping things under control. He was not slow to lash out when he felt like it, and no one wanted to be on the end of one of Thicko's backhanders.

That was first thing, when the climb up Ben Rosimore had been going smoothly. Now Alan Dickson had more urgent things to worry about. After the breather he had allowed the boys, the path became much rockier and narrower. As the first of them negotiated a sharp turn near a frighteningly long drop, the sky lit up for ten seconds or so, as bright as a flashbulb. Then, just as quickly it turned a deep grey, as if someone had taken the battery out, and a heavy rain started.

They were all rapidly drenched through. Any of the boys who were without proper walking boots began to find the going more and more difficult. The wind picked up, at first in gusts and then steadily, blowing hard enough to drive the rain into their faces.

Visibility dropped just as suddenly. Dickson, who was somewhere in the middle of the line, could no longer see beyond the five or six boys closest to him. He shouted 'Boys! Here!' but the wind whisked his words away almost as soon as they had left his mouth. Almost at the same time he heard a shriek from someone whose voice had not quite finished breaking, somewhere below them.

Edgell, one of his hockey eleven, was hurled by an even stronger burst of wind straight into Dickson's midriff. The games teacher grabbed a handful of wiry hair and hauled the boy to his feet. 'Be more bloody careful, moron!' he bellowed, his face not more than a foot from Edgell's ear. 'It was the wind, sir,' the indignant boy replied. 'I just lifted one foot up and . . .' At that moment another gust nearly took them both over.

A sudden shaft of sunlight appeared, just long enough for two or three boys to be visible up ahead of them. 'Gary,' shouted Thicko Dickson to his son, who looked round in surprise: the teacher was usually scrupulous in addressing him only by his surname while they were in school. He sounded rattled. 'Go on up ahead. Gather up everyone up there, and tell them just to hold still, until we catch up with them. You two' – gesturing with his head at Bedingfield and Dunne – 'come back down with me. You others, keep going, until you catch up with Dickson again, then wait up there until I find you all. And be careful, understand?'

As the rest of the boys disappeared up the path, the games master peered back down the hillside. He could see several indistinct shapes, but with the cloud cover constantly lifting and lowering again, it was impossible to tell one from the other, or even to be sure how many boys were left down behind them.

'Come on, then,' Mr Dickson said to Bedingfield and the smaller but almost equally sturdy Dunne, and the three of them started picking their way over rocks which were now shiny, bright coloured and very slippery.

\*     \*     \*

They were just off the path in a slight hollow where the ground above them gave a little shelter from the wind. The rain had dropped in intensity, although visibility was no better than before. Mr Dickson and Bedingfield stood over a seated form, slumped against a rucksack.

'But I can't, sir.'

The boy had started off whining but now sounded straight-forwardly desperate, his voice cracking as if he was about to cry. Thick black hair was plastered on to his forehead, from where drops of rain were falling down to his nose and chin.

'My bag's soaked through so it's too heavy now, and I keep slipping and falling over, and I might have twisted my ankle. I don't think we should even have come up here.'

'What d'you mean, "can't"?' Without realizing it, the teacher found himself imitating the trembling voice of the exhausted Gold.

'Sir . . .' Bedingfield interjected; but Thicko ignored him, instead keeping his glare fixed on Gold, who looked up at him pleadingly.

Bedingfield tried again. 'Sir, I can take Gold's bag, mine doesn't weigh that much, and then I'll go on up with him slowly, until we find Dickson and you and the others.'

Mr Dickson's gaze didn't budge. '*You little parasite!*' he screamed, suddenly. '*Get up, now!*' He reached down and dragged the boy up by his ear. 'You're all like that, all you lot. Whining and wheedling, waiting for someone else to do the honest work for you.'

Gold's eyes were open wide behind his rain-smeared glasses. 'I'm not a parasite! I'm not wheedling, that's not fair! I just keep slipping over and you blame me. You're an . . .' He swallowed, thinking better of it.

'*I'm a what, you little Yid bastard? What am I? Come on!*' Dickson's features were contorted, his face bright red but no redder than the quivering boy standing in front of him.

'You're an anti-Semite. That's what my dad says you are. An ignorant anti-Semite.'

'You dirty little toerag, I'll give you "ignorant"!' Dickson reached down to grab Gold by the neck, but somehow the boy squirmed free, nearly losing his balance in the process. He threw his arms up, to protect himself or possibly just to keep from falling. The back of his right hand connected with the teacher's face, one of his fingernails catching in the man's cheek an inch or so from his mouth.

'You just scratched me, you dirty little bastard!' Dickson smacked the boy with the back of his hand, hard across his forehead, and then again. A trickle of blood that had been spreading across the teacher's cheek reached the corner of his mouth. He wiped his face and saw the red stain on the back of his hand, his face furious, fist now clenched ready to strike the boy again.

'Sir!' Bedingfield held the master's arm in both of his hands, and for a second none of the three moved. Then, at the same time, Gold moved unsteadily back a step, Dickson relaxed his fist and Bedingfield dropped his hands. At that moment Dunne came running up.

'What's happening, sir?' he asked, a grin on his face. 'Was there a fight?'

Thicko Dickson had seemed almost in a dream but now he whirled around again. 'You stay out of it, you grinning little oaf.'

'I'm not grinning, sir!' Dunne protested. 'I only said—'

The games master, who was definitely starting to get angry again, turned on him. 'I told you once already – *stay – out – of – it!*' He walked towards Dunne who took a step back, down through a clump of bog grass, as Dickson extended his hand towards him. Although he had intended to connect with the boy's chest, the heel of his palm caught the end of Dunne's nose, which promptly started to bleed as he swayed forward against the teacher. For a moment they stood chest to chest, like two boxers in a clinch.

Bedingfield caught Dickson's arm again but the sight of blood on Dunne's face seemed to have calmed the man down at last. 'Go over to that pool and wash it off until the bleeding stops,' he told Dunne. 'Then come back up the path carefully. OK?'

Without replying, the stocky, fair-haired Dunne stomped off through the heather in the direction of a small pond, thirty metres or so away. Mr Dickson looked around to see Gold passing his sodden rucksack to Bedingfield. '*No!*' he roared, apparently enraged again by the sight. 'I told you to carry the bloody thing yourself.'

'But Bedingfield said he'd do it! You're mad!' shouted Gold, his normal (and hard-learned) circumspection in the face of physical danger almost literally blown away.

'What did you say?'

The master advanced on him again, knocking him nearly to his knees with one blow to his shoulder. Gold scrambled to his feet as Dickson stood over him, the boy's hands flying wildly up at the man's face. Bedingfield started towards them again but he was encumbered by two bags and was slow to move. Dickson shoved Gold again and kicked at the same time. Gold fell heavily on to his right side and kept going, the momentum of the blow taking him over a large rock and down towards a scree-covered slope.

His arms flailing in panic, Gold somehow managed to grab the front of the master's shirt as Dickson leant down. Bedingfield couldn't tell if the teacher intended to rescue Gold or attack him again. He too flung himself on Dickson, taking all three of them closer to the edge of what they could now see was a very deep gully. Stones dislodged by their struggles flew past Gold's face. Dunne had looked up and started to run back towards them.

Up above, no more than twenty metres away but unobserved by them all, stood another boy, a lopsided smile on his face. All they've got to do, Michael Fisher thought, is to stop pratting around, and they'll all be fine. The clouds had dropped again so that at times even at that distance it was hard for him to see which limb was whose.

One thing was clear to all of them: the body which slid over the cliff, arcing in mid-air before it began to bounce off the rock face on its long descent, was too big to belong to anyone but Mr Dickson.

# Glasby

*Derived from Gillespie, a surname common in Ireland and Scotland. Anglicisation.*

*Cf. Dizzy Gillespie, American jazz musician, Jason Gillespie, Australian cricketer, Gary Gillespie, Scottish footballer.*

*Derived from Irish and Scottish Gaelic, meaning 'Bishop's servant'.*

*'A garden, lately in the holding of William Glasby' – from the book of the Abbot of Combermere, 1469.*

*From the notebook of Michael Fisher*

# Two

**London, June 200—**

She woke at five thirty, sun streaming in through the gap at the top of the curtains. Outside, some birds were enthusiastically competing with the early traffic for top spot in the noise pollution stakes. Alison Glasby had always been a light sleeper, and there were mornings when she would lie in bed listening to the city's early sounds and marvelling that she was in the middle of it all, feeling excited to be young and alive in twenty-first-century London. Today wasn't one of them.

The headache which she'd taken to bed with her seemed to have acquired residence somewhere deep inside her forehead, and her jaw was aching which meant that she had been grinding her teeth in the night.

It was a little over six weeks since Glasby had split up with her boyfriend, John Redgrave. One of the good things – one of the many good things, she told herself – about being single again was that there was no one to complain about this, or any other unappealing habit which she might have.

Glasby and Redgrave had been introduced by friends. He was a detective sergeant in Scotland Yard's murder squad, she a journalist with a strong interest in crime.

Redgrave had made his attraction to her known right from the start; she, as was her nature, was more cautious, but there was no doubt that they were a well-matched couple. Glasby was rather taller than medium height and lean, with an intelligent, watchful face. She had the determined, almost driven, look of someone who still felt – and quite probably would always feel – that she had plenty to prove. Although in many ways similar physically, Redgrave was more self-confident and more relaxed. Neither of them paid much attention to fashion or any other type of display, barring a weakness of Redgrave's for rather flashy cars.

A perceptive observer might have seen from the start that the overlap in their professional pre-occupations would do as much to pull them apart as it had to bring them together in the first place.

In her first year on the *Sunday Herald*, when her long struggle to make it as a crime reporter had not even begun and she was still buried without trace on soft features, Glasby had done an article on self-hypnosis. Since this required emptying your brain of all thoughts, she was about as unlikely a candidate for it as you could get. The first stage involved lying with muscles relaxed and allowing only calm feelings, and she gave this a try now in the hope that it would persuade the headache to go away somewhere else. After a few minutes of occasional calmness, punctuated frequently by self-doubt, anxiety, bad temper and indignation, she gave up and went to the kitchen in search of caffeine instead.

There wasn't much of a mystery to the cause of her pain. Even by her usual standards, life was tough for Glasby at the moment.

It was expected and even acceptable for an investigative journalist to get the odd complaint. These days, this as likely as not involved the Press Complaints Commission, which meant an official enquiry and might end with the newspaper having to publish an apology. But the problem that she now had was a fair bit worse than that.

When the Metropolitan Police had launched Operation Longhammer to root out corruption in their own ranks, they couldn't have foreseen that the investigation would still be going on, more than a year later. Or, probably, that Henry Dunne and the tight little team known as the Godsquad that he had gathered around him would have been quite as energetic and effective. The first batch of rotten apples had quickly been found, but instead of quietly consigning them to the compost heap of early retirement on health grounds, Dunne was persistent and thorough enough to get convictions against two police constables and an inspector.

A wave of voluntary departures from the Met had followed but obviously that hadn't been enough for Dunne and the Godsquad. Twelve people were now serving prison terms as a direct result of Longhammer, ten of them former police officers.

Press access to the investigation team had been nailed down tight, right from the off. No one was allowed to talk on the record, but Glasby had a source well enough placed to know who the Godsquad were looking at next. When things were going well this had worked perfectly.

The drawback was that Glasby's source had remained hidden behind an anonymous email account. She had been doing her best to corroborate everything, but that wasn't easy. In truth, at times there hadn't been much more to rely on than her own instincts.

A more experienced journalist than Glasby would probably never have taken the risk of using information supplied in this way, and a more competent editorial team than the *Herald* could currently muster would certainly have vetoed it anyway. Instead, she had got herself into a situation where whoever it was that had taken the trouble to register long.hammer as a hotmail address could cut himself off from Glasby any time that he wanted. Unfortunately for her, he had now done just that.

Having sent her a whole string of inside track information, stuff that she had turned into really good pieces which had been proved right every time, he'd given Glasby two more names. His last tip-off concerned two police constables named Salmon and Shipp. Predictably they were in Central Vice, which had already lost two inspectors, a sergeant and several PCs in the first wave of Longhammer.

What she had been told was that this pair had gone a bit further than the usual shake downs of street girls and massage parlours and were actually running girls themselves, hooked up with a pimp known as 'the Albanian'.

She had written up the story and as before had got it past her editor, Mark Ellington. He didn't seem to have noticed the complete lack of any corroboration this time and presumably he hadn't made that clear to the *Herald*'s lawyer either. Be that as it may, they had agreed that she could name the two coppers as the latest suspects.

But when the trouble started her source simply disappeared. The email address which until a month ago had been her only contact point with him – she thought of long.hammer as 'him', but in fact she didn't even know this for certain – simply stopped yielding any replies.

Now Fish and Chips (as Mike Marshall, the *Herald*'s self-appointed resident wit, had christened Salmon and Shipp) had got hold of lawyers themselves and were threatening to bring a big defamation case, not just against the paper but its editor and Glasby personally as well. That was enough to give Mark Ellington a major attack of spinelessness, naturally.

Not only had Glasby's main source of information on Longhammer gone to ground, any other chances that she had to get hold of useful information had dried up too, just when she really needed them. Dunne himself didn't return her calls. She'd had the impression before that the chief superintendent quite liked her, but that didn't seem to count for anything now.

Not that long ago she would have thought of turning to Mick Doherty. But that was out of the question now, since their disastrous evening out together.

Mick Doherty was Dunne's sergeant on Longhammer and his right arm in the Godsquad. He was a quiet guy, but he had a way of looking at her that had sometimes made her feel a bit uncomfortable. Doherty's relationship with Dunne gave him real potential as a source but although she had tried more than once, she'd never before succeeded in getting particularly close to him. So when he had suggested that they have a conversation over dinner, she was rather surprised, but she still accepted readily enough.

Glasby was feeling a bit frustrated. It was getting late – Doherty had suggested dinner at nine, apparently unable to get off work any earlier – and she was tired. This wouldn't have bothered her if Doherty had been telling her anything useful, but every time she had steered the conversation around to Longhammer he simply changed the subject. She seemed to have done most of the talking and she had learned nothing of any worth at all. Meanwhile he was well into the second bottle of red wine and he kept trying to encourage her to drink more quickly with him.

The direct approach was all she had left to try.

'So was there anything particular that you wanted us to talk about?' she asked him, trying to sound casual but firm as well.

Doherty looked straight at her. Although not much past his mid-thirties he looked older, with grey hair receding across an already deeply lined forehead. He was spare in stature, taut rather than fit, with bags under his eyes as if he had been sleeping badly for some time. Glasby had heard that he had a wife and child but had been separated from them for some time.

He continued to hold her gaze. 'I just want us to have the chance to get to know each other, Alison. And that's what you want too, isn't it?' Before she could answer he reached across the table and closed his hand over hers.

Startled, Glasby looked down, staring at his hand for long enough to notice that he bit his nails, before coming to her senses. 'Mick, I think that there's been some misunder-standing.'

She pulled her hand away. He left his arm lying across the table where it was, almost threateningly close to her. 'I mean, when you asked me for dinner—'

He interrupted. 'Misunderstanding? Those looks you gave me?' He put his other arm on the table, leaning across towards her now. '"If you've got time for a private chat some time, Mick . . ."' – the pitch of his voice raised in what was supposed to be a copy of hers – 'How am I supposed to understand that, eh? What's all that supposed to mean?'

Glasby glanced around her, feeling thoroughly uncomfortable. She could feel that her face was hot with anger, and humiliation as well. It was nearly eleven but the Italian restaurant that Doherty had chosen was still quite full. No one seemed to have noticed anything, though. She took a deep breath.

'Mick, we are both professionals. I don't know what you thought, but if anything hasn't been clear between us I'm sorry.' She stopped herself; why was she apologizing? 'You know that John Redgrave and I . . . that we're . . . in a relationship, I mean. You know that!'

Doherty leant back in his chair, which at least had the effect of taking him further from her. 'I can see that you're a professional all right! A real pro!' He was shouting now, loudly enough for one of the waiters to notice. The couple at the next table looked up from their conversation.

'As for you and Redgrave, you don't let that stop you coming on to me, do you? Not to mention rolling over for Henry Dunne, which you'd do in a flash if you got the idea that it would suit you!'

Glasby was too shocked to reply. Doherty stood up, threw some twenty-pound notes on to the table and strode out of the restaurant, saying something to himself which she preferred not to hear.

Back home, she was on the phone to Redgrave before she'd even got her coat off, perched on the edge of the uncomfortable sofa in her rented flat. Like her he was shocked, but seemingly almost as much by her behaviour as Doherty's.

'Mick Doherty? What the . . . what *were* you thinking of?' he demanded. 'And Alison, why didn't you tell me? You never said that you were going out with Doherty! What else am I going to find out about, that you've been up to behind my back?'

'John!' She was on her feet now, pacing around her living room. It was true, she hadn't told Redgrave what she was doing that evening. It had been a quite deliberate decision. She thought that she had no option, since she had been hoping that Doherty might have become a source of information to her. Surely he should understand that!

'You're acting like this is my fault,' she told him, indignantly.

'No, I'm not. Although plenty of blokes would, you know.' Redgrave gave himself a moment to calm down. 'What did all that mean, about you and Dunne?'

'How would I know? You should be asking Mick, not me. Do you think that's how I work as well, then?'

'No, but why do I keep getting the feeling that you're more bothered about your bloody job than you are about us? Do you have any idea what people are saying? If I want to get my promotion to inspector, I need to start choosing my girlfriend more carefully, stuff like that? And then you go and do – *this*!'

She didn't remember everything that she said next. It certainly included accusing him of caring more about what his mates at the Yard thought about him than he did about her. He let her talk, until the point where she called him a 'typical emotionally-retarded throw-back copper', and then he got angry too. It was she who'd put the phone down, and he who'd tried calling, several times that night and again over the next few days. Then he gave up.

Glasby was nothing if not independent, but she missed Redgrave's company even while she was still angry with him. After a week or so she began to admit to herself that she might have overreacted. But she was too proud, and possibly not experienced enough in the ways of men, to take the steps needed to repair the damage.

She wanted to get him back, but she simply didn't know how.

That put Glasby where she was now, with a headache that wasn't going away any time soon. She had been ordered to see her editor in his office at nine thirty to tell him how they were going to defend themselves against Fish and Chips' lawsuit. And at the moment she had absolutely nothing to offer him. She badly needed Redgrave's support now.

She sat at her kitchen table, gloomily sipping at a mug of instant coffee. Alison Glasby was twenty-six, with rather large eyes under a mop of perennially untidy brown hair. When there was something on her mind, and there usually was, she could seem severe and a bit thin-lipped, but there were plenty of men who found her interesting enough to look at, and to be with if they got the chance. Not that Glasby usually thought very often about that sort of thing. Nor, many who knew her would say, about anything else that went much beyond her work.

Life at the *Herald* had never been easy. She loved the job, of course. Bloody Joe – 'call me Jack' – Daniels liked to make obscene jokes about what she should do with a rolled up copy of the *Herald* in order to fully express her feelings for it. (She'd had a drunken fling with Daniels after work one night, an idiotic and most uncharacteristic incident that Glasby had regretted the instant she woke up the next morning.)

She had endured three and a half years of having to prove herself, stuck for most of that time doing articles on dating or new trends in dieting, all the time desperate to do . . . well, to do what she was still trying to do now. Crime, stories you had to take risks on, making contacts and working them, putting scraps of information together, being patient (not one of her greater virtues, even Glasby would admit that) and moving fast when you got hold of a solid story.

But even now, despite all the promises she'd been given

that the *Herald* understood where her talents lay, that they recognized the contribution she could make to investigations and reporting hard news, even now she was still officially part of the features team. That meant that she was supposed to seek permission from her boss, Thomas Lear, more or less on a case by case basis, if she wanted to cover a crime story.

Her coffee finished, she glanced at the clock. It was six fifteen, way earlier than she needed to be. She'd already checked her email and drawn a blank, barring yet another solicitation from a particularly persistent dating agency which she'd registered with in pursuit of a series she'd been working on for the paper a year or two ago.

Well, there wasn't much point in sitting miserably at home; she could go and sit miserably in the office instead. Either way, barring a last minute rescue by Mr long.hammer, she was stuffed. Worse, Mark Ellington was stuffed with her, as he no doubt intended to point out at their meeting. Unless she could talk him round, it was going to be a short conversation and a bad one, that was obvious.

'Alison, please! This isn't a question of trust, it's . . .' Ellington stopped, lost for words as usual. Not a characteristic that you would look for in the editor of a national newspaper, but everyone knew that he had been put in to raise advertising revenues and cut costs, and wasn't a real newsman at all.

As was often the case, Glasby thought that Mike Marshall had summed things up best: their editor was living proof that cream isn't the only thing that rises to the top.

Ellington looked as if for assistance over to Thomas Lear, who had been very quiet since the meeting began. Known universally (except to his face) as the Leer, he was Glasby's immediate boss. Since he was head of features news, which she spent much of her energy trying to avoid so that she could cover crime stories instead, Glasby did her best to treat this as a purely nominal arrangement.

His presence here must mean that Ellington thought otherwise; be that as it may, the Leer had hardly said a word. He had put on a lot of weight lately. Unfortunately his dress sense, which could politely be described as garish, made things worse. His plumage was as bright as ever – today it included a mauve shirt and electric blue tie, knotted loosely in an attempt to disguise the fact that his collar could no longer comfortably be buttoned up. But under it, Lear looked pale, grey and generally as if he'd rather be somewhere else.

Glasby pressed home her advantage. 'Mark, whenever you've decided to question one of my stories – needed to question it, I mean – it's always stood up. And it will do this time.'

Ellington looked expectantly at her from across the large empty space of his desktop. 'What do your sources say?'

That, of course, was just the problem. Her sources weren't saying anything – not to her at any rate. Even the wretched press office at the Met would hardly pass the time of day with her.

She blew whatever slim chance she'd had. 'I'll just need to talk to a few more people, so that I can try to shake things up a bit, that's all.'

Rising to his feet, Ellington gazed out of the window. His office was on the twenty-seventh floor and, unlike the bit of corridor on the floor below where Glasby had her desk, it was on the prestigious west side of the building. There were spectacular views across the Isle of Dogs, past the Gherkin and other more prosaic office blocks in the City, across to the London Eye, Big Ben and beyond. Her view was of the office block next door, just about far enough away so you couldn't make out what was going on inside it. Given that it was the headquarters of the country's largest bank, possibly you wouldn't bother, even if you could.

There was a silence. Then: 'Alison . . .' Ellington paused again. Glasby looked up at him. Not only was he not facing her, he was actually standing behind her so that she had to twist around in her chair even to see the back of his head. As she did, she noticed that Lear's forehead was covered in beads of sweat. She wondered if he was coming down with flu.

Ellington started again, with an obvious effort. 'You've been with the *Herald* for nearly four years now. And you know how much I value your contribution. Everyone on twenty-seven does. Even the Longhammer stuff.'

Another pause. Glasby, who needed to know what was coming next, had to stop herself from jumping in – what did he mean, *even* Longhammer? The *Herald* had got three major exclusives out of Longhammer, all down to her. Under the table she dug her nails into the palms of her hands. They were jagged in places where she had been chewing at them again.

'You remember the note I sent round last week.' It was a statement, not a question, which was a good job as she hadn't the faintest idea what Ellington was talking about. 'Record-keeping and so on.' That did remind her of something, an email to all staff, but she certainly hadn't bothered reading any of it and couldn't imagine what it had to do with their current conversation.

'As I mentioned, one of the most important duties of my position is general employee welfare. There are studies, you know, about people who don't take their holidays.' Ellington reached for the pocket of his tweed jacket and drew out his PDA. It was strange that someone who dressed like a country solicitor also loved every high-tech toy he could find.

'According to our records, you have not taken a single day off this year, and you've carried over twenty-two days from last year. I assume that you were aware of that, Thomas?'

Lear looked startled to hear his name, as if he hadn't been paying attention. 'Well, Mark, what with pressure of work lately . . .' He tailed off, not making it clear whether he was talking about Glasby's workload or his own. Ellington sighed, loudly.

'Leaving aside – for the moment, I mean – Herald Group rules on vacation accrual waiver, you are nearly six weeks behind schedule. Now these rules are put in place, not just to protect the quality of your life – your social life I mean' – Glasby felt herself going pink, for no reason that she could think of – 'we also have to protect ourselves, against burn-out and all that could be brought with it. So the best thing will be for you to take two weeks, immediately, from today. No' – this with a hand raised as she opened her mouth to protest – 'you don't need to worry about your current assignments. Thomas has assured me that he's got everything covered already.'

Glasby left his office mortified. She had been banished from the newspaper, supposedly for her own good. Which made no sense whatsoever: all of her Longhammer problems would still be there when she came back. She had even been forced to agree not to make any calls while she was off work.

And that was the worst of it really. Two weeks off. What the hell was she going to do with herself?

*I am sad but you'll be sadder*
*I am mad and you'll get madder*
*Running trying to catch a shadow*
*Up the snakes and down the ladder*

*From the notebook of Michael Fisher*

# Three

'Well, dear, we would like you to come to Harold and Julie's with us. They're a lovely couple, very friendly, and their daughter's only a year younger than you. Of course, she's married already, and doing very well for herself. She's got a place at one of these City solicitors' companies. Julie told me that she gets a very good salary and a car as well. She met her husband at the firm, too.'

Alison Glasby's mother looked over at her daughter, who was scowling down at the Chinese carpet in her parents' living room, and thought better of it. 'Well, if you're sure you won't come . . . I just hope you don't get too bored while we're out. We'll be back after lunch, and you can always call on Dad's mobile phone.'

Bored? How could anyone possibly get bored here? Her parents' library ran practically into double figures (not counting golf books, of which there were plenty); the TV had five channels of terrestrial; and if even that wasn't enough to keep an active brain fully entertained, there was always her father's extensive collection of holiday photos. Or, as an alternative, she could go to the local Spar store and buy some glue for a good old sniffing session. What could be more fun?

Glasby settled back into the off-white sofa and reached for the pile of newspapers next to her. It was the third day of her exile in Hertfordshire, and this was the only pleasure left to her by the cruel and unusual punishment that the *Herald* had imposed. To start off with, she had decided just to stay in her flat in unfashionable Stockwell (an area which no estate agent had yet been bold enough to describe as 'up and coming'). Maybe she could tidy up a bit, get some food in and even do some cooking. It would do her good to relax at home, catch up on some reading and possibly get back in touch with a friend.

That had lasted her the rest of Monday, after she had left the office, until about Tuesday lunchtime. Her thoughts kept turning to John Redgrave and she had to fight the temptation to call him.

Glasby had never been the most sociable of people; her circle of friends would have needed several more points to make up the full 360 degrees. The problems of the last few weeks had made her more withdrawn than usual. Of those few people that she had kept in touch with from her university or her schooldays in Norwich, there was simply no one who she felt like sharing her predicament with.

It was obvious that she had to get out of the flat if she was to keep her self-respect for the rest of her so-called holiday. Her relationship with her parents was distant at best; they knew almost nothing about her life and didn't generally seem very concerned to find out more, but this was a positive under current circumstances.

Now it was Thursday, getting towards what should have been the busiest time of her week with impending copy deadlines for the Sunday edition, and here she was, doing nothing.

She had never lived in the redbrick house, on a little Home Counties estate that her parents had moved to a few years ago. In fact, other than one photo of an unsmiling Alison in a brown suit that her mother had made her buy, half hidden behind the golfing trophies on the sideboard in the sitting room, a visitor could be forgiven for not realizing that Mr and Mrs Glasby had a daughter. And yet, within twenty-four hours of coming to stay, Glasby had fallen into exactly the sort of sullen routine that had taken up a large part of her teenage years.

She was getting up as late as she could manage (why did her mother have to hoover, every morning?). That didn't mean that she was actually sleeping in, of course; that would be too much to ask for. But she lay in bed for hours after she woke up until driven out by hunger or guilt, miserably checking her email or just staring blankly at the ceiling. Then breakfast on the Formica-topped table in the kitchen, which still bore scratches that she had been responsible for as a child, followed by a trip to the nearest newsagent and others too if necessary, to make sure that she got every national and the locals as well, just in case.

As soon as she got them back she would zip through the
news pages once, fast, to make sure that she wasn't missing
anything important. By then, it was probably half past eleven
or so, and she only had another twelve hours to fill before it
was time for bed.

Glasby looked at her watch: eleven thirty, on the dot. The
urge to call Redgrave came to her yet again. Maybe if she
said sorry for some of the things she'd said . . . But he had as
good as told her that he didn't trust her. And it was pretty
clear that he cared more about whatever juvenile gossip went
around the Scotland Yard cafeteria than he did about her.

Talking about it to her parents was absolutely not an option.
For a start, before telling them that she'd broken up with
Redgrave she would have to tell them that she had a boyfriend
in the first place, something which more than a year after their
relationship began she hadn't got around to doing. And she
could just imagine her father's comments about not being able
to hold on to her man, and her mother's sympathetic look
which somehow would be nearly as unbearable.

She sat miserably, head in hands, for several minutes, feeling
that she had to do something. Then she reached for her phone
and called a familiar number.

Chief Superintendent Dunne had had a difficult meeting with
his boss. Assistant Commissioner Horgan was a genuine
product of the ranks, with an almost religious belief in the
need for the police service to achieve the standards of integrity
that its name implied. Horgan was about the last person in
the world to give any comfort to anyone bent or on the make,
and neither his Masonic connections nor his sentimental affection for the ordinary policemen on the beat would change that
one bit.

But, Dunne reflected, elbows on his desk and head resting
on his hands – there was always a 'but' in his work, nowadays
– you didn't get to Horgan's position without an understanding
of the politics of the job. And Longhammer, which at one time
had the fairest of winds behind it, was starting to feel like it
was, in Horgan's phrase, running out of puff.

'It's the Federation, Henry,' Horgan told him, and he was
right, of course.

No one with half a brain could ignore the power of the

Police Federation, a trade union in all but name that represented all 135,000 police officers below the rank of Superintendent, and who included amongst their members Bill Shipp and George Salmon. They had kicked up an almighty stink when some idiot had given their names to Glasby, and now the fumes had reached as far as Alec Horgan.

'No one's trying to sell you short, Henry. If you've got work to do, wherever it leads, you know that you've got my blessing. But we've got to keep the men with us. Crucifying police officers in the press, men with twenty years' service each, that isn't the way to do it.'

Dunne looked at the older man, but made no reply.

'Are you any closer to knowing who the mole is? Which one of your famous Godsquad has yielded to temptation?'

'If I knew that . . .' Dunne trailed off. Really there was nothing for him to say, but he felt the need to add more. 'It could be anyone, you know. I've no right to suspect any man above any other. Anyone close enough to Longhammer could be doing it, anybody who wanted to make themselves a few quid extra.'

Horgan wouldn't even let him deny leaking the names himself – 'No one could think that you'd be behind a stupid play like that, Henry' – but Dunne was left with the uncomfortable feeling that this was exactly what everyone did think.

He had no great wish for a high profile or fondness for journalists in general, but his position on Longhammer occasionally required him to attend press conferences, and Glasby had showed up at some of them. He'd even met her in the pub once or twice with John Redgrave, although he'd heard that they had split up since then. So far as he could remember, she was a nice enough girl and not bad looking either, but she was also the cause of a Premier League-sized headache for him.

Dunne had no idea how Glasby had got hold of those two names, but now she had published them, it was made absolutely clear to him that he had two options, and not much time to choose: get something on them, or clear their names, publicly. And in the meantime, any further operations were paralysed; Longhammer was suspended in all but name.

The problem was, if he had to backtrack on these two, it would probably be the end. Longhammer might still have

Horgan's support but there were plenty in the Met –
including, it was rumoured, Commissioner Andrews himself
– who felt that the whole thing was becoming a liability.
And him with it.

As usual he'd had far too much coffee already but Dunne
found himself stomping along the corridor to get some more
anyway. His rubber-soled shoes squeaked as he walked across
the glistening lino – Alec Horgan was a stickler for cleanli-
ness as well, and the whole of their wing of the building
smelled permanently of floor polish. As he pushed open the
swing doors to the canteen he heard a familiar name spoken.

'. . . Glasby. It's always her. Or one of them other bastards.
Frigging bitch, trying to bring down good coppers like Billy
Shipp and George Salmon.'

Dunne didn't recognize Glasby's accuser but he knew one
of the other men at the table, a uniformed PC who'd worked
under him a few years previously.

There was a general murmur of agreement. 'What the bloody
hell does she want?' – this from one of the other uniforms
sitting nearby. 'If some slag goes and scratches her car or
something and we don't catch him, there's God only knows
what to pay. Since when can we get the bad guys without
bending a rule or two?'

Even if Dunne didn't know most of them, they clearly recognized him. A silence fell over the group. Not feeling like
coffee any more, he turned on his heel and left them to their
conversation.

'Hello Alison, I was hoping that it might be you.' There was
real warmth in his voice, a warmth borne from shared experiences and perhaps a little from the loneliness that they were
both suffering from these days as well.

'Hello Bill.' Bill Davenport, Fleet Street legend, the man
who had started Glasby's career as a crime journalist – a real
journalist, according to her way of thinking. They'd worked
together on his last story, saving his reputation and making
hers, such as it was, in the process. Now he was retired and
seemed happy to put her up in her hour of need. So happy,
in fact, that it wasn't all that clear whether his need was greater
than hers.

Davenport had been pushed out – eased out, as Mark

Ellington preferred to put it – from the *Herald*, two years over the normal retirement age but at a point where he still felt that he had plenty to give. He was a proud man and independent to a fault, with a calm, easy manner that served him well in all sorts of situations. Even though he was popular with women – something of a flirt, in fact – Davenport had never married and was living on his own, in a small house on the South Downs, with only his two cats for company.

Glasby scribbled a hasty note to her parents. Soon she was in her car and on the way to Davenport's cottage. As usual she felt guilty about how she was treating her parents, and as usual the weight of her father's disappointment started to lift from her shoulders the further she got from their house. He never tried to hide that he would have preferred a son, and certainly not a daughter like her, one who wore jeans rather than dresses and who didn't look like getting married any time soon.

Davenport had moved away from London after the *Herald* had finally eased him out, a victim of the ever-increasing need to save overheads as much as any decline in the quality of his journalism. A man who lived his job rather than worked it, retirement didn't look like it would suit him well, and so far as Glasby could tell it hadn't. Anyway, he was one of the few people in her life whose advice she always valued. She was really looking forward to seeing him.

Passers-by didn't tend to remember him. His eyes were his only notable feature, eyes that were hungry enough to swallow someone up. The eyes told you something, about a man with a hole inside him, a man looking for someone or something to fill it. The eyes were enough to make most people look away.

He was thin, enough to emphasize his height but not so much that you'd notice. A bit scruffy but no more than that, and not altogether unfashionable. Armani jeans, expensive looking trainers and a turtle-necked jumper were his standard, worn today without a jacket in honour of the early June sunshine.

He liked to walk from his flat in Euston, sometimes all the way to the river and beyond. When he saw something that struck him he noted it down in a small black book which he carried with him. Yesterday he had come across a café called 'S&M', which stood for sausage and mash. He had written the name down and its address, although he had no particular intention of going back there.

Mostly on his walks he liked to look at people. If someone took his interest he might follow them for a while and jot down a few notes about them after he had let them go. Usually he chose women, but not always. His interest wasn't invariably sexual. He just liked to observe things.

Of course this habit of watchfulness could come in very useful at times.

Today he was walking with a purpose. There was still time to look around, there was always that, but his pace was faster than usual, anxious to get back to the flat and go through the bundle he had under his arm. Glasby was not the only person bulk-buying newspapers that day, and his interests were remarkably similar to hers; he wanted to see what, if anything, was happening on Longhammer.

The man reached into his pocket as he approached the gate which some of his neighbours had successfully lobbied for, at the foot of the stairwell. It hadn't lasted long before being jemmied open, presumably by someone who had returned home one night drunk having forgotten their key. Part of the frame was now hanging clear from the brown tiled wall to which it had been fixed. He hadn't expressed a view one way or the other when asked about the new security measures, but when the gate was up, he did notice that the local practice of using the stairway as a urinal seemed to have stopped.

Back in his immaculately tidy flat, he glanced around carefully. Everything seemed to be in its normal place, including the small piece of paper he had left balanced on the top of the sitting-room door. For a middle-aged man he had few possessions other than a large collection of books, jammed on to shelves which had been built into the alcoves either side of a blackened metal fireplace. A closer inspection of these would have shown that many of them carried the imprint of university or public libraries, although whether they had been legitimately purchased or simply stolen would not, of course, have been clear.

There were three chairs in the room, each of them in matching brown leather, arranged around a large antique rosewood coffee table. Two threadbare oriental rugs were next to it, on bare floorboards that had been stripped and polished many years before. A mirror hung above the fireplace. The sole ornament in the room was a framed photograph of an elderly woman, placed in the middle of the mantelpiece. A set of fire irons sat below, functional rather than decorative. A long, low, dark oak cupboard was the only other piece of furniture, two locked wooden doors either side of three drawers.

The man looked through each of his newspapers with growing impatience. Failing to find what he was looking for, he reached for his mobile phone and called a number that he had programmed in a few days before.

Parked outside, just underneath the graffiti-covered sign that read 'Amelia Street, NW1' was a white van. It had no signs on the side. The windows at the rear were mirrored, so that the two bulky men inside it were invisible from the street. They both looked up as a light began to blink on the electronic panel placed between them. With no need to say anything, each of them reached for a set of headphones.

But the man inside the flat knew nothing of this. 'Hello, is that Alison Glasby?' he began. 'My name is Michael Fisher.'

Davenport's front door, which was bare wood when she'd last seen it, had been painted a rather majestic dark blue and was almost encircled by roses and some other climbing plant which she didn't recognize. It was also surrounded by scaffolding, meaning that the building work needed to make the cottage habitable was now more than a year overdue.

The doorbell worked, though; she could hear the two cats approaching followed at a slightly slower pace by their keeper. A dusty mountain bike was leant against the front wall without even a lock to guard it, not something that Davenport could have thought of doing at his other house in south London. Just as the door handle turned Glasby's phone rang.

Whoever was calling her did not want to disclose his number. Michael Fisher, he said his name was, which meant nothing at all to Glasby, and neither did what he said next: 'Unman, Wittering and Zigo.'

'Sorry, what did you say?' she asked. Davenport was framed in the doorway, giving her a welcoming look.

'Unman, Wittering and Zigo. Don't you know who they are?'

'No,' said Glasby, impatience rapidly winning out over curiosity. She hadn't reached the point of needing a frustrated pub quizmaster for company.

'Then go away and look them up. And then look up Alan Dickson. He was a teacher. He made the news in 1974. Oh, and in this case, Wittering goes by the name of Dunne. I'll call you back in an hour or so.'

'What was all that about?' Davenport asked her. He looked to have lost weight since they'd last met. Compact, not much taller than Glasby in fact, and the best part of forty years older than her, he had the same inquisitive face and searching eyes that she'd noticed in him when they first met. His jacket looked the same as well, a mixture of tweed and cat fur.

But his hair was mostly grey by now, and thinning, more than she had remembered. Age, from what she could see, was beginning to catch up on him, and he seemed scruffy, smaller and more vulnerable..

'I've no idea what it was, actually.' She told him what the caller had said. There was something in the man's voice – whiny and nasal, as if he had a cold or bad catarrh – that made her instinctively doubt him.

'Dunne? Your Dunne, Longhammer?'

'He's not *my* Dunne,' she snapped, remembering Mick Doherty's accusations. 'I mean, I'm sorry Bill, yes, that's who I think he meant. But what all the rest of it's about I have no idea.'

'Well one bit's easy; *Unman, Wittering and Zigo*. It's a film, from the Seventies. Rather a good one really, although I suppose it might be a bit dated now. You know what?' He stopped and grinned at her, his smile as ever taking years off him.

'No, what?'

'If you actually come in instead of standing on my doorstep, I might even tell you about it.'

Davenport had been the *Herald*'s only real journalistic star name for decades. His book, *Children Carried Away*, about a series of child killings which had shocked the country in the late 1960s, was a classic that was still studied in journalism colleges.

Glasby had worked as his assistant just before he retired. Their relationship had at first been coloured by mutual misunderstanding and suspicion, but gradually each had seen something very similar in the other, an absolute determination to reach for the truth, no matter what – or who – might be in the way. From this foundation, there had developed not just trust but a genuine affection that spanned the considerable divide in their ages.

A little later, Glasby was perched on a seat built into a window, on the other side of which was a pretty little garden which sloped down from the house. The view was magnificent; green hills, one after another, and in the distance the sea.

The room she was sitting in was almost identical to the sitting room she remembered from Davenport's south London home, with the same furniture covered in the same dusty piles of paper, as if it had all been carefully lifted out and reassembled. In between the papers everything seemed clean enough, and the garden was positively manicured. Either Davenport was looking after himself or, more likely, he had as usual been successful in finding someone else to do it for him.

Davenport had what looked like a whisky and ginger – although it was a little early in the day for strong liquor – and Glasby was sipping at a cup of mint tea, bought in her honour during her last visit.

'How's the book going, Bill?' In theory, he was writing a novel, but having talked quite a lot about some ideas he had before he started, Davenport was strangely quiet on the subject these days.

He looked downright shifty. 'Oh, you know . . .' he said, meaninglessly.

Glasby had the thought that, despite the beautiful surroundings, Davenport was bored and a bit depressed and was now hoping that she might provide something to get him interested in life again.

'Let's get back to your little mystery,' he said, as if to confirm her suspicion. 'The point of Wittering and his colleagues is that they were public-school boys who killed their teacher.'

Glasby had her laptop out, connected to the wireless network which she had previously helped Davenport to install. 'And Alan Dickson was a teacher, as this Michael Fisher character said to me. He died in a climbing accident, in 1974. It looks like he was taking part in some sort of outward-bound event for his class. He was the games teacher at Burstone School, apparently.'

'Burstone? Isn't that near Oxford, in the Cotswolds? There's some rather fine antiques shops there as I remember, but you'd have a job to find a hill big enough to fall off.'

Glasby smiled. 'It was in the Highlands, Bill, in Scotland. That's where the accident happened. It must have been some sort of school trip. There was a class of fourteen-year-old boys. So is this Fisher saying that the teacher's death wasn't an accident, that he was murdered?'

'How old is Dunne, Alison?'

She lifted her head from the computer, a look of understanding spreading over her face. 'I'm getting slow, aren't I? 1974, fourteen years old – that would mean that now they would be . . . Forty-eight, Bill, that's how old Dunne is. Forty-eight years old.'

Her phone rang again. The number was withheld, as before.

Thirty minutes later she was in her car and heading back to London, leaving her erstwhile host behind her.

In the white van, the older of the two men wiped some sweat from his forehead with his sleeve and reached for his phone. 'He's arranged a meet with Glasby, guv'nor. Looks like he's decided to cash in his chips.'

At the other end of the line, a weary looking man removed his glasses and raised his thumb and forefinger to the bridge of his nose. He rubbed thoughtfully at two red marks there, and slowly closed his eyes.

*On a huge hill,*
*Cragged, and steep,*
*Truth stands,*
*and he that will Reach her,*
*about must, and about must go*
*John Donne*

*From the notebook of Michael Fisher*

# Four

It was a beautiful day for a drive, the summer sun high in the cloudless sky, a pleasant breath of air moving the trees which were heavy with leaves as Glasby drove past. Her blue Punto formed part of an endless stream of vehicles on London's orbital motorway, notorious as one of the most expensive car parks in motoring history but today flowing as smoothly as any transport planner could have wished.

Glasby's informant had specified a café on Upper Street for them to meet at. This involved her driving into town from the south and then through the Congestion Charging zone and up to Islington, in north London. She didn't know the café but didn't think it would be hard to find. This turned out to be right; she spotted it on the other side of the road as she drove past, just a couple of minutes before their allotted meeting time.

Even in the middle of a Thursday afternoon Islington was busy, the road choked with traffic in both directions, leaving her stuck in a jam with no parking place in sight. Happily the next turn served her better, a tight space into which, feeling rather pleased with herself, she performed a neat parallel manoeuvre. Then she found that she had nothing smaller than a ten-pound note.

She ran back around the corner into a small newsagent's. It was empty except for a small, elderly man who looked Turkish or possibly Middle Eastern. 'I'm really sorry, but could you help me please?' she asked. He looked impassively at her. 'I'm parked just around the corner, and I just need some change.'

She held out a note to him. Without saying a word he stretched out his index finger to her, making sure that he had her attention, and moved it slowly until it was pointing at a handwritten sign propped up against the till: 'Please, do not ask credit, do not ask change. We do not give it!'

Embarrassed, Glasby turned and grabbed a bar of chocolate from a nearby shelf and thrust it at the man, who reached down to his till and handed her a five-pound note, four pound coins and some smaller change, all in the most complete silence.

'Camomile tea, please.' Glasby was sitting at a table near the door, her handbag propped up in front of her as she had been instructed to do. There were a few other tables occupied, at one of which sat a rather lanky man on his own who she supposed could have been Fisher. She glanced again at her watch: if she'd been late, he was later. It was now past four thirty. With no way of contacting him, she resigned herself to waiting . . .

Her cup was empty by now, the waitress had looked over at her for a second time, and still there was no sign of Fisher. Glasby was starting to wonder if he had sent her on a wild goose chase. The tall man who she had noticed before was finishing paying his bill. He stopped next to her table, speaking into his phone, just loudly enough for her to hear: 'Walk down to the Angel Tube, go to King's Cross, and wait at the Victoria Line platform, going south. I'm Michael Fisher.'

Startled, Glasby looked up and was about to speak, but the man was already past her and on his way out of the door, apparently heading in the other direction to the one which he had instructed her to follow.

There didn't seem to be anything for it except to do as she was told. She hurried to pay her bill and walked briskly down to the Tube station, which was just starting to fill up with the early part of the London rush-hour. Less than fifteen minutes after her first encounter with Fisher, Glasby was stood on the still fairly empty platform at King's Cross, wondering what was going to happen next.

A couple in their thirties were next to her, cuddling a baby between them. They could have been Mediterranean or from somewhere in the Middle East. The man said something in a language which Glasby didn't understand and they both laughed, and then kissed, before turning their attention back to their baby.

A train drew up, disgorging quite a few passengers. All of the people who had been standing around her on the platform got on to the train. Feeling self-conscious, Glasby remained where she was. The train, which was about half full, stood still, doors remaining open. She peered into the carriage nearest her but could see no one who looked at all like Fisher. A hand grabbed her from behind and she was half pushed, half lifted into the train, just as the doors began to close.

A voice hissed in her ear: 'That's it – we should have lost them now.'

It was Fisher. Glasby tried hard to dispel the awful feeling that the man might be completely deranged.

One of the things that George Pincher's men had always liked about him was that he was predictable. If you did a good job, he would be generous with his praise, and in other more tangible ways as well. Screw up, and you'd get it in the neck. Right now, George Pincher was not a happy man.

He roared down the phone line: 'What do you mean, you lost them? What are you, muppets? What do you think the client is paying for, for you two to play *bloody tiddlywinks*?' The last two words were loud enough to distort the sound on the telephone.

The large man winced. 'They split up, guv'nor. He went north, she went south. Different Tubes, different lines. We stuck with him, but he jumped trains. If we'd gone with him, he'd have to have spotted us, and you said that couldn't happen. It's not like when we was in the Branch. You know we ain't got the back-up. Not now we're just civilians.'

'Don't you go telling me what I know. My bloody *milkman* could have done a better job than that, you jokers!'

The man at the other end of the line relaxed. Pincher's multi-talented milkman often put in an appearance. At times likes this, it tended to signify that any unpleasant stuff was over. The conversation moved on to other issues; specifically, next steps.

After all the messing around on the Underground, Glasby finally had the chance to see Michael Fisher face to face. What she saw didn't give her any great comfort. He looked to be in his middle or late forties, which was about right if he was claiming to be a contemporary of Dunne's, tall and skinny with piercing eyes.

It was the eyes that were worrying her in fact, darting around as if their owner had them under only partial control. He had brought her to a different branch of Café Rouge, across in west London now, and despite Fisher's claim to have shaken off their pursuers (real or imaginary) he still seemed to be on the jittery side of nervous. He was certainly not a man (as Davenport, who'd done his National Service with the army, liked to say) that you would want to go into the jungle with.

Still, she was here now, so she might as well hear the man out. 'So, Mr Fisher – Michael, shall we start with some background on yourself?'

'No,' was the unpromising response. 'That won't be necessary. We're here to talk about a certain policeman of your and my acquaintance, not Michael Fisher. We'll call him "Seddon"; that was his nickname, at Burstone.'

Before leaving Davenport's house she had taken a quick look at Burstone School's website. It was one of a number across the country that had been founded in the sixteenth century and named in a piece of Tudor spin-doctoring after the boy king Edward VI.

'Seddon?' Then she got it: Seddon Dunne – 'said and done'.

Burstone's premier educational establishment had, so far as she had discovered, lasted for something like 500 years without ever achieving any great distinction, and feeble public school humour seemed to suit it rather well.

'OK, so you'd rather talk about, um, Seddon then, first. But you do understand that I'll need to know something about you too, for credibility, don't you?'

'Credibility? Oh yes, you'll want proof, and Michael Fisher can give you that, all right.'

Glasby groaned, inwardly only she hoped. Not only was the man borderline paranoid, he referred to himself in the third person. That was always a bad sign.

He was waving a black notebook in her face now. 'It's all in here, everything you'll need.'

She made an effort to get things under control. 'Mr Fisher, why don't you just start at the beginning and tell me what happened. We can go back over the details afterwards.'

Fisher's story was simple enough, and telling it seem to calm him down. 'You already know what I'm going to say, from what I told you on the phone,' he began. 'Seddon, the other two, and me, we were all boys at Burstone in the Seventies. They all hated the games master, Mr Dickson. Everyone called him "Thicko" Dickson, but it was Seddon who started it, I think. Bedingfield was his friend, they were really tight. He went on to be head boy, Bedingfield. It was him who protected Gold the most.'

Glasby had plenty that she wanted to ask but decided to let Fisher continue.

'We were on a school trip, climbing in the Highlands. It was supposed to be character building, that's how they sold it to the parents. The weather was foul. We had no proper equipment and there was only one master. It was completely irresponsible of them to put us in danger like that. Do you know anything about the school? The *alma mater*?' (This last with heavy sarcasm).

Glasby preferred to hear what Fisher might want to tell her, so professed complete ignorance.

'It was a con trick, a complete rip-off.' Fisher seemed to be getting agitated again. 'They claimed that we were getting a superior education, with all this public school snobbery, but it was nothing more than a rip-off. Half of the masters didn't even have the proper qualifications. Of course, places like that, they've got the fix in where it matters, the old school tie, that game. You people know all about that, don't you? The sort of connections those places have got, they're above the law – places like that *make* the laws, to suit themselves.'

Glasby had already noticed that there was a vein bulging from Fisher's forehead. It was twitching slightly now. He seemed to realize that he needed to get himself back under control.

'So the weather came down, and the three of them, they must have agreed it in advance, to take their chance if they got it. He was a big man, Mr Dickson, but with three of them on him he didn't have much of a hope. He fought for a while, luckily for you and me as it turned out, but our friend Seddon did for him eventually, he just threw himself at him, and down went old Thicko. At the inquest they said he'd fallen more than a thousand feet. You don't get much deader than that.'

He paused. Glasby waited, guessing correctly that there was more. 'You see, the great thing is, that they would have got away with it, except for one person. Yours truly. They didn't know that I saw the whole thing. And after they'd run off, thinking that they'd accomplished their murderous little design, Fisher moved in and went to work. He was serving the needs of justice, you see. I've got evidence of the whole thing! Now, tell me, what do you need to know?'

Glasby had about a thousand questions to ask, not least why Mr Fisher would think that justice was best served by waiting thirty years to tell his story to a newspaper, rather than talking to the police at the time. Justice might even have demanded that he had made some effort at the time to intervene, and save the unfortunate teacher's life.

But she had more pressing concerns. Was the guy a nutter, was he a chancer out to fool the *Herald* into parting with some cash, was he a put-up job by somebody out to smear Dunne? Or, just possibly, might he actually be telling the truth?

'OK, Mr Fisher,' she began. 'Let's start with talking about this evidence that you've got.'

'We went over the details as much as I could get him to,' Glasby told Davenport. She was back home in south London, having rescued her car from where she'd parked it up in Islington.

John Redgrave had dropped hints from time to time about them finding somewhere to live together and it was hard not to remember this, coming back to the quiet flat filled with furniture that wasn't hers. Glasby had been living on her own for more than two years now. She enjoyed her own company, most of the time at least, but there were days, and occasionally nights, when she switched the radio on to a channel where people were talking and carried it from room to room, not listening to what was being said but simply to hear the sound of human life going on around her.

Her landlord had let her keep the few pieces of furniture which he'd put into the flat in order to entice potential tenants, and she'd been grateful for them at the time. Most had come from the very bottom of Ikea's range, and Glasby had promised herself that she would change it all as soon as she could.

Two years on, her student debts were well on the way to being paid off, her car was still in one piece and her finances were generally a bit more solid, but the badly stuffed purple sofa was still the only remotely comfortable thing she had to sit on other than the bed.

'Let's hear it, then,' said Davenport, cautiously. 'I'm sure you will, but just remember who you're talking about here. Your informant is accusing a senior police officer of murder, after all. Not to mention two other people – who are they, by the way?'

'Their names are Richard Bedingfield and David Gold. According to Fisher, Bedingfield is an army major. Or was, rather. He was killed in Afghanistan a few months ago.'

'Well, that's convenient for Mr Fisher – or is it? I assume that his conspiracy theories don't encompass the Taliban as well?'

'Not yet, anyway. Actually his story fits around Bedingfield's death as well. Let me explain, I'll get there.'

'Ride on then, my dear, and don't spare the horses,' was the response. 'Take your time – I've got plenty, and I'm starting to enjoy this.'

She gave it to him in as logical an order as she had been able to gather from Fisher's ramblings. The teacher had been something of a brute, apparently, an anti-Semite who picked on David Gold and encouraged the other boys to do the same. Mr Dickson had a down on Bedingfield and Dunne as well, possibly seeing them as a threat to his authority, and that, together with solidarity with their friend Gold, might account for their wish to be rid of him.

Gold's motivations were clear enough, but other than that he was a complete mystery. He had stayed on at Burstone, as practically everyone did, until he was eighteen, but after that he had simply vanished. It was clear that Fisher had gone to a fair bit of trouble trying to find him, even hiring a private detective a little while ago, but without any success at all.

Fisher had left Dunne alone, having seen him at a Burstone School reunion a short time after Bedingfield's death but not before or since. 'He's not a complete noodle, then,' was Davenport's comment. 'Or at least he hasn't got the balls to try putting the squeeze on a chief superintendent of the Metropolitan Police.'

As for evidence, unless the man was a flat-out fantasist or a complete liar, it sounded like he did have something.

'Before you say it,' she told Davenport, 'I can't write off the fantasist theory just yet. But listen to this.'

Fisher had told her that Bedingfield had been paying him for many years, right up until his death. 'Justice money' was how Fisher had described it; blackmail certainly sounded closer to the mark, but more importantly from Glasby's point of view, he claimed to have bank records relating to these payments. He also said that he had DNA evidence which proved that Henry Dunne himself had been actively involved.

'The trouble is, he won't show me anything yet. He kept shoving this black notebook under my nose and saying that everything I'd need was in it, but he wants money, or at least a written guarantee of pay on proof from the *Herald*, before we go any further.'

'Hmm,' was the response. 'So, as we thought, he might be a nutter, but he's not a fool?'

'I think that's right,' agreed Glasby. 'But where does that leave me, Bill?'

'Well, it's pretty straightforward, isn't it? You go to Ellington – and Lear as well, I suppose – and tell it to them the same way as you have to me, and see if you can get them to stump up some cash. Ellington's easy, really, you just have to play him. It'll be a question of his appetite for the whole thing, and what he makes of Fisher's credibility. And' – he paused – 'yours as well, I suppose, Alison.'

'So it's really looking black, is it, boss?'

Mick Doherty was in Henry Dunne's office, leaning against the wall. The door was closed, as it usually was when these two got together, but both men were keeping their voices low, aware of the thin walls and the keen interest all around them in what they might be saying.

They had known each other for many years, years which had been kinder to Dunne than Doherty, ten years his junior but many places below him in the hierarchy. Dunne had always done his best to repay the loyalty which the younger man had shown him, but a prominent role in Longhammer no longer looked as if would bring with it any real prospect of advancement. If that was of concern to Doherty, it was something which he certainly never voiced.

'Black as the darkest night, Mick. Someone's trying to have us, this time. And they're trying damned hard.'

Dunne, a sturdy man whose fair hair had receded only a

little and was only lightly touched with grey, waltzed through the Met's annual medical, which was compulsory for senior officers, but his shoulders were getting rounded and his face lined, seemingly more and more as each day went by.

Doherty hesitated, then spoke. 'Boss? You know, you always say to go by the rule book, with no cutting corners. Don't you think, this time, we might need to do something, something a bit . . . *drastic*?'

Dunne looked down at the floor. Without speaking, he nodded his head, three times. 'You know what, Mick? I'm going for a walk.'

Doherty, who thought that he knew Dunne as well as anyone, was surprised. 'A walk? Where to?'

'Just a walk, that's all. In the park. Cover for me, will you?'

Glasby had decided to tackle the Leer first. Her plan was to treat him with great respect, as if he really was her boss, which she hoped he would respond to positively by supporting her with Ellington.

Lear's office door was open but she knocked anyway and then looked around it. He was slumped over his desk, head held in one hand, apparently studying a single piece of paper in front of him. He looked in Glasby's direction but his expression didn't change. Glasby wondered if he had been drinking, although she didn't think that he was the type.

'Um, Tom,' she began. 'I hope you don't mind, but something has come up which I should, I mean I want, to discuss with you. To get your advice, and direction, I mean.'

Still Lear gave no real reaction. Then a look of surprise came over his face, as if he had only just noticed her. 'What are you doing here, Alison? I thought that Ellington put you on leave, didn't he?'

'Well, yes, he did, sort of. But,' Glasby countered, 'something's come up, as I said, and I knew that you and Mark would want to hear about it as soon as possible.'

'But Alison, you don't understand.' He sounded put out, but plaintive rather than angry. 'As team leader, I have to plan assignments, and priorities, and so on. I can't do things properly, not if people just wander in and out, willy-nilly, you do see that?'

Lear leant back in his chair, which tilted underneath him.

His stomach was held in by a shiny crocodile-skin belt which had clearly been let out to its widest notch; marks showed where the buckle had bit into the leather before his recent weight gain. There were white stains under the arms of his shirt and damp patches where he had been sweating.

Glasby had anticipated some resistance, even antipathy, but she hadn't foreseen this at all. The Leer, who usually had confidence to spare, seemed out of his depth, almost pathetic. 'Of course I want to be a good team member, Tom,' she murmured, hoping that she sounded reassuring.

For the first time he looked more cheerful, giving her a grateful smile. 'Oh, do you? Well that's OK then. Can you help on a story that Jack Daniels is working up, do you think? I'm sure he could use your assistance, now that you're here.'

Game plan now completely abandoned, Glasby snapped at him. 'I haven't come in off my holiday to do Jack's legwork for him! I'm on to a real story, something huge if I can develop it, and I need to see Ellington on it, now!'

Lear flinched, as if she had hit him. He looked hurt now and a bit bewildered, like a dog who knew he was being punished but wasn't sure why. 'I don't know then, Alison. What do you want me to do? If you have to see Mark, you'd better go and see him, OK?'

In some strange way she had more or less got the result that she wanted, but Glasby had no idea what on earth was going on. She turned to look back at Lear as she left his office. His head was propped up on his right hand again. For a moment she thought that she could see tears in his eyes. It was all very odd.

# Counter-surveillance

*Disguise – if you leave from your residence they will be expecting you and will get sight of you. If disguise is to be utilized effectively it should be used as part of other avoidance strategies. Consider changing appearance in a bathroom in a hotel, railway station or store to confuse pursuit.*

*Evasion – particularly if your pursuers do not want to be identified themselves, physical evasion is a realistic method to utilize. Always split up from other potential surveillance targets. Use public places with multiple exit points such as large stores or stations. Be unpredictable. Do not buy tickets to specific locations. Vary routes.*

*Crowded places give opportunities to confuse pursuers but also give cover under which surveillance can operate without detection by the target. If the pursuers are professional you will not be able to detect them in these circumstances.*

*Using the London Underground could be very effective, particularly if the pursuers do not have a large team up against you. Underground stations have multiple exit points, especially large interchanges such as King's Cross or Victoria. They are often crowded. When a train arrives wait and look around the platform. It may be possible to jump on at the last moment which would require pursuers to identify themselves if they continue the surveillance by following you on to the train.*

*If they are following you by car you will not detect them if they are professionals. They will have enough vehicles and good enough coordination to be able to keep you in sight without revealing any of them. If their resources are more limited it may be possible to make pursuit difficult. Consider switching from one means of transport to another (e.g. taxi then jump quickly to Tube or through department store on foot).*

*It will be difficult to see if the target's home has been searched if they are professional. Place a small piece of paper or thread where it will be dislodged by a searcher. Check carefully when returning that nothing has been disturbed.*

*How effective their telephone surveillance is will depend on what technology they have available. Their activities may be undetectable.*

*From the notebook of Michael Fisher*

# Five

She had spent well over three years on the job at the *Herald* and, Glasby was reflecting, all she had to show for it was the same poky little cubicle, the same junior level moth-eared desk and the same office chair, covered in an indeterminate beige and stained with coffee and who knows what else.

When they took her on it was as part of Thomas Lear's group, and that's where she still was, with Jack Daniels, who was rapidly carving himself a niche writing (in her opinion) the worst type of celebrity drivel, and Mike Marshall who she got on well with personally but who seemed content to be something of a dogsbody. They had been joined by Hetal Singh, who was almost straight out of college, only a few weeks ago. Glasby had been too self-absorbed to form any real opinion of her during this time. A shapely and pleasant looking young woman, Hetal hadn't lacked for male attention since her arrival but had done little to encourage it, being reserved and rather serious in her attitude to her work.

The sound screens that marked out the boundaries of Glasby's little world were largely empty; she had once thought of pinning up a photo she had of John Redgrave, grinning drunkenly at her on Brighton beach, but had never quite got around to it.

Thus saving herself the trouble of taking it down now, of course, a thought which made her feel suddenly sorry for herself. Glasby had no great experience of relationships before John. Ignoring an episode of teenage fumbling and her shameful encounter with the appalling Jack Daniels about which the little that she could remember was still far too much, a single relationship at university was the sum total of her emotional history.

Lester Dolland was his name, a philosophy student with unkempt curly brown hair and a relaxed attitude to his studies, and indeed to the rest of his life, including (it had to be admitted) her; he was gregarious, impulsive, unreliable – everything that she wasn't, in fact. Most of all, he knew how to make her have *fun*, something that was almost as much beyond John Redgrave as it was Glasby herself. She'd bumped into Lester by chance eighteen months or so ago and they had kept in touch since, on and off.

But she and Lester were friends only, she told herself, and that was how things should stay. Life was quite complicated enough as it was. What she needed was a bit of support, counsel and some practical assistance. Michael Fisher's story was extreme, to say the least: extremely explosive, extremely far-fetched, and extremely hard to substantiate, if by some chance it turned out to be true.

It would have been great for Glasby to be able to talk it over with Redgrave, the way that they used to do, but since that wasn't going to happen she got herself settled down to work.

In her usual methodical way she started to set out the holes in what Fisher had told her, holes that she would need to fill if she stood any chance at all of getting any of it to print. The school reunion would be a good place to start; she could see if Dunne had indeed been there, as Fisher claimed.

Coming up with some background on Richard Bedingfield shouldn't be too hard either. British soldiers were getting killed overseas with depressing frequency these days, but at the very least their names got reported, and their regiment. Armed with this information it shouldn't be hard for Glasby to find out more about him and possibly get an in to his family. Fisher had suggested that Bedingfield had a wife and children, but he hadn't revealed their whereabouts, if indeed he knew.

Beyond that, a lot would depend on what records she could unearth, which given the amount of time that had passed might not be easy. Fisher had mentioned that an inquiry had taken place into the teacher's death but other than a vague concern that they might do things differently in Scotland compared with the English inquest procedure (which she already had some familiarity with) Glasby had no idea what details might now exist.

Most important, of course, were the pieces of evidence which Fisher claimed would back up his story. If whatever

he had didn't materialize, or didn't add up to what he claimed
it did, she could forget all the rest. So, Fisher himself held
the key and her path towards it led straight to Mark Ellington
and in all probability the *Herald*'s chequebook. She steeled
herself to prepare for what would probably not be an easy
encounter.

The man paused at the foot of the stairwell that led to Michael
Fisher's front door. He saw that the security gate, which had
always been locked in place on his previous visits, was now
broken and hanging open. He stomped up the stairs, allowing
himself the pleasure of making each step vibrate under his
solid frame.

That was as much satisfaction as he would get from his
visit, though. Fisher either wasn't in or – you wouldn't rule
it out – was lying low. He banged his fist on the door several
times and, for no reason except that it made him feel better,
swung a size fourteen boot at it too, once and then a second
and third time. After muttering a short description of Michael
Fisher's character to himself he cursed again more loudly and
went heavily back down the stairs and on his way.

He planned on coming back soon.

Henry Dunne slipped his key into the front door. It fit. He had
joked to his wife, Patsy, a while ago that this was the only way
that he knew that it was still his home. The joke didn't sound
very funny; Patsy didn't laugh, and neither did he.

Besides a border terrier that barely recognized him, the other
inhabitants were the two children that even in these more plural-
istic times were typical for the family of a senior police officer.
In his case, they were teenagers who'd grown up largely without
him, together with a wife who no longer seemed to be trying
to hide her drinking.

He'd had an ugly scene with Patsy the night before and, if
he was honest, his decision to take the air in St James's Park
was partly aimed at putting off having to see her again. It had
centred, not for the first time, on their daughter Chloe, who
at sixteen was combining his determination and single-
mindedness with the self-destructive tendencies of her mother.

Chloe had started hanging round with a guy called Goldie
who any father, even one with less experience of the bad

things in life than Dunne, might take against; he was several years older than her, with a large gold earring and a tattoo of a smiley face on one arm that he occasionally forgot to cover when visiting her at home.

For reasons that Dunne thought might include deliberately annoying him, his wife seemed to get on famously with Goldie. He had tried to discuss his concerns with her after they'd had dinner together, but it ended in an argument; everything seemed to, nowadays. 'For God's sake, Chloe's only sixteen, Patsy! I've checked his record – he's called Keith, by the way, not Goldie—'

'You've been running checks on your own daughter's boyfriend? What century do you think you're living in, Henry? Or are we all supposed to call you "Chief Super" at home now?'

'I'm just trying to protect the girl, Patsy,' he protested. 'The boy's clean, I'll give him that, but—'

'But what? But he wants to have sex with your little girl, and you don't want anyone to have her if you can't? Is that your problem, *Daddy*?'

'Patsy! For Christ's sake, think about what you're saying! Where do you get this filth from? Are you drunk? I almost hope you are, this time!'

'It's not filth, it's a well known psychological phenomenon. You seem to have plenty of spare time these days, so look it up. The reverse Electra complex, that's what they call it. And if you think I could get drunk on one little bottle of wine, where've you been living for the last few years?'

That was how their last conversation had ended and he wasn't particularly looking forward to their next. As he pushed the door open Patsy came down the stairs and hurried towards him. She looked worried.

'Where have you been, Henry? I've been trying to get you! Your mobile's switched off and Mick said that he didn't know where to find you.'

'What is it? Is something up with Chloe?'

'Chloe? She's fine, I told you she is. It's Mattie. You know that he went on that demonstration about the war in Iraq?' Dunne didn't, or had forgotten if he did, but nodded anyway. 'They say that he was spray-painting an anti-war slogan. Penny called me to tell me, a couple of hours ago.'

'Penny? Penny Logan? What's it got to do with her?'

'Think, Henry. You know that Jack Logan's in charge of Orange Street nick now, in Westminster. That's where they've taken Mattie.'

'Well, if Mattie's done something stupid they'll slap his wrist and that'll be the end of it. What do you want me to do, pick him up from the station?'

'Henry! This is your family, *think* please! I told you that he has to have a clean record to get his place at medical school. Mattie's worked so hard for that, for years now – he'll be devastated if he loses it. Penny understood; she said that Jack can just caution him, and then it won't show up on the criminal records check. She said that all you have to do is call Jack, and he'll sort it.'

Dunne looked past his wife at the ornate banister rail, all twists and curls, one of the original features of his Edwardian house that an estate agent would love so much. Some years ago Patsy and he had painted it together. It had yellowed now and bare wood was showing through in places where the paint had been chipped.

'Henry! This time, you *are* going to put your family first. Aren't you?'

If only, Glasby was thinking. Counterfactuals, they called them. If only she hadn't agreed to go to dinner with Mick Doherty or he hadn't behaved the way he did; if only she had waited until she had calmed down a bit instead of calling John right away afterwards. And if only he hadn't reacted, and she hadn't reacted . . . Then she would have been able to call Redgrave and as well as giving her his advice, which was always good, he would have helped her feel calm and self-confident, ready and able to enlist the support from Ellington that she needed.

She found herself looking in the direction of her mobile phone, as if daring herself to call him. And have to swallow her pride, she told herself. No, she was going to have to pull this off by herself.

Her phone rang. It wasn't Redgrave, but the next best thing: Bill Davenport.

His name was showing on the screen but when Glasby spoke there was no answer. She was just about to put the phone down, thinking that Davenport had dialled her number by mistake when she heard something. It sounded like Bill's voice, but it was so faint that she couldn't hear what he was saying.

'Bill? Can you speak up please? Bill?'

'Ditch . . .'

'Bill? Are you OK? Did you say something about a ditch?'

'Ditch,' he said again. 'Accident, my head . . . Ditchling, near a place called Ditchling. Ambulance, I need the ambulance. I think I'm badly hurt.'

'I remember that ruddy bike,' said Mark Ellington. Glasby was back in his office again, grateful at least that the Leer hadn't been called into the conversation this time. 'Bill wanted it as part of his retirement presentation, and then he insisted on riding it around the whole damned ballroom. It wasn't really quite the thing, if we're being honest. So what's he done, taken a tumble and come off it?'

'He was still a bit woozy when I spoke to him at the hospital, but from what I can gather, he seems to have been out on the South Downs, and he swerved to avoid something and hit his head on a rock as he fell off. They're keeping him overnight with concussion.'

'Well, I suppose that's what comes of charging around like a schoolboy at his age.' Then, perhaps realizing that this sounded more unsympathetic than he intended, Ellington added, 'Poor old Bill. I'll have Janet organize some flowers, if you wouldn't mind giving her the details. Now, that wasn't why you came to see me, was it?'

Here goes, said Glasby to herself. All she had to do was play Ellington, just like Bill told her.

He was predictably unimpressed. 'Alison, in my job it's necessary not only to consider substance, but also process. In this organization we have processes, policies in fact.' Glasby groaned inwardly while doing her best to look attentive, concerned and eager to learn from her editor.

'Now, first we have the issue of your, um, unauthorized, or at least unexpected, presence.'

'Is there a policy against that, coming into the office on my holiday, Mark?'

Ellington was starting to look irritated. 'Well, furthermore, there's also your discussion with Constance.'

Jonathan Constance was the *Herald*'s lawyer. His main function was to keep the paper and its journalists on the right side of the many laws to which they were subject. A former barrister with soft, rather appealing eyes and a ready smile, he was usually helpful, especially to Glasby, towards whom he seemed to have something of a soft spot. This was rather more than she had a right to expect, considering the amount of trouble she had put him to of late. Like all lawyers, he had a tendency to speak in long phrases punctuated by brackets, but Glasby rather enjoyed these verbal perambulations.

She had called him earlier to see whether he thought it possible to sign a contract with Fisher that would commit the *Herald* to paying him if, and only if, he produced enough evidence to allow them to run a genuine exclusive on the teacher's death and Dunne's involvement in it. Constance had counselled her that the contract would be complex. Issues would need to be covered such as whether Fisher's evidence had been legitimately obtained and who decided whether it was strong enough, as well as the usual shut-out clauses to prevent him from talking to another newspaper.

Glasby had decided not to trouble Ellington with these details for the moment, preferring just to give him the impression that the legal position was generally positive.

'The correct processes, as I say, are a fundamental prerequisite of . . . What I mean is, it's very clear, that any new instructions for Constance are supposed to come through me first. If you had any idea what these fellows cost, you would understand.'

'But I thought that Jonathan was on the staff, Mark? Surely we don't pay him by the hour, do we?'

Ellington wasn't looking any happier. 'That's not the point, Alison.' He sighed, and then, pleased with the effect, sighed again a bit more loudly.

'If by any chance, later in your career, I mean—' He stopped, looked at her without especially seeming to like what he saw, and started again. 'If you imagine yourself, one day, in a position of responsibility on a newspaper – not necessarily this one, of course – you would understand that we have to balance up costs, priorities, and our duties, to our owners I mean, and of course to the readers. And . . .'

'Isn't one of our duties to carry original stories and investigative work?'

'Yes, originality, entertainment and cost effectiveness. Now' – his face brightened and for the first time Glasby felt a pang of optimism – 'has Thomas Lear explained to you the lead that Jack Daniels is working on?'

Glasby felt the temperature soar. What the hell did Daniels have to do with anything? She wasn't sure that she could trust herself to speak, but managed a muttered 'No.'

Ellington looked surprised. 'No? That's strange, because I specifically asked him to get you up to speed before you and I met. Well, Jack can brief you himself. He's had a tip – from one of our boys in blue, you know, out of the back door of the police station – that Senty Mayback's son is in trouble. Somehow he's got himself involved with illegal substances. Drugs, in fact. The boy has just finished Uni, and it seems that he's been picked up getting these *things* imported into the country for him. Jack's done awfully well, he's got himself in tight with Senty's publicist . . .'

Senty Mayback had been a game show host and all-round TV entertainer for as long as Glasby could remember and more, so Glasby could understand the news value of anything that concerned his family. It was the sort of story she despised, and typical of Daniels to latch on to; trivial, eye-catching and . . .

'Are you following me, Alison?' She snapped back to attention. 'You can put together a backgrounder, the curse of drugs today, how their pull reaches even the best families, some statistics, you know what I mean. You're jolly good at those sort of things.'

Her blood temperature hit boiling point. 'Mark, you're not saying that all I'm good for is doing Jack Daniels' research for him? I've brought more heavyweight stories to this newspaper in the last year than he will in his whole bloody career!' She stopped, suddenly horribly aware that this wasn't how Davenport would have been 'playing' Ellington.

It was too late. He looked furious. 'Alison! You are a professional like all of us, and if you want to remain here you need to play the part that management assigns to you. I have no idea why Thomas hasn't already made that clear to you, and I intend to find out. I want you on the Senty Mayback story now. It's totally under wraps at this stage – Jack, Thomas, you and I are the only people in the know.'

His face softened, just a little, and his voice dropped. 'And in the meantime, you can keep talking to this Fisher' – he wrinkled his nose, as if the man's name somehow smelled bad – 'and see what you can find to corroborate his tales. Then go back to Thomas – no, better make that me – and until you've done that, we can't agree to pay him at all.'

As if that wasn't enough, he had the final word as she was on her way out of his office and off to become Jack Daniels' assistant. 'Alison.'

She turned, hopeful that she might be getting a reprieve.

'I don't want to see anything in the paper about Henry Dunne and Longhammer, unless I have specifically approved it. Is that clear?'

It was as clear as a glass of white vinegar, and to Glasby it tasted just as sour.

# SMS

*In a big cup steve. Feel jazz, wont get heroic!*
*Will in good room, he can. Lips.*
*In a big bus queue. Feel lazy, wont get hernia!*
*Will be home soon, if can. Kiss.*

*From the notebook of Michael Fisher*

# Six

In the office the next morning at a little before eight thirty as usual, Glasby spent the time while she was waiting for Daniels to arrive by looking up statistics on drugs finds. Even for the factually-inclined Glasby the pleasure of this wore off rather quickly, so she amused herself by reading up on Senty Mayback – 'the doyen of Irish entertainers', as one breathless article dubbed him, which rather put Bono in the shade, not to mention Sir Terry Wogan, Sir Bob Geldof and the whole of Boyzone.

The most recent article, 'Senty's Golden Fifty Years on TV', referred to him as 'Ireland's first eight-figure television star' which even if it meant Euros not pounds (it came from an Irish newspaper) suggested a salary which would probably cover, in these austere times for the newspaper industry, the *Herald*'s entire annual wage bill.

As for Senty's private life, she couldn't discover much, except for a progression of wives (Glasby found pictures of four), the dimensions of whose breasts seemed to increase as their age decreased. The latest one looked about twenty and a fair chunk of the entertainer's salary must have gone on the bejewelled dress she was pictured in, not to mention the two balloon-like objects on her chest that were fighting their way out of it.

There didn't seem to be any references at all to a son, for whom Glasby was beginning to feel a little sorry. No doubt Mr Journalism Daniels would know all about him, anyway, and would equally certainly be happy to show off to her every scrap of knowledge that he had.

Given the lecture she had received from Ellington the day before, she didn't have much choice but to work with Daniels – and, she told herself, she would do a damned good job of it too. But she wasn't expecting to enjoy it much.

'What's that look for, Ali?' enquired Mike Marshall, whose easy-going attitude to the job Glasby sometimes wished she could emulate. He was one of those people whose character exactly matched his appearance; blond, freckled, and open-faced with a quick (if occasionally pointed) sense of humour and generally a good word to say about everyone.

'Did you hear the one about the horse that went in to a bar, and the barman asked—'

'"Why the long face?" You tell me that one every time you think I'm in a bad mood, remember? Where do you get them from, Christmas crackers?'

'You should know better than to ask a journalist to reveal his sources. How about this: a man walks into a bar with a cabbage on his head, and . . .' – then, seeing his audience's expression, Marshall thought better of it.

'So you've come back in to work with us again, anyway, Ali? I thought that you were supposed to have been sent to the salt mines – I mean, on a well-deserved holiday?'

'Oh,' replied Glasby, vaguely, 'Ellington had one or two projects that he needed me on, you know. Do you know where Jack is, anyway?'

'Jack? Off buttering up Senty Mayback and his agent, I think. I saw him yesterday evening, he said that he'd asked Ellington for you to help him out. I guess that's one of your projects, is it? Jack's exclusive, with Senty's son?'

Glasby was surprised. 'Ellington told me that no one except him and the Leer knew about the Mayback story, Mike. Did Jack tell you?'

Marshall looked a bit embarrassed. 'Well, Jack does share some things with me, you know, because he knows I can keep my mouth shut.'

'You've never told me that before, Mike. I didn't know that you and Jack were so tight these days.'

'Well, that's the point, that he can tell me things in confidence. The same as you do. And I don't go gossiping about it. I only mentioned the Mayback thing to you now because he said that you'd be in on it. He was really keen to get you, you know.'

Glasby wasn't sure whether to be pleased or angry about this piece of news. She had assumed that Ellington had assigned her to work with Jack, not that he had specifically requested her assistance. The way things had been going for her, recognition of any kind was welcome – although it certainly came at a price, if it meant being valued only as a useful assistant to Jack.

She also was unsettled by the news that Mike and Jack shared confidences that she was not privy to. Mike was as much of a friend as she had in the office, and other than Davenport (and Redgrave, who she really needed to get in the habit of forgetting about) he was the only person whom she could really trust to discuss her all too frequent concerns with.

Diplomatically, Marshall changed the subject. 'Did I tell you that I've found a new ghosting job? I'm doing another autobiography, a cricketer this time.' He had a Brazilian wife and twin boys to support and was moonlighting wherever he could to add to his salary. As usual, Glasby warmed to him the more they spoke. He really was a decent guy. Maybe if she could be more like him, life might be a bit easier for her.

From what she could gather Jack wouldn't be in until the afternoon, so Glasby decided to pursue what leads she could on Michael Fisher's story. She reached Roger Bushell, the organizer of the school reunion whose details Fisher had given her.

'I'm working on a piece about Richard Bedingfield,' she extemporized, 'and I want to understand some more about school life at Burstone, and what it all meant to him. How it built his character, and so on.'

This was the best cover story she had managed to come up with. Luckily Mr Bushell seemed to swallow it.

'Well, naturally, as President of the BOBs – that's Burstone Old Boys, naturally – I should be delighted to assist you in your researches. Where did you say you were based? I'm in the City, of course.'

Despite the fact that their offices were nearby, Mr Bushell insisted on meeting at his club in St James, which was miles across town for them both. Glasby booked herself a taxi on the *Herald*'s account, vaguely remembering but deciding to ignore a missive from Ellington some time ago about how such things were supposed to be authorized.

There seemed to be some sort of trouble in Parliament Square, something to do with the war from the look of it,

which jammed the traffic solid, so she got out next to Big
Ben and walked for ten minutes or so before arriving at a
large imposing doorway at the top of an equally impressive
flight of stairs, where an embossed sign announced 'The
Independent Club'.

The doorman, if that was a good enough word for such a
magnificently liveried creature, greeted her with frosty civility.
'We don't have a dress code for, ah, *lady* guests, naturally,'
he told her, sounding very much as if he wished that they did,
so that she could fail it. Glasby was wearing a pair of her
better chinos and a perfectly respectable top, although in retro-
spect she thought that her rather scruffy training shoes might
have let her outfit down a little.

She was ushered into a small room at the side of a wide
polished wood staircase, marked 'Ladies' Waiting Room'. In
it were four wing-backed chairs, a portrait of Her Majesty the
Queen circa 1970, and an oval table fashioned from walnut
and bearing copies, naturally, of *The Lady* magazine. Not
needing advice on how to run a successful shooting weekend
or how best to vet potential domestic servants, Glasby decided
that these were not for her.

Eventually Mr Bushell appeared, turning out to be one of
those people who look nothing like they sound on the phone.
Underneath his thick red hair he had an almost perfectly
round face and a large frame that seemed somehow not fully
developed. He looked like a fourteen-year-old, Glasby decided,
as if that had been his golden period and he had managed to
desist from further mental or physical growth at that point.

He stood aside politely to let her leave the waiting room
and she started towards the stairs, until she felt a polite tug
at her sleeve. 'The ladies' stairs are this way,' Bushell told
her, indicating a door on their left. 'Ladies are allowed in the
dining room for luncheon but not on the main staircase, except
on Her Majesty's birthday. Or in the library, naturally.'

'You don't have any women members, then?' asked Glasby,
beginning to feel as if she'd wandered into a comedy sketch.

'Oh no, the Independent doesn't admit *lady* members,'
said Bushell (for whom the 'w' word was obviously a little
too modern). 'It's for public-school men only, you see. The
steak and kidney pudding is top notch; I do thoroughly
recommend it.'

Not without a certain amount of effort, Glasby managed to steer her host on to the matter at hand. 'Poor old Bedbug,' he told her. 'Bedbug, you see, was Bedingfield's nickname, naturally.'

'Naturally,' Glasby replied, without realizing that she was echoing him; it must have been catching.

He had printed out for her a list of Burstone Old Boys members, with Dunne and Bedingfield's year highlighted for her, and also a register of attendees of the last reunion. It started: 'Allington Major, Allington Minor' (who Glasby supposed might well be elderly gentlemen but who would for ever be referred to like this in the strange world of Mr Bushell and his BOBs), and included both Dunne and Fisher, just as he had told her. Michael Fisher might have all sorts of ulterior reasons for attending the reunion, but what Henry Dunne had been doing there Glasby couldn't imagine. He absolutely did not seem the type.

She noticed another name on the list. 'Is the "Dickson" here anything to do with the teacher . . . ?' she hazarded, not wanting to reveal any particular interest in the games master's death.

'Oh, you *have* been thorough in your research,' Bushell said, beaming at her, apparently delighted at her knowledge of Burstone School history. 'Yes, that's old Sicko, Thicko Dickson's son. It was a pleasant surprise to see him, as a matter of fact. Gary Dickson is one of the few who stayed on in the town. He's quite the bigwig now, you know, leader of the District Council, which is frightfully important locally. He left Burstone at sixteen. It was a crying shame about his father. He was a military man as well, you know, like poor old Bedbug. *Dulce et decorum est, pro patria mori*, you know.'

Glasby nodded, not entirely sure what he was on about. Having got what she needed she left as soon as decently possible. Down the ladies' stairs, naturally.

'Great to have you on my team, Ali,' Jack Daniels met her with. There was a time when he dressed in sub-Lear mode, loud Prince of Wales checks and golfing loafers, but this didn't seem to be tasteless enough for him these days. He had on a black jacket with a shiny black leopard-skin pattern, matched (if that was the word) with a salmon-coloured shirt and a black-and-white stripy tie. He had taken to wearing his hair heavily gelled back, like the compere of a seaside review.

Not trusting herself to give a civil reply (*his* team, indeed!) Glasby was silent.

Daniels seemed to take that as encouragement. 'This is going to be H.U.G.E.!' he announced, loudly enough to make heads turn around them. Having achieved the desired effect he hissed at her, 'Let's go into the office. Need to know, you understand. Our eyes only.'

Daniels turned out to have appropriated as his own a small conference room next to Lear's corner office. Having accepted his gracious invitation to sit, Glasby gritted her teeth hard enough to hurt while he regaled her with his own brilliance.

'So Nemo' – this, Glasby gathered, was Senty Mayback's equally exotically named agent – 'said to me, "Jackie" – that's what I'm known as by the way, not Jack any more – "if it was anyone else we'd be asking for the earth on this one. But as it's you . . ."'

Flattery, Glasby thought, clearly worked a treat on 'Jackie'. No matter how obvious it was.

Something of this must have shown on her face because Daniels abruptly stopped what he was saying. 'Look, Ali, I know that this isn't your world. But this is a real coup and I'll make sure that you get a piece of it. What I need from you is some back-up stuff, something that'll show young Ryan's little postal escapade in its true context.'

'What exactly did young Ryan's escapade consist of?' Glasby asked.

'Well, they always say that Senty's the shrewdest man in showbiz,' said Daniels, 'and some of it has obviously rubbed off on Ryan. It was quite a smart little gig he had going. What he did, was to get some stuff posted to him from a mate in Amsterdam – nothing hard, you know, just stuff – and he had it sent under a false name, to a house where some other mates of his used to live. This old Paki couple had just moved in' – he glanced at his notes, which were written in purple ink – 'Mr and Mrs Gunarathna.'

'Isn't Gunarathna a Sri Lankan name?' Glasby interrupted. 'I don't think that you should be calling them "Paki", anyway.'

'Whatever,' said Daniels, impatiently. 'That's how Nemo described them. But you're the details girl, so I expect you're right. Anyway, so he went round there, introduced himself under the false name, said he used to live in the house and told them that he might get the odd parcel delivered from a mate that didn't know he'd moved, and would they hold them for him. Then he turned up once a week or so to pick his packages up.'

'Brilliant. And what was this stuff that he was importing?'

'Oh, ecstasy, and some old-fashioned LSD, and a bit of coke I think. Like I said, nothing hard.'

'Compared, say, with heroin laced with rat poison, I suppose you're right. And not much harm in it, bar the occasional accidental death and an innocent elderly couple getting mixed up with the police. How did he get caught?'

'One of the packets was split open when it arrived at the' – he stopped and gave Glasby a look – 'OK, *Asians'* house. The old couple showed it to their son, who's a doctor, and he called the police. After that, they just kept a watch on the house, and when Ryan turned up they nabbed him.' Daniels hastened on before Glasby could say anything more. 'So what you could do now, is to come up with some overall numbers for ecstasy in the UK – you know, put it all in context. You can see the line that Nemo will want us to play: a minor youthful transgression, no harm done, no tears need be shed, that sort of thing.'

'I'm sure he will,' replied Glasby. 'But last time I looked, Senty Mayback's agent didn't run the editorial line of this newspaper. I'll check, but I think about ten kids died from ecstasy or cocaine in this country last year. Do you want me to estimate the chances that Ryan Mayback will be responsible for the next one?'

'Look, Ali, get real,' Daniels threw back at her. 'Ellington is gagging for this exclusive, and the way the story gets spun is just part of the price. Get it?'

'What does Thomas say?'

'The Leer?' Daniels was surprised. 'So far as I know, he hasn't said anything. I don't know what it is with him, but have you not noticed that he seems a bit distant nowadays? Go and ask him, if you want. I'm sure he'll back me up, but please yourself. Oh, and I'll need your stuff by the end of tomorrow.'

\*     \*     \*

Glasby had arranged to see Davenport that evening. He had been released from hospital and was back for recuperation in his London home, a beautiful little Victorian terraced house on the Merceaux Estate in Kennington.

He had told her where the spare key was so she could let herself in. You might suppose, she thought, that someone with a lifetime's experience of crime would come up with somewhere better than 'under the mat' for where to keep it.

She pushed open the black front door, bearing a bunch of flowers, to be met by Lady Penelope and Lord Jim, Davenport's cats who must have made the journey up from the South Downs with him. 'Is that you, Ali?' he shouted. 'Come on up!'

Standing at the foot of the stairs Glasby glanced into Davenport's sitting room. Cardboard boxes were stacked up in it, papers bulging from a few of them. Glasby thought that she recognized some of the items from his old office at the *Herald*, when the contents of what he liked to refer to as his 'filing system' had led her into danger and ultimately to the solution of a decades-old mystery.

If only the same could be true now. This time, she really was on her own. She heard Davenport call again, and hastened up to find the invalid.

He was propped up on several pillows, wearing slightly incongruous candy-striped pyjamas. A large bandage was wrapped around his head. For a man stuck in bed on doctors' orders, he seemed cheerful enough.

A cabinet next to the bed held six or eight books which were folded around each other as if several were being read simultaneously. Next to them was a glass containing an amber-coloured liquid; Glasby wondered if it was whisky.

'So what happened, Bill?'

'It was one of those blasted hang-gliders,' he said, pretending to be indignant but from the sparkle in his eyes clearly seeing the funny side of his predicament. 'I was bowling along the South Downs Way, near Ditchling – the suspension over the front wheel is terrific you know – and then before I knew it these feet appeared out of nowhere, heading straight for my bonce. I swerved and managed to miss him, but took a tumble from there. They're a menace, those people, a blasted menace. If God had meant us to fly, he'd have told us to take our ruddy boots off first!'

'And if God had meant us to whiz along on two wheels, maybe he would have told us to wear a helmet – like the one I bought for you?' suggested Glasby.

'Yes, well, it was a hot day . . .' protested Davenport, sheepishly.

Glasby took pity on him. 'You're being well looked after, anyway?' she asked.

'Oh yes, the neighbours here are very helpful and kind,' he told her. 'There's Betty, and Lisbeth, and Elspeth . . .' Glasby noticed that all of his kind helpers seemed to be female and wondered if Davenport had them competing for his affections.

'How's your Henry Dunne mystery going along?' he asked her.

'Not too well right now. Ellington's all taken up with a big celebrity story which the *Herald*'s hoping to get. All he's let me do is to corroborate what Fisher told me. So far, it stacks up. Dunne and Fisher both were at the school reunion, just as Fisher claimed. And the man who organized the event has given me contact details for the other attendees, and a number for Bedingfield's widow, so I can see what I can get from her.'

'But without Fisher's so-called evidence, it doesn't amount to much, does it?' said Davenport. 'The thing is, Ali, are you not a bit worried about your own relationships here? I mean, Dunne himself, and your source on Longhammer whoever he is, and of course there's your friend John Redgrave? I mean, none of them are going to be too happy if what you're getting involved with is an attempt to smear Dunne, are they?'

Glasby protested. 'Don't you remember that TV campaign the *Herald* ran? "In no one's pocket, on everyone's table"? Well, if we are supposed to be the home of independent thinking and reporting without concern for powerful interests, surely that includes the police, Henry Dunne and everyone else. And John Redgrave,' she added quickly, not wanting to discuss the state of her private life, or the lack of it, with Davenport.

Davenport smiled benignly at her. 'As usual, Alison, you're right. Any good journalist should be beholden to no one. But at the end of it, a newspaper is about two things: inches and pennies. Column inches, and one pound ten, or whatever it is they're charging for it now. Your job is to fill the inches up with stuff that'll bring the pennies in, and if you're going to carry on doing that, you need to keep your relationships in place and in shape. Just be very careful what you're getting yourself involved in, that's all. Softly, softly, that's the watchword.'

So Mark Ellington, and Bill Davenport both wanted to tell her the same thing. Glasby decided that it must be time to change the subject.

'So you've all these women looking after you then, Bill?'

He grinned rather wolfishly from underneath the bandage around his forehead. 'Well, there are certain compensations in being a gentleman of leisure, I suppose. I don't ask for help, you understand. Betty absolutely insisted on bringing the cats and me back up to London, for example. You know what people are like; sometimes they just won't take no for an answer.'

'You don't ask . . . but you allow one of your ladies to offer, hmm?'

'They're not "my ladies",' he protested, but a bit feebly. 'They are just good neighbours, that's all. It's one of the nicer things about the Merceaux Estate, you know. We've all known each other for a long time.'

'Aren't any of them married?' Glasby asked, wondering what the husbands might feel about having Davenport in their midst.

'Oh, well that depends on who you mean, of course. Lisbeth was widowed when she was young, and Betty's husband passed away a couple of years ago too. Elspeth was never married . . .'

'And neither were you,' Glasby interrupted. 'Don't you ever think that you might be happier with one special person, instead of having all these unattached ladies hanging round you?'

Davenport thought for a moment, the smile fading from his face.

'The job. It was the job, Alison. You know, a woman wants to feel that she's the most important thing in your life, but when you're on a story nothing else matters, it takes every-thing you've got . . .'

He looked at Glasby, the story of her break-up with Redgrave written on her face, a deep sense of loneliness hanging unspoken between them.

The doorbell rang – 'That'll be Lisbeth,' said Davenport happily. 'Dinner time!'

Realizing that she had forgotten to replace the spare key, Glasby rushed to open the door, to be faced by a fierce-looking lady of a certain age, rather heavily made-up and smelling strongly of perfume. She was carrying a wicker picnic basket which presumably contained Davenport's dinner.

'I suppose you didn't think to put the door key back,' was Lisbeth's opening shot. 'Are you this Alison girl he mentioned? I can't think why Bill would have phoned for you, when what he needed was an ambulance.'

For some reason Glasby felt it necessary to explain. 'I think he must have had my number saved as a speed dial, and just got it mixed up with an emergency call.'

Lisbeth didn't look any more impressed by this.

'Come and see the beautiful flowers young Alison has brought me,' shouted Bill. Catching another look from Lisbeth, Glasby decided that it was time to leave.

It was a bit late by the time she got home. Typically for Glasby, she thought about food only when she noticed that she was hungry. By this time it was after ten. The Indian shop downstairs would be shut, and she couldn't be bothered to drive up to the twenty-four-hour supermarket, a mile or so away.

That left her with a choice of the chip shop just along the road or baked beans on toast. She opted for the latter and had spooned the baked beans into a bowl and put the bowl inside the microwave before she discovered that the packet of bread which had been sitting on the work surface in her kitchen for the last week or so had now gone mouldy. At the bottom of the freezer compartment she found an elderly pita bread, half buried in the ice like an arctic explorer who had been overwhelmed by the elements. It was dry, but just about still edible.

After a brief and not very satisfying dinner, Glasby called Michael Fisher, assuming that he was not a man who kept office hours.

'I've talked to Roger Bushell about the Burstone Old Boys' reunion that you mentioned, the one which Henry Dunne attended,' she told him. 'There are a couple of things I'd like to ask you about it.'

He sounded panic stricken. 'Not on an open phone line!

They'll be listening in. That name you just mentioned, I never said it to you, never!' The man was positively squeaking. She could hear someone say something in the background, a girl with a foreign accent, but she couldn't make out what.

'What are you scared of, Michael?' Glasby asked. 'I need to understand.' But he had cut her off.

George Pincher was talking to his employer. 'Our man Mr Fisher is definitely up to something, sir. He's in motion now. It looks like he could be seeing that young tart again. We're on him. And this time we'll stay on him, don't you worry about that.'

Glasby rode up in the elevator at a little after eight fifteen the next day. It was empty at that hour, as were the offices and desks around hers, except for one: the Leer's. Glasby was surprised. She thought about going to see him to raise her concerns about the way that Daniels was handling the Mayback drugs story, but decided that her position would be stronger if she put some work in on the story beforehand. First she would complete her research on overall drugs imports into the UK, and then she intended to look for particular stories of people damaged by drugs of the type Ryan Mayback had been trafficking in.

Deep in her research as she was, she only gradually became aware of the Leer's voice. She heard him say 'Mark' a couple of times, so presumably he was talking to Ellington. Then all of a sudden he was shouting, sounding not just angry but cornered, desperate, almost at bay. 'But you've got Jack and Alison running around all over the place on news stories. I'm a features man, not news! How the hell do you expect me to keep track of them? It's not fair, Mark, *it is not on!*'

There was a slam as the receiver went down and then just the sound of Lear's breathing, easily loud enough for her to hear from across the corridor. Glasby had no idea what to do. She decided that the best thing was to say nothing, to Lear or anyone else. She went back to her work on use of illegal drugs.

The office gradually filled up. Mike Marshall arrived, shortly followed by Hetal Singh, well groomed and neatly turned out as usual in tailored trouser suit and heels, which made her quite a contrast with Marshall and Glasby herself.

A few minutes later Hetal came over to Glasby's desk. She had a worried expression on her face. 'Hi,' said Glasby, looking up from a particularly depressing tale of a girl who had died from dehydration after taking ecstasy for the first time at her eighteenth birthday party.

'May I interrupt you, please, Alison?' Hetal hadn't yet got the hang of the level of informality that prevailed in the lower reaches at least of journalistic life. 'I'm very sorry to bother you, but I was wondering if you had any assignments which I could help you with.'

Glasby had the impression – not least from the Leer's outburst earlier – that the whole group was under pressure. 'Hasn't Thomas given you anything to do? Why don't you ask him, if not?'

Hetal looked even more ill at ease. 'I did try to speak to him, but his door was closed, and he sort of, well, waved me away. I don't think he wants to be interrupted.'

Surprised, but not altogether displeased, Glasby explained what she needed to accomplish and how, and they split up the material that she was working through between them. The quicker she got the Mayback project done, the sooner she could get her teeth back into Michael Fisher, Henry Dunne and Longhammer.

They were back in their familiar places, Doherty leant against the wall, Dunne slumped behind his desk. The door, of course, was closed.

'It's not as if he's a bad kid, Mick. I don't know if I ever told you, but my parents educated me at a very posh place, a pukka public school, actually.'

Doherty responded with a neutral grunt. An increasingly successful graduate-entry scheme was changing the traditionally working-class social make-up of the police service, but very slowly. Dunne's relatively privileged origins were common knowledge around the canteen and indeed were held against him by many, but Doherty didn't see the need to go into this with him.

'I probably could have got Mattie into Burstone. But I always thought that the boy had to make his own way. And that's what he's done, fair play to him. Until this . . .'

'It's not that tough a nut to crack, is it boss? Jack Logan's a straight shooter, and he's pretty much served it up for you on a plate. Or his missus has, any rate.' He smiled, a crooked affair that showed up a hole where a couple of teeth should have been. 'It's the wives that run this place, that's what the boys say. Your missus and his have sorted it already, and all you've got to do is show him a bit of respect.'

'You mean acknowledge that I owe him one, don't you?'

Doherty nodded.

'So next time there's some little bit of bending of the rules to be done, it'll be me who will be doing it. No!'

Dunne was animated now, standing and waving a finger at his deputy. 'We don't work like that. Some sort of "Godsquad" we'd be if we did!'

To his surprise, the normally quietly spoken Doherty replied every bit as vehemently: 'You don't get it, Henry. You've got to look out for numero uno. You've just got to. No one else is going to, not in this world. Definitely not in the job, and that's a fact.'

# Spam

*To thee is not slept friend? Thee look at a lap of the sun, facing by gate in an unknown world of sex? Thee all in dreams of the fine goddess. By love, which one will reduce thee from mind. I shall help thee to forget about all. I shall enter thee in a world love. Thee will fly in clouds of beatificate all night, having made her for itself by most indelible. You see in this life all in thy hands and I shall be only guiding star on to unknown back streets.*

From the notebook of Michael Fisher

# Seven

Michael Fisher's sitting room wasn't tidy any more. Books were scattered all over the flat, some with the spines torn open. An oak cupboard was splintered in places, one of the doors ripped clean off, the other hanging drunkenly on a single remaining hinge. Papers were strewn around, mixed in places with shards broken from a large mirror, the frame of which was smashed into pieces.

In the middle of all this lay the owner of these objects, on his back, with an angry expression on his face, as if objecting to the chaos that he now found himself surrounded by. An ugly bruise covered part of the left side of his face and his cheekbone may well have been broken.

This wasn't going to inconvenience him at all, however. The back of Michael Fisher's skull was the worst mess of all. Someone had smashed it into so many pieces that the pathologist would later determine that it was not practical to try to identify them all.

George Pincher was on the telephone to his employer again.

'So I think that you could say that something went bump in the night for our Mr Fisher. Yes, no worries, sir, my men are pros. They're well away.'

Glasby had more or less given up trying to persuade herself to phone Redgrave, and no longer had any real hope that he was planning to call her. When he did, it was not so much a surprise, as a shock.

'This is John Redgrave,' he began, as if she might not have realized.

'I know, John. I can see it's your number. Why are you sounding so formal? Anyway, how have you been?'

'Alison, this isn't a personal call. I'm calling you about a police matter.'

Without realizing it, Glasby had half risen from her chair when she got his call. Now she sat back down again, a feeling that something awful had happened coming over her.

'What is it, John? Nothing's happened to Bill, has it? Or Mum and Dad?'

His voice was just as expressionless as before. 'It concerns a man called Michael Fisher. Do you know him?'

Different scenarios flashed through her mind. Had Fisher gone crazy and attacked Henry Dunne? Or more likely, he had been caught out in some sordid blackmail scheme. Was he trying to implicate her in some way? And if so, what did it have to do with Redgrave, whose job was . . .

'He's dead, Alison.'

'Dead?' she echoed him, foolishly, her voice going up a pitch. 'He can't be. I spoke to him last night!'

'The investigating officers found your call on his mobile phone, and traced the number back to you. Yours was the last call that he received, at just before eleven. His death is being treated as suspicious. So you understand that I need to ask you what the nature of your business was with Mr Fisher and specifically, what was said when you spoke to him last night.'

'Suspicious? How did he die?'

There was a slight pause. 'Look, Alison, in this sort of situation people like me ask questions, and people like you answer them, not the other way round. We're talking about murder here, not a newspaper story. But I'll tell you this one thing, just so you understand what we're dealing with. Michael Fisher was beaten over the head, brained is what you could call it. He suffered a very violent death. Now let's have your part of the story, please.'

A shiver started in Glasby's forehead and travelled all the way around her skull and down into her spine. She made herself breathe: in, out, in, out.

Someone was dead – not just dead, savagely murdered – and she was mixed up – no, *involved* – in it. Fisher had obviously been scared when she called him; quite possibly, he had been killed because of her call. And now, of all terrible things, she was mixed up in one of John Redgrave's murder inquiries. Worse still, she wasn't able ethically to reveal what Fisher,

her source, had said to her; only a judge could order her to do that.

Glasby did her best to sound like a seasoned professional, although it would have been easy for her to give way to tears. 'John, you know how things work as well as I do. All I can tell you is that Mr Fisher was a source of mine. I can't tell you anything more than that.'

Another pause. For the first time, he sounded more like himself, and less like a detective sergeant in the murder squad. 'Alison, I already told you, this is murder. I know that you take your work very seriously, and you know how much I respect that. But this isn't you and me, it's police work. You don't want to be in a position where you're obstructing a murder investigation – trust me on that one.'

'"Trust me," said the policeman,' said Glasby, and instantly wished that she hadn't. 'Oh, I'm sorry, John, I didn't mean that. Look, can you give me a bit of time on this please? So that I'm sure that I'm doing the right thing?'

There was no response. She tried again. 'John, I really wanted to talk to you. But not like this, for God's sake! I'll try to help you, if I can, you know I will.'

What she now recognized as his official voice had returned.

'Alison, I have to warn you. When your name came up, well, you know that you're not flavour of the month in certain parts of Scotland Yard. One train of thought was to bring you down to the station and treat you to the heavy squad. You mustn't think of this as you helping me. I persuaded people to let me make this call, to help *you*. I've done my best, and now it's up to you. If you want to get back to me, do. If not, you'll hear from the investigating team, be sure of it.'

His voice softened again. 'And until then, well, there's not too much else that we can talk about. Sorry, Alison. Look after yourself. Bye.'

Sometimes when you need a shoulder to lean on, none is in sight. Ellington, so his PA told Glasby, was in conference, whatever that meant, and was unlikely to be reachable for the rest of the day. She tried Davenport, first on his mobile, which was switched off, and then, after some hesitation in case he was having an invalid's nap, on his London home number. It just rang unanswered. Even Mike Marshall had the day off, probably to catch up on his second job writing other people's autobiographies.

Then she had a brainwave, and found the number of the Journalists' Union. 'I need some help please, on an ethical issue,' she told the switchboard operator.

She was asked for her membership number. 'I don't know what it is, sorry. I'm on the *Sunday Herald*. I'm sure I must be a member. Can you put me through to someone please?'

'Can I have your membership number?'

Feeling that she was stuck in some sort of a tape loop, Glasby tried again. 'Look, I don't have a membership number. Isn't there someone I can talk to, someone who can offer me some help?'

Apparently there was, although first she had to suffer the inevitable and, to Glasby's impatient ears, overlong, burst of on-hold music: 'New members' enquiries, is there something that I can help you with?'

'Yes please,' said Glasby, pleased to be talking to someone who showed signs of having more than one option for replies. 'I have a query about what level of assistance I need to give to police who are investigating something relevant to a story I've been working on. Is that the sort of thing which you can help me with?'

'Yes, of course. We have a unit dedicated to offering professional assistance exactly of this nature.' The woman's voice was calmly reassuring. It was exactly what Glasby needed.

'Can you put me through to them please, then?' Glasby asked.

'Yes, of course. As soon as your membership has been actioned and ratified, we'd be pleased to help. Would you like me to take you through the costs involved, and some of the major benefits which we are able to offer to our members?'

'No, that's OK.' Glasby felt that the conversation was in danger of slipping out of control again. 'Can we just get my membership dealt with now, so I can talk to your colleagues as soon as possible?'

The voice was starting to sound a bit unsure. 'Well, there are some things that I am definitely required to inform you about, the compensation fund, and of course there are the insurance elements of your membership subscription. Although I can send it all to you by post if you prefer. So long as you

get the forms back to us before the next membership ratifi-
cation committee, in three weeks, it won't cause any delay.'

'You mean my membership won't be activated for another
three weeks?' asked Glasby, on the edge of losing her temper.
'And I suppose that I can't get any advice on my police issue
until after I'm a member?'

'Oh yes,' responded the voice, sounding a little shocked
that anyone might think otherwise. 'We offer a membership
service only, not advice to the general public. You can't imagine
the legal problems that we could face otherwise.'

'Do you need any help with your legal problems?' asked
Glasby, 'Because if so, don't bother asking me!' She put the
phone down, feeling worse than when she had started the
conversation.

At last she had a brainwave, and went to see Jonathan
Constance, the *Herald*'s lawyer whose office was along the
corridor from Ellington's on twenty-seven. Constance heard
her out in silence.

'You always seem to be one of my more interesting clients,
Alison,' he told her, after a pause to gather his thoughts.

'Is that a good thing, or not?' she asked, smiling at him.

'Well, that rather depends. Let's just say that you provide
good brain food for me. Well, I think that we can keep you
out of prison this time, anyway. This Mr Fisher, as you tell
me the story, he was a source, but of course at this moment,
he's rather in the nature of an ex-source, as you might say.
Being deceased, I mean.'

Glasby agreed that this seemed logical.

'Now I don't think that I'm clear in my mind that you actually owe him any duty of confidence, based on the relatively
little that he had to say to you so far. None of it was expressed
to be off the record, or in confidence as such?'

Glasby agreed that it wasn't. She liked the way that this
seemed to be going.

'And,' Constance continued, rolling a pair of gold-rimmed
glasses between the index finger and thumb of his right hand,
'if we ever needed to (which by the way from what you know
of Mr Fisher's possible *proclivities* to underhand behaviour,
and his seeming lack of close family connections, I think is
unlikely) that is to say, if we ever needed to argue it, I think

that we could say that any duties you owed to Mr Fisher were indeed personal to him, and so would perish at precisely that point in time that marked his own sad demise. If you take my point?'

Glasby had never heard him in courtroom mode before; he was rather impressive, she thought. 'So I'm free to respond to the police's request for information, then?'

'Indeed I believe you are, yes. And as a public-spirited citizen (or should I say subject?) and a representative of a responsible organ like ours, I think that you should.'

As Glasby got up to leave, Constance indicated with a polite clearing of his throat that there was another issue that he wished to raise with her.

'Since we are both here, perhaps I can touch upon our other extant matter. "In re Fish and Chips", as we might call it.'

Seeing Glasby's blank face, he translated from legalese into English for her benefit.

'Your aggrieved policemen, I mean. I thought you might be reassured to hear that, in my view, there is little chance of a case coming to court. As I understand it, the two gentlemen in question may have a few – shall we say, questionable? – business dealings which they would not enjoy being cross-examined upon. An apology, perhaps a nominal payment to cover legal expenses, and I would see this one going away. Perhaps you can take comfort from that. And if you do, maybe you could persuade the good Mr Ellington to see it the same way – I have tried, but so far with no success at all.'

Glasby returned to her desk and was straight back on the phone to Redgrave. He picked up immediately, as if he had been waiting for her call. This time he sounded much more relaxed. She gave him the slightly edited version of events that she had decided was appropriate.

'I thought about your advice, John, and decided that I can take it. Michael Fisher approached me out of the blue so far as I know, with a cock and bull story about Henry Dunne and something he'd done when he was at school. I met Fisher once, that's all, a few days ago. I think that he might have been a bit crazy. He kept waving a black notebook at me and saying that there was all sorts of vital stuff in it, but then he wouldn't show anything to me.'

'A black notebook. OK, I'll pass that on to the investigating team. We'll see if one was found. What was he after from you – money?'

'Yes, of course. He wanted paying by the *Herald*, and I called him last night to tell him that we'd have to get a lot more information from him before that could even be considered. He didn't want to talk, and the call was just a few seconds long. He sounded very agitated, but to be honest, he was like that the time before, when I met him, as well. Like I say, I think that probably he was a bit nutty. And that's about it.'

'OK, Alison. Thanks for getting back to me,' was Redgrave's only reply. After the pressure he'd put her under when he had called her, now he sounded almost uninterested. Something didn't seem at all right to Glasby.

'John? Aren't you bothered about this any more? What's going on?'

'No, it's helpful, thanks. Actually I've been told that the boys in charge of the case are pretty much sure now that it was just a burglary, you know, a break-in gone wrong. They think that it was probably opportunistic – some junkie tried knocking on the door, Fisher answered, and the junkie would have just grabbed what he could.'

Now Glasby was getting curious. 'A burglary? What was taken?'

'I really don't have the details, Alison. It's not my case. Look, if you want to know about the Fisher case, try Paul Mallam. He's the investigating officer.'

Antennae a-twitching, Glasby did just that. Inspector Mallam wasn't available but another officer promised to have him return her call, which he duly did, a while later.

'Hello, Alison. We've met once, you were with John Redgrave, remember?' Glasby didn't remember much about him but could picture him, a tall man in his fifties who wore tinted glasses which, together with his shaved head, gave him something of an air of foreboding. He seemed friendly enough now, though.

'Of course, hi Paul. I was hoping you could fill me in on the Michael Fisher murder.'

'Well, there's not much to tell, really. The neighbours didn't hear anything, no one knew him well, you know the score. "He was a quiet man, kept himself to himself", that sort of thing. There was a security gate in the stairwell but it had been broken some time before. And his door hadn't been forced so he must have opened up, which is just the sort of stupid thing that people will do, as you know, and from then on it's all nasty. His head was beaten in, stuff all over the floor, you know the story. Some drugged-up head case, odds on.'

'So you think it was a burglar. What was taken?'

Mallam was sounding somewhat more cautious now. 'It's a bit hard to be sure, as you know, what with the mess the place is in, and him living on his own. We had one of the neighbours take a peek, but he's an old guy and didn't know the place well so he wasn't much help. But you told John Redgrave that he had some sort of notebook. I've checked, and that seems to be missing. We can't find a wallet either.'

Glasby persisted: 'I can understand the wallet, but why would a drugged-up burglar want to take his notebook?'

Mallam didn't sound particularly concerned. 'With these junkies, Alison, there's no accounting for them, as you know.'

That was as far as she got.

She remained motionless at her desk, a good thirty minutes after the call, playing it over and over in her mind. Fisher had been frightened. His enemies might or might not have been imaginary, but his death was real enough. It was natural enough for the police to want to get a quick solution to a crime as serious as this, but this Mallam seemed almost uninterested. Something just didn't feel right.

Decision made, Glasby slipped out of the office, glancing around her almost furtively. Daniels was nowhere to be seen. From the look of it Hetal was still buried in the work that Glasby had given her the day before. She didn't notice Glasby leave and neither did anyone else.

She went back down in the elevator, through the glass-walled atrium and along the wide expanse of featureless concrete which the developers had thought fitting to channel people in and out of the Tube station. Only when she got to the barrier did she remember that her travel card had expired.

She doubled back. 'I need a ticket for Euston, please, return.'

*The Camden Town Murder*
*Emily Dimmock, 29 St Paul's Road (Agar Grove),*
*1907*
*Walter Sickert, The Camden Town Nudes*
*Courtauld Gallery, 020 7872 0220*

*From the notebook of Michael Fisher*

# Eight

It was easy enough to spot Michael Fisher's front door, covered as it was in tape marked with the name and logo of the Metropolitan Police, warning anyone thinking of crossing it not to do so. The security gate in the stairwell, which was broken and hanging open, looked to have been dusted for fingerprints. Other than that there was no sign of any police activity at all.

The block of flats where Fisher had made his home seemed decent enough, barring a patch of what smelled like urine just inside the street door. There was only one other apartment next to his on the first floor. Guessing that this would belong to the neighbour who had discovered the body, Glasby first put her ear to the door and then knocked.

Nothing happened. She leant towards the door again. Unlike Fisher's, which was made from solid wood with only a small spy-hole to see through to the outside, his neighbour's door had a frosted glass window in its centre, made more secure with squares of wire built into it. Glasby peered through it as best she could, but her view through the glass was too distorted for her to make out anything more than a few blurs on the other side of the door.

It was obvious that someone was in, however, because she could hear a television which was apparently turned up very loud. Some sort of game show was taking place. Every now and again the audience burst into applause, and so did the occupant of the flat, clapping loudly even after the sound from the television had died down again.

Glasby tried again to get the neighbour's attention, this time hammering her fist against the glass hard enough to hurt her hand. She waited, and a few seconds later the noise from the television disappeared. Nothing else happened, however. No one came to the door.

Impatient by now, she beat her fist on the glass again and this time was rewarded by a shuffling sound from inside, and an annoyed sounding bellow of, 'All right then, all right then!' The shuffling noise drew closer and finally, with much turning of locks and bolts, the door opened.

'All right then, all right,' Fisher's neighbour repeated, more loudly than was necessary given that Glasby was stood less than a metre from him. 'I'm not deaf, you know! Who are you, then?'

Standing in front of her was a man who looked at least in his eighties and might have been older, bent slightly so that the top of his head was angled towards her. It was an interesting head, almost perfectly round and shiny with just the occasional wisp of white hair, and covered in freckles. On either side of it two large ears stood out, almost at right angles to the head, and at the top of the downward slope of the face Glasby could see two bushy white eyebrows.

The face tilted up towards her, causing its owner some effort from the look of it, and two bloodshot eyes looked suspiciously at her. 'Well?' the old man asked again.

Conversation was obviously going to be difficult so Glasby decided to launch straight in. 'It's about your neighbour, Michael Fisher,' she began, but didn't get any further.

'Eh? Why are you muttering to yourself? What did you say?'

'I want to talk to you about Michael Fisher,' she shouted in the direction of the nearer of the two large ears.

'First you're muttering everything to yourself and now you're shouting in my ear. If you're another of them lot, you'd better come in, hadn't you?'

Without waiting for an answer, the old man turned his back on her and shuffled down a corridor in which hung three almost identical dark woollen overcoats. Surprisingly, she found herself squeezing past a huge old black bicycle which looked as if it had been made sometime around the Second World War.

She followed him into a sitting room in which stood the television and two armchairs, one of which had been positioned no more than a metre away from the screen. He sat carefully down and gestured her towards the other with a wave of his hand.

'I already told the other officers everything, more'n once, so I don't know why they sent you as well,' he complained. Glasby decided not to dispel his impression that she was attached to the police investigation, at this stage at least.

He wasn't the easiest of interview subjects but she managed, with patience and at the risk of a sore throat from shouting at him, to evince the following. His name was Eric Whiteside, *Mr* Whiteside to her as he emphasized, and he had lived in the flat since 1951. (Everything had changed since then, and there was all sorts in the area now, not like it used to be at all, so it was no wonder he didn't get out as much as he used to.) Michael Fisher was a rum sort, he never seemed to be working, and he always had this funny look to him and odd ways, what with girls visiting him at all hours, *foreigners* (this with his face screwed up for added meaning) from the look of them.

He had seen nothing and heard nothing the night before (which given his deafness, Glasby hardly found surprising) but he had noticed that Fisher's door had been left ajar that morning. Putting his face around the door he had seen something of the wreckage that Inspector Mallam had described to her, and phoned for the police.

'I heard that he was all bashed about, with blood and everything spattered all over,' Mr Whiteside told her, with some relish. He seemed disappointed not to have witnessed the grisly sight himself and was a little peeved when she refused to add any further details of the brutality that had been visited on his neighbour.

Nonetheless, he had a theory of how Fisher had met his death: 'It'll be like on *Midsomer Murders*, it was them foreign girls!' Given what Mallam had described of the force used by the murderer this seemed unlikely to Glasby, unless Fisher had been consorting with retired weightlifters, but she promised to pass this back to the investigating officer.

Then he gave her a real surprise. 'Them two big fellers that were hanging around, were they on your detective force as well? How come they was here these last few days, and now they've gone?'

It took Glasby a bit of questioning to try to be sure that this too wasn't part of Mr Whiteside's television-fed imagination, but he was clear enough. There was a small window set at right angles to his front door which she hadn't noticed before, high up in the wall. It had been placed there to let some light into the corridor rather than to see through, but it overlooked the stairwell and Whiteside, who had obviously taken quite a strong interest in his neighbour, had positioned a wooden crate underneath. He hauled himself up on to it to demonstrate his vantage point to Glasby.

What he had seen were two men of military or police appearance who had been staking the place out, on and off, and particularly over the last few days. When Fisher left the building, they had followed him.

He even gave her a fairly good description. They were both large; one in particular was overweight with thinning dark hair and sweated a lot. The other was taller but a bit thinner, with curly brown hair. As to their age, according to Whiteside they were 'young, thirty or forty', but Glasby wasn't sure how accurate his perception would be on this point.

Having got as much as she thought she could, Glasby gave him a business card which he put in his pocket without looking at, and her thanks. He left her to show herself out. Before she had reached the front door the television was already switched back on.

Glasby walked briskly around the corner towards Euston Station, fishing in her bag for her phone. She stopped outside a run-down looking office building, paint peeling off metal window frames, improbably named Greater London House. It was distinctly decrepit but must have been in use, judging by the cigarette butts scattered around the entry.

'Is that Inspector Mallam? Paul Mallam? It's Alison Glasby here. I've just been talking to a Mr Eric Whiteside, the man who rung in the Michael Fisher murder, his next-door neighbour.'

Mallam didn't sound best pleased. 'Look, love, Johnny Redgrave told me all about you, and I know you're very thorough. But do us both a favour, don't go making something out of nothing, will you?'

If 'Johnny' had indeed briefed Mallam about Alison Glasby, he should have told him a couple of things. She did not take well to being patronized, and the more she was told not to do something, the more likely she was to press right ahead with it. A very determined look indeed came over her face.

'I'm sure that you're not taking the brutal murder of Mr Fisher as "nothing", Inspector,' she replied. 'And I am also sure that you will be following up on Mr Whiteside's description of two men of military appearance who seem to have been staking Mr Fisher out. Won't you?'

Inspector Mallam seemed to realize his error. 'No offence, Alison. Of course we'll take it all on board, but at the end of the day, what there is, that's all there is, you know how it goes. There's always someone who saw something, and then my lads look into it and it turns into a big fat nothing, know what I mean? But we'll have another word with this Mr Whiteside, all right? And if there's anything to it, we'll be on to it, quick as you like, we will.'

Glasby headed for the office, looking even more thoughtful than when she left it. As she walked back towards her desk she heard her phone ringing. Jack Daniels was walking past, resplendent in pale yellow shirt and black-and-white kipper tie. She broke into a trot and reached it just before it cut to voicemail.

It was Mr Whiteside, sounding unhappy. 'You told me that you was a copper,' he bellowed. 'I ain't talking to no journalist. I didn't see nothing and I don't know nothing. Did you hear that, did you? Don't you bother coming round with your questions again, and don't you go printing nothing what I said, or I'll have you up!'

'Mr Whiteside,' she began, but he had already hung up.

So she was back where she'd been a few hours earlier, sitting at her desk, turning it all over in her mind. Fisher had a story to tell; Fisher had been very frightened; now Fisher was dead.

The police's attitude was very strange, as well. To start off with, they were all over her, even to the point of getting Redgrave involved. It wasn't so surprising that they would want to know what Glasby's interest in Fisher had been; what was more odd was that almost immediately they seemed to have changed their minds and could hardly be bothered to investigate the murder at all.

Fisher said that he was being followed, but she hadn't really believed him. Now, from what Mr Whiteside had told her, Fisher really *was* being followed, by two heavies who had disappeared from view once he was murdered. She told the police about this, and within minutes her informant withdrew everything he had told her.

Forcing herself to consider all the possibilities, she had to admit that she might just be making something out of nothing, as Inspector Mallam had put it. But she didn't think so. Unless she was mistaken, there was no other word for it: something was very fishy.

Unlike Glasby, Jack Daniels was suffering from no doubts whatsoever.

'Since Hetal and you helped out a bit,' he offered generously, 'I thought I'd give you an advance preview. Mark will give it the final blessing in a few minutes. Read and enjoy!'

She did as bidden. Well, she read it anyway. Admittedly being forced to witness Daniels' greatest career moment so far would have been hard for Glasby to stomach had he written an exposé worthy of a double Pulitzer with bar. This piece wasn't going to win any prizes, except maybe for cynicism.

It started unpromisingly enough, under the heading 'TV Personality's Son Ensnared in Drugs Sting' – it having apparently escaped Daniels that a sting was a situation where the bad guys got caught in a trap engineered by the good guys, not as a consequence of their own stupidity.

> Britain's favourite star of the small screen and devoted family man Senty Mayback, pictured here with our own Jackie Daniels – *pictured here? Daniels was planning to get his own photo in as part of the story?* – was reeling last night as tragedy hit his son Ryan, 21.
>
> Senty fought back tears as he told of how Ryan, fresh from a degree in pan-cultural studies at De Montfort University, had apparently become caught up in what started as a student jape but which could easily have ended in tragedy.

Bubbling with disbelief, Glasby continued, as 'Jackie' really got into his stride:

> Ryan then realized that he was in way over his head. He found himself in a situation where he was the fall guy, as some immigrants from Sri Lanka, whose status in the UK as we write could not be fully ascertained, turned him in to the police. Similarly their role in the whole

conspiracy cannot yet be determined but it is believed that drugs had been received at their address and allegedly passed by them to Ryan.

If any of this found its way into this Sunday's *Herald*, thought Glasby, she was going to tear it up, add some mustard and vinegar, and eat it on toast.

Some of the rest of the piece wasn't too bad, being basically a rehash of her and Hetal's background work, albeit with a heavy spin on how much drug use went on amongst the young, and the relatively low casualties associated with it. But Daniels (or, probably more accurately, Senty Mayback's publicity machine) hadn't finished yet:

'These people,' big-hearted Senty was quoted as saying, 'need to learn the British way if they want to stay in this country. Unlike them, we don't want to live in a police state.'

Daniels was looking eager for praise, of course. 'So what do you think, Ali? Mark's going to cream himself, isn't he?'

She couldn't trust herself to look at him but she managed a response. 'Absolutely, Jack. Oh, by the way, what did Constance make of it?'

Daniels looked slightly puzzled. 'Constance? You mean Jonathan Constance, the lawyer? Oh, Mark will have him run the rule over it I'm sure. For form's sake. Got to go now, so *ciao bella*, ladies!'

He actually blew a kiss in Hetal's direction and for half a moment appeared to be thinking of doing the same to Glasby, as he swept by on his way to glory.

Hetal had been looking rather hard at Glasby and now she came over. Always quietly spoken, her voice this time was so low that Glasby had to strain to catch it. 'What do you think, Alison? Will the editor be happy with Jack's piece? Only I was wondering . . .' She tailed off.

'What were you going to say, Hetal?' Glasby encouraged her.

'Well, I wondered if there might be any legal problems, for example.'

'Hetal, unless this place has gone collectively mad, I think you might just be right. Contempt of court, for starters, and almost certainly defamation of the Gunarathnas. Despite the blatantly anti-immigrant line, I suppose that Jack might just about get away without being accused of incitement to racial hatred, but the *Herald*'s new line in condoning illegal drug importation and use should be a real winner with advertisers, don't you think?'

The two women smiled at each other. As the smile faded from Glasby's face, her thoughtful look returned. If Ellington was going to be taken up with the delectable little treat that Daniels had served up for him, he probably wouldn't have time to pay any attention to a small piece that she had started thinking about. She'd been banned from writing anything on Longhammer without his permission, but nobody had said that she couldn't cover Michael Fisher's murder.

Glasby started typing:

> Police are now understood to be investigating whether a brutal murder may have been the work of a professional hit man. Michael Fisher, 47, was found beaten to death in his own apartment two days ago. The crime, which was at first thought to be the work of a burglar, bore all the hallmarks of a gangland execution.
>
> Witnesses are said to have seen two men of military appearance shadowing Mr Fisher's north London home in the days leading up to the killing. Murder squad detectives have so far refused to make any comment.

For a moment she had a vision of Bill Davenport's face, looking less than impressed. She banished it, reeread her piece and nodded her satisfaction with her own efforts.

Still, the image of a disapproving Davenport wouldn't quite go away. There didn't seem to be much point in asking his opinion, even if she could get hold of him. Yes, Bill, her story was based on little more than her own speculation and yes, her 'police sources' didn't, technically speaking, actually exist. This was not the standard of journalism that he would expect of her. He didn't have much hesitation in setting her straight on things like this, despite being officially retired these days.

But a cloud of police complacency or worse seemed to be descending over what, to anyone who knew what she did, was a very suspicious set of circumstances. It was up to her to do something to stir things up.

Nonetheless, since Mark Ellington was unhappy enough with her already, Glasby thought that it might make sense to give herself a bit of cover by making the effort to run the article past the Leer before it went to press.

What happened next was an incident that no one was supposed to know about, and no one who did know was supposed to talk about. Soon, of course, the whole office was gossiping about nothing else.

Even as she walked into his office Glasby, who it has to be admitted was not always the most sensitive to other people's problems, felt that something was wrong with Thomas Lear. He was hunched over his desk, arms wrapped around himself as if trying on a straitjacket for size. She thought at first that he was rocking back and forth but saw as she got nearer that in fact his whole body was shaking.

He looked up but did not otherwise acknowledge her.

'Um, Thomas, do you mind if I show you a short piece that I want to put in this Sunday?'

He carried on looking at her with tired, almost reproachful eyes, but said nothing.

'Thomas,' she tried again, 'is there anything wrong?'

Then it happened. To her horror, she realized that her boss was crying, first a few drops that leaked down his face and then loud sobs, erupting from deep inside him.

'Alison, Alison,' was all he replied, in a voice that was haunted and full of pain.

Glasby had no idea what she should do. Of all people, Thomas Lear, the Leer, for whom the word 'cocksure' might have been coined, the Leer on whom Jack Daniels had modelled himself!

Feeling useless, she asked, 'Can I help, Thomas? Maybe you need some water?'

That seemed to calm him a little. 'Yes, Alison, I want you to help me please.' He had stopped shaking now but his voice was flat and his face was unnaturally blank, lacking in expression and glassy, like something from a terrible dream.

Still with no idea of what she was supposed to do, Glasby offered water again and then – idiotically, she thought afterwards – remembered that she had seen some chocolate on Hetal's desk and asked if he would like that.

Speaking with great precision, as if he had hand-carved each word before uttering it, Lear said, 'Please call an ambulance. I think that I am very unwell. Please help me get out of here. I don't want anyone to see me.' Then, sounding suddenly panic-stricken, he shouted at her, '*I don't want anyone to see me!*'

The ambulance arrived less than ten minutes later, although it felt a lot longer to Glasby. Lear resumed his near-catatonic state, rocking backwards and forwards in his black leather chair and occasionally muttering something to himself that she could not catch.

Glasby had given her name to the emergency operator. When she heard her phone ringing she bolted back to her desk.

By chance or simply because it was Friday lunchtime, the office was largely empty. She had asked the paramedics to wait by the lift to try to fulfil Lear's request that no one see him leave, and Glasby walked the few metres from his office, him half leaning on her shoulder, before turning him over to their care.

Afterwards she told no one but Mike Marshall, and only the bare minimum at that, having first sworn him to secrecy. Later that day she was called to brief Ellington and someone who she didn't recognize from Human Resources.

For a while Glasby found herself in the unusual position of being the most popular person in the office, as all sorts of people who usually ignored her tried pumping her for sala-cious details. She told none of them anything further – not even Davenport, who was as keen as anyone – but one way or another, the story of Thomas Lear's collapse spread rapidly around the building anyway.

George Pincher knew how to reassure his men.

'There's no problem, you're sound. This young journalist, Glasby, she's a bit of a limpet, I can't deny that. From what I hear, she's dug up one of the neighbours, an old geezer who saw you two once or twice, outside Fisher's place. But this old bloke, he's somewhere on the far side of senile and half-blind with it, and Mallam's not interested in him. He knows the score, does old Mallam, know what I mean?

'So you two stand by for the moment and we'll see who makes a move next. All right?'

*Crossword Clue*
*GSGE (9,4)*

*From the notebook of Michael Fisher*

# Nine

Mark Ellington disappeared from Glasby's view again, wandering around his office in his usual manner. She shifted in her chair, trying to avoid a blinding beam of sunlight that was glinting off the curved glass near the top of the Gherkin office building and into her eyes.

Daniels' exclusive on Senty Mayback had been rewritten almost out of existence. Appearing the previous Sunday under the bland headline 'Celebrity's Shock at Son's Arrest', it consisted of not much more than a photograph of Senty (looking appropriately shocked), a quote which his agent would no doubt have given to any newspaper that had asked for it, and a few lines of background on the son's arrest. Jack Daniels was nowhere to be seen, with not even a by-line, let alone the photograph which he had obviously been hoping for.

Right now, however, Daniels was very much in sight and probably, like Glasby, wishing that he wasn't. They were gathered at one end of the long chromium-framed conference table in Ellington's office.

Daniels had chosen to tone down his finery for a change, opting for understated chic in black polo-neck and matching goatee. Mike Marshall was his usual calm and relaxed self. Hetal, immaculately suited again, was sitting very close to Glasby as if for comfort and smiling more than was really fitting, presumably from nerves. Glasby herself was in her normal uniform of jeans and a shirt which, she realized too late, had several grease spots across the front that the washing machine hadn't managed to remove.

Thomas Lear, of course, was not there.

Ellington presumably had a point that he wanted to make – he would hardly have called Lear's team in to see him otherwise – and Thomas Lear's unscheduled absence seemed to be it. But it was taking him an awful long while to get there.

Glasby found her attention wavering, somewhere around the part where Ellington was informing them that a newspaper was not just a people business, but a newspaper *was* its staff.

'And, of course, its reputation. As you and I have had cause to consider of late, haven't we, Alison?' The editor appeared again in her line of sight as he made what was presumably a reference to her ongoing difficulties with Longhammer. Glasby flushed, and then was annoyed with herself for letting her discomfort show.

She said nothing and he continued: 'Now you may have noticed that Thomas Lear couldn't join us today.' He paused again, bizarrely seeming to expect an answer to this, as if it might only now have occurred to them that their boss wasn't in the room.

All four of them squirmed uncomfortably; even Hetal had heard the rumours that were sweeping the building about the Leer's odd behaviour last week. Glasby had given nothing further away to any of her colleagues, resisting even Marshall's famous and much proclaimed ability (by him, naturally) to charm a secret out of anyone no matter how tight-lipped they might be.

'Well, yes,' Ellington carried on, after an awkward pause in which they all concentrated on avoiding his eye. 'As you will probably have heard, Thomas is taking a well-earned break. He's a very conscientious chap, as all of you know, and he's thoroughly earned this' – he hesitated again, searching for the *mot juste* and as usual failing to find it – 'this *break*.'

To Glasby's right, Hetal's smile had grown even broader; she was nodding her agreement enthusiastically. Ellington, noticing this, beamed back at her and seemed about to say something before stopping, possibly because he couldn't remember her name.

'Now, we need to get some rigour and discipline back in to this area of the *Herald*'s operations.' This time, Glasby was pleased to note, Ellington was looking squarely at Jack Daniels, who met his gaze momentarily but then flinched and looked down at the table.

'As you will all know very well from my staff newsletters, I am a great believer in the importance of management structures. The strongest structure that nature has to offer is a pyramid, so it's no accident that this is the paradigm shape for our organization.'

His audience were looking even more blank than before, but Ellington didn't seem to notice. 'So, in Thomas' absence, we need to reconfigure, don't we?'

Ellington strode across to his desk, empty of papers as ever, and spoke into his phone. 'You can send him in now, thank you.'

Glasby could have fallen off her chair. With a cheeky smile in her direction and a pronounced limp, in walked none other than Bill Davenport.

Henry Dunne hadn't been a cop for twenty-five years without being able to spot a put-up job. Unusually enough, a meal had been arranged and the dining table laid ready for his return from work. It was stranger still for his son Mattie to be present. As Dunne picked the bones out of the steamed sea bass and wondered whether he was supposed to eat the mixed herb garnish that accompanied it – Patsy really *had* made an effort this time – he noted the boy's attempts to make polite conversation and Patsy's rather obvious efforts to help him.

He was sure that he knew what was coming next, but tried hard not to think about it, not wanting to spoil the unexpected pleasure of a family dinnertime. When his offer to help with the dishes was firmly refused and Mattie remained at the table with him while Patsy ostentatiously disappeared to the kitchen next door, it was clear that he couldn't put it off any longer.

'Was there something in particular that you wanted to tell me about?' he asked his son, thinking that he could at least make it easier for them to get started. Mattie kept his head down, eyes hidden by a long floppy fringe that Dunne had to try hard not to feel irritated by.

'I want to . . .' he started, then lifted his head and looked his father in the eyes with a steady gaze that made Dunne proud of him. 'I want to ask for your help, Dad. Please. I think I made a mistake, doing what I did, and I've already gone and cleaned the paint off the wall. I mean, I feel strongly about it all, the war and stuff, but I was wrong to break the law, and it won't happen again, you know?'

Dunne thought that he did know, as it happened. The boy obviously had morals and beliefs, and he was pretty sure that if Mattie said that he wouldn't re-offend, he meant it and could be trusted to keep his word. He was hard-working, serious-minded and was the sort of son that anyone would take pride in. In fact, he was exactly the type of person who deserved the second chance that a police caution, rather than a formal criminal conviction, was designed to offer.

'I'm sure you won't get into trouble again, Mattie,' he replied. He noticed deep worry lines underneath his son's fringe, lines that he didn't remember having seen before. 'If I was the officer in charge of your case, I don't think I'd have any trouble in issuing you with a caution. That's what you need, isn't it?'

The teenager's posture relaxed and some of the lines faded from his forehead. 'So you'll talk to the inspector, then? Mum says that if you do, he'll be cool about it. And then I've still got the chance to get in to Imperial.'

Dunne hated himself as he replied. 'Mattie, you know that at the Met, I'm in charge of an internal anti-corruption unit, don't you?' The boy nodded, now looking worried once again. 'Well, it wouldn't be right for someone to be charged with that sort of duty, and then to take advantage of their position in the force to get preferential treatment for their own family, would it? Do you see what I mean?'

'Yes, Dad.'

Mattie was staring at the dining table now, his face reflected in the polished mahogany top. Patsy and he had rescued it from a junk shop and had it restored, back when the children were only just big enough to sit and eat at it. 'So you can't help then?'

This time it was Dunne who looked down, and by the time he looked up it was at his son's departing back. 'I've got to make a phone call,' the teenager muttered, and stomped loudly upstairs.

Dunne wasn't alone for long.

'You self-righteous sanctimonious bastard!' his wife hissed at him. Clearly she had been listening in through the serving hatch which joined the two rooms. 'You and your duty that you've been *charged* with – who do you think you are, the sodding Queen? As for preferential treatment, who was it whose parents sent him to an expensive school, and who insisted that his own son had to go to the local comprehensive? Well?'

Before Dunne had a chance to think of anything to say,

Patsy continued, shouting now. 'Let me tell you how it's going to be, Mr Chief Superintendent. Your son – our son – has worked his bloody socks off at that shitty school that you made us send him to, to get into the toughest course in one of the top medical schools in the country. And if he doesn't get a caution for the only tiny little mistake the boy's made in all that time, then you'd better set about finding yourself a new family and a new home. You won't be welcome in this one, and that's a fact.'

'And so,' Ellington wrapped up, at last, 'I'm looking to each and every one of you to pull together and step up to the plate. Understood?'

They nodded affirmatively with the air of people who would have agreed to anything if it meant that they could escape. All four of what had until a few days earlier been Thomas Lear's team started to get up. Hetal, Mike Marshall and Jack Daniels duly left the editor's office but Glasby was not to be so fortunate.

'If you would, please, Alison.' Ellington motioned her back to the uncomfortable leather chair in which she had been trapped for what felt like several hours. Davenport, opposite, grinned at her sympathetically but said nothing.

Ellington sat down at the head of the table. 'You placed a story in the last edition, Alison. About a death, a murder.' His PDA was in his hand; he peered into its small screen. 'A Mr Michael Fisher. Who you had some acquaintance with, just before his death, I recall.'

He looked over at Glasby. 'That's right, Mark,' she began, intending to say more, but the editor, unusually clear in what he wanted to say, pressed on.

'"Police are now understood to be investigating whether a brutal murder may have been the work of a professional hit man",' he quoted. 'But I don't know how you could substantiate that. If called upon to do so, of course. I was contacted, by a source. A *trusted* source, who occupies a certain position, in public affairs. This source seems to have very different information from the allusions which you make. He suggested that the inspector in charge of this inquiry' – he consulted his handheld computer again – 'Inspector Mallam, thinks no such thing. And furthermore, he gave me to believe that this

Inspector Mallam made the position very clear to you, before the story went in.'

Glasby was mortified. Unfortunately this was not the first time that she'd had this experience in her editor's office. Ellington had stood up and was on walkabout again, speaking from somewhere behind her left shoulder. Davenport was studiously fiddling with a loose thread on his jacket, of which fortunately for present purposes there were plenty to choose from. 'But . . .' she started, but again got no further.

'So we are clear then,' Ellington said, a statement not a question. 'There will be no more coverage of Michael Fisher, unless it's done with full responsibility and with proper discretion. That's what our source expects of us, and that's what we will do.'

'Right, Mark,' said Davenport cheerily, the first words he had uttered in some time. He led Glasby down to the small conference room next to the empty office which Thomas Lear had inhabited. Daniels had clearly been expelled back to his normal cubicle and Davenport had set up shop instead, his presence established by a disorderly pile of papers and a coffee maker, complete with spilled grounds and two dirty cups.

Glasby might have wondered how Davenport had managed to gather this detritus around him, seemingly without actually doing anything to make it appear, but she had no time for such thoughts. As soon as the door was closed, she exploded.

'Source? What the hell is Ellington on about, Bill? What source has he got, who is it that knows so much about everything that I have doing?'

Davenport looked at her and spoke gently. 'All newspaper editors have a line through to certain elements in the government, Alison. You've heard of the "D-Notice" system?'

Glasby nodded. 'Yes, of course. But that's supposed to be used to censor information that might damage national security. You're not telling me that Fisher was a spy, are you?'

'No, I'm not. And I'm not really saying that Ellington's been approached under a D-Notice. Just that when someone who knows how to do it wants a story killed, or soft-soaped at any rate, maybe just to avoid embarrassment in the wrong places, then the right person picks the phone up to some other well-connected person, and they have a word with Ellington, or maybe someone on the board, and it's done.'

'But that's outrageous! Who would it have been?'

Davenport laughed. 'Alison, what can I say? You've obviously got under someone's skin. And the last thing that you should do is start trying to work out who it might have been. Just remember, I'm the head honcho now for you and your young colleagues, and I'd just as soon not have any of you picked up by a government death squad on my watch.'

Glasby didn't laugh.

'Just joking, Alison,' he tried again, a bit sarcastically. 'But you've been given a message to stop playing games, back off, and find yourself something else to write about. It couldn't really be any clearer, could it? And maybe just for once, you could do what you're told. If your boss asks you, nicely?'

Her expression went from unhappy to positively bad-tempered, but Davenport ignored it. His voice dropped to a conspiratorial level. 'Now, Thomas Lear, that was a bad business, wasn't it? A man like that, what is he, in his thirties, maybe early forties, with a wife, and a child I hear . . . What exactly happened, Alison?'

Team Davenport, Ellington had insisted on calling it, and Bill was clearly taking pleasure from using the description. 'So, team, are we sure that we all know what we're doing?' They said that they did, smilingly in Mike's and Hetal's case, Daniels' less so. Glasby was totally grim.

Davenport's big idea for the rest of the week turned out to be the problems of commuting – starting off, of course, with cycling. Glasby was going to be working on this with him; Davenport himself would take the point of view of the older cyclist returning back to the mode of transport of their childhood, while Glasby got to research cycle lanes, wet weather clothing and other such fascinating practicalities. She was not much short of livid, but managed to wait until the others had left before saying so.

'Bill! You know that I should be working crime stories, not bloody soft features! Of all people, you know that perfectly well!'

He was surprisingly unapologetic. '"Should" isn't in it, Alison, and it doesn't matter what I know or I don't know. The *Herald* pays your wages, and they're being kind enough to pay mine too. For that, in my book, they get the best that we can offer, and if they need human interest features from us, that's what they're getting.'

Glasby did her best to calm down. She thought for a few moments. 'It was human interest, that's what you said?'

Davenport waited warily, having learned to recognize a particular look that had come over her face. 'Yes . . .'

'How about the plight of a soldier's family, you know, widowed and orphaned by the war, for example?'

He was rather sure that he knew where she was heading. 'And was there any particular soldier's family that you had in mind?'

Glasby smiled at him, knowing that she'd been rumbled. 'Well, I did hear of one example. Richard Bedingfield died a real hero's death, apparently, rescuing two of his troops who'd been badly injured. He got them out, and managed to hold off the Taliban who were pursuing them but he died of his wounds back at base. I contacted his regiment and they said that there's talk of a Victoria Cross being awarded, for his bravery.'

'So you'd like to interview his widow, of course. To get the full story of his heroism. Do you know whether she'll even talk to you?'

'Well, I did speak to her yesterday, and it turns out that she's very involved in army welfare, and she said that she'd give me an interview if it gave her the chance to publicize some of the issues that bereaved service families have to go through.'

Davenport was smiling too now, approvingly, although pretending to be exasperated. 'And while you're doing that, you might just see if she knows anything, something that might just be relevant to the stories told to you by, and the untimely death of, one Michael Fisher, Esquire?'

Glasby felt that dignity required her to keep a straight face, and she just about carried it off. 'Well, I might, yes,' she admitted.

He thought for a moment, and made a decision. Knowing her as he did, he could more or less guarantee that she'd get herself into trouble somehow. This seemed like a fairly safe bet.

'OK. But not a word goes in the paper that I haven't given the nod to. No uncorroborated stories from anonymous inform-ants or unnamed police sources, not on my watch. We got our marching orders from Ellington, and we'll stick to them. We'll pull together, just as he told us. And step up to the plate.' He grinned at her again. 'Once we've worked out what exactly Mark thinks that it means, anyway.'

The black notebook almost fit into his palm, so large were the man's hands. He was flicking impatiently from page to page, trying to decipher the scratchy handwriting which covered them.

Eventually he found something which caught his attention, but from his demeanour it didn't seem to please him at all. Seconds later he gave up, holding the book with a look of disgust as if it smelled bad, and then flinging it away from him across the room.

The notebook hit the opposite wall and came to rest next to a muddy pair of boots. The man leant back scowling and slowly cracked his knuckles, one by one. Then he ran his fingers through his shock of blond hair and pulled, hard enough to hurt.

Anne Bedingfield was tall, well-spoken, of good background, and so utterly charming and devoid of artificial airs that not even the often thin-skinned Glasby felt in any way patronized or looked down upon. She had welcomed Glasby into a sunlit room that was decorated with photographs of two auburn-haired girls at various stages of childhood and adolescence. A piano stood in the bay window with a cello propped up against it.

Glasby had finished her second cup of tea and learned everything that she might need to know about the various charities that Mrs Bedingfield worked with, and the hardships which they tried to mitigate. For the last few minutes she had been wondering how to turn the subject round to matters that she considered more pertinent.

Her hostess did it for her; fixing Glasby with a smile and a pair of bright blue eyes, Anne Bedingfield asked quietly, 'And now, would you like to explain what you really came here for?'

Thinking about it later, Glasby thought that she hadn't done too badly, neither getting flustered nor trying to keep up a bluff which had obviously been called.

'Roger Bushell is a bit of an oddball,' Mrs Bedingfield helped her, 'with his Old Boys and that ridiculously outdated gentlemen's club which he insists on inviting one to. But he has a very senior position in the City, d'you know, and really he's nobody's fool at all. So you were asking him all about Richard's schooldays, and you did seem rather well-informed about Burstone. He made a point of mentioning that to me. Now I confess that I'm not normally a *Sunday Herald* reader, but I did look at it last week, and I noticed your article. About Michael Fisher, I mean, who of course was another Burstone boy. But I'm sure you know that already?'

Glasby leant forward. 'Off the record, Mrs Bedingfield, I wanted to ask you something about Richard, something that Michael Fisher told me.'

'You talked to Michael Fisher, before he died? Good gracious, I didn't know that you knew him. Wasn't he a bit of a sneaky sort of chap? Not that he deserved the end that he met, of course.'

'He approached me, trying to sell a story, just before he was killed. It . . .' She hesitated, trying to think of the most diplomatic way to put it.

Again Mrs Bedingfield helped her out. 'Obviously this story concerned Richard, and you must think that it's important, or you wouldn't have gone to all this trouble over it. Let me ask you one thing: you are going to publish, aren't you? About the Forces Families in Need, and so on, I mean?'

Glasby promised that of course she was, hoping that neither Davenport nor Ellington would veto it.

Mrs Bedingfield looked at her for a moment as if to assess the truthfulness of what she had just been told, but seemed satisfied.

'So you tell me everything, and I'll answer anything I can. But this is not to be written about in the newspaper, that's what "off the record" means for you people, isn't it?'

Since she was banned from on high from doing any such thing, this time Glasby could give the assurance requested with a clear conscience. It took a while to tell. The more she told it, the more improbable Fisher's story sounded, and the more unworthy and cheap she felt, sitting in the lovely sunlit room with a photograph of a tall, clear-eyed soldier looking down at her.

'So I was wondering if Richard ever said anything, about the teacher's death, or about being blackmailed by Fisher, or giving him money for some reason . . .'

This time Mrs Bedingfield didn't do much to ease her guest's feelings. 'You've obviously talked to people who knew Richard, and of course you won't find anyone who knew him better than I did. You can look as much as you like, and you won't find anyone to say that he ever did a single dishonourable deed in his life. He just wasn't capable of it, even if – for some reason that I can't imagine – he'd have wanted to. You really are wasting your time, Miss Glasby. And mine as well, I'm beginning to think. Now, unless there was something else?'

Back in the office, she filled in an only partly interested Davenport on the rest of the interview.

'She told me that she and her husband kept separate finances, so she couldn't say definitively that Bedingfield hadn't been giving Fisher money, which was what Fisher claimed; you know, he said that it was hush money to stop him spilling the beans on Bedingfield's part in the teacher's murder. In fact, she said that he often helped out old colleagues from the army, so she thought it was quite possible that he might have done the same for a former school-mate like Fisher.'

'So it's another dead end, then, really,' was Davenport's conclusion. He didn't look at all unhappy about it. 'Now, about this issue of cycle paths in city centres. Have you ever thought that they could raise them above head height, right up above the pavement I mean?'

Glasby's mobile rang, possibly saving her from saying something which she might later have regretted.

The girl sounded young. She had a strong accent; something from eastern Europe, Glasby thought, probably Russia. Like Fisher, what she wanted from Glasby was very clear. 'Michael, he say if I phone you, you give me money.' She giggled. 'He say, lot of money, you must give me, and then I must give you something. From him. Something from Michael.'

Glasby tried hard not to let herself get over-excited. 'What did he give you? And what's your name, by the way? You were a friend of Michael Fisher?'

'Yes, I am friend of Michael,' was as much as she got in reply, together with another nervous-sounding giggle.

Glasby tried another approach. 'When did you last see him?'

'I see him, the night he dead. He come to visit me, he really scared. And he give me these things, in a bag, he say they very valuable to you, and if anything happens to him, I must call you. So how much money you will give me?'

'Well,' Glasby improvised, wondering how on earth she would ever convince Ellington to write a cheque for her, what with the Senty Mayback fiasco, all the Longhammer problems, and the little matter of a warning that had been delivered along secret back-channels instructing her to keep away from the Michael Fisher story altogether. 'First we'd have to meet. I really need your name to get things started first, and some details of how you knew Fisher. Michael, I mean.'

The girl didn't laugh this time. 'Why you want my name?' she asked, sounding suspicious.

'I have to check all of the facts, you see, before the *Herald* can give someone money for a story. It's perfectly normal, all the newspapers would do that sort of thing in the same way.'

There was a silence. Then, 'Maybe I call you again.'

'Wait!' said Glasby, but she was too late. The girl had rung off, leaving Glasby with no way to contact her again. She kicked the air in frustration, connecting accidentally with the metal leg of her desk. 'Oh, bugger!' she shouted, as the little toe of her right foot began to throb.

# The Knowledge

**221b Baker Street to Great Scotland Yard**
*L on R Baker Street*
*L Blandford Street*
*R Marylebone High Street*
*F Thayer Street*
*F Mandeville Place*
*L Wigmore Street*
*F Cavendish Place*
*R and B/R Regent Street*
*L Coventry Street*
*R Haymarket*
*L Cockspur Street*
*F Pall Mall East*
*L Cockspur Street*
*COM Trafalgar Square*
*L/BY Whitehall*
*L Great Scotland Yard*

*From the notebook of Michael Fisher*

# Ten

Glasby was having another bad week. Her old friend Kate Hall had phoned to give her the news that she was engaged to be married. Kate was rather evasive as to who had actually proposed, which Glasby suspected meant that Simon, her live-in boyfriend – by whom in Glasby's view the word 'supercilious' might be defined – thought that the traditional getting down on one knee thing was a bit beneath him, and had found some way of manoeuvring Kate into taking the initiative.

Later that evening Lester Dolland, Glasby's ex-boyfriend from her university days, phoned her. They'd been getting on surprisingly well since their chance encounter eighteen months or so ago, which had led to him almost unwittingly helping her to a crucial breakthrough in a story she was trying to run down. It had also led to a long drunken evening with Lester and some friends, and almost to something rather more intimate when she found herself alone with him later that night.

Lester had matured to the point that his rather dissolute ways and eclectic artistic interests now formed part of his lifestyle rather than *being* his life, and was now engaged in running something called a community publisher. And she . . . well, maybe she'd loosened up a bit, and found it easier to accept that with his unreliability and carelessness came an unpredictable intelligence and almost unlimited tolerance.

But she'd come back to London and begun what had turned out to be a troubled relationship with John Redgrave, and Lester had stayed up in Norwich with all the junkie artists, jazz poets and other exotic friends that he'd made there.

With her break-up from John Redgrave now seeming more and more irrevocable, and her limited to nonexistent social circle containing no other eligible man of any description, Glasby's thoughts had been turning more and more to Lester and the possibility that she might find a bit more than old friendship with him.

He was coming down to London quite often these days, which was why he'd phoned her, in fact; he had a trip coming up, to a festival of anarchist poetry in Hackney. It was normal for Lester to mention various of his exotic acquaintances as if Glasby had known them all her life, so when someone called Naomi cropped up, even for the second and third time, she didn't think much of it. But when he started saying "we", and in particular "we dropped by to see the old folks", it was rather clear that whoever Naomi might be, she wasn't just another member of the Lester academy of oddballs.

Not that either Kate's engagement or Lester's love life were any of her concern, of course. Or so Glasby told herself, more than once, as the week dragged by. She had much more obvious concerns than the almost complete lack of any personal life.

Things at the *Herald* seemed to get a little worse as each day went by. For a start, Jack Daniels seemed to be prospering under the new regime instituted by Bill Davenport. Given the mission of working up a series on the inanities of the celebrity lifestyle, Daniels was positively overflowing with ideas and enthusiasm. 'How much does it cost to look like this?' was his theme for the week, complete with in-depth research into membership of the coolest clubs, the hottest beauty treatments and the loudest tailoring.

Meanwhile Glasby's knowledge of commuting, especially cycling and its rewards and perils, grew by the day. The on-off strikes on the London Underground which left her stuck in crowds of overheated and frustrated commuters only increased Davenport's enthusiasm for her new specialist subject.

Just to remind her why she had been condemned to this two-wheeled Siberia, a further letter had arrived from solicitors acting for Salmon and Shipp, the two police constables she had named as being the next focus for the Longhammer investigation into corruption. They had decided that now was the time to turn up the pressure and were demanding a front-page apology together with a proposal for 'very substantial' financial recompense within the next twenty-one days, failing which the *Herald*, its editor and its erstwhile crime reporter could expect to find themselves in the dock. Without further notice.

The letter had appeared on her desk around lunchtime. Glasby, having lost any appetite completely, sat staring at the single piece of premium weight paper, admiring the quality of the embossment and the watermark, and wondering why convention demanded that even the most unpleasant of messages began with the writer addressing her as 'Dear' and ended with him declaring himself sincerely beholden to her . . .

She looked up; it was after five. She'd let a whole afternoon pass in useless daydreams. It was surprising that Ellington hadn't called her. She checked with his PA, Jan, to see if he was out of the office.

'Oh no, he's been here all afternoon. I think he's dealing with top-level admin matters today. But he's got all his post, including that letter on Fish and Chips.'

It seemed that the office nickname for her nemeses (if that's what the plural of nemesis was – Glasby wasn't sure) had reached as far as the editor's suite. 'I'm sure if Mark wants to talk to you about it, he'll let you know.'

This left Glasby unable to decide if she was more worried by the thought of having to face Ellington, or by the fact that he didn't seem to want to see her. She tried to concentrate on something more constructive instead.

Unfortunately her thoughts kept returning to Michael Fisher, scared to the point of paranoia one day, dead the next. Somewhere there was some detail, something connected to his wild story or his violent death, that would open up the whole Longhammer debacle. But what?

Unlike his sometime protégée, Bill Davenport was rather enjoying life. His return to the professional fold was all the more satisfying for being totally unexpected. And what was more, given that he seemed to be learning some new tricks, he clearly wasn't such an old dog after all.

Never in his long career had he worked on features. In itself that was no big deal – as a newsman, he'd always suspected that dreaming up some light relief to space out the real point of a newspaper couldn't be too much like hard work. So far, he was still of that view.

The hard thing was the people. He'd made his career as a lone operator; sociable and socially adept, of course, but he'd never been given or wanted any responsibility for anybody other than himself. Now the eponymous head of Team Davenport had four young people to manage, an experience that was as perplexing as it was stimulating.

Daniels, for example, could easily have reacted badly to his appointment. The boy had got a bit out of control, and Ellington had made it clear that he needed to be roped in and kept there. In fact he was performing splendidly, either enjoying the sense of direction he was getting or doing a damned good job of pretending if he didn't.

Marshall was a clock-watcher and was going nowhere fast, but once you'd accepted that, you got a solid enough day's work from him. The young Indian girl, Hetal, was a pleasure to have around (and a real looker – he was honest enough to admit that to himself) but really too junior to do much more than help the others out.

Which left Glasby, his friend and former collaborator, whom Davenport had actually disliked quite a lot when he had first been thrown into working with her. Unfortunately he was now beginning to remember why. She was the most talented of the lot of them, himself included possibly, but stubborn and temperamental with it to the point where she took you to the pain barrier and beyond. Somewhere between Lear and Ellington, they'd failed even to keep her to basic standards of professionalism. How could they have let her run those Longhammer pieces based on information from a source who she couldn't even identify herself? Some of the stories had paid off, to be fair, but if you hurtled along taking every fence with your eyes closed you were riding for a fall, and it was only a matter of time before you got one.

'Bill?' Here she was in his office doorway, with exactly the look on her face that he knew that he should be worried about. What was she up to now?

'Bill, I remember that you mentioned a South African guy to me once, a sort of security consultant?'

She pushed the buzzer to let him in through the door at the foot of the stairs, and waited, anxiously. Mr Smith – not the most original of pseudonyms if that's what it was – had been abrupt almost to the point of rudeness when they had spoken on the phone earlier. The conversation was too short for her to get any impression of him, bar an accent that sounded harsh to her ears and a lot of pauses and loud intakes of breath between words, as if he had a heavy cold.

Annoyed with herself for a childish attack of nerves, she forced herself to wait in the kitchen until he was actually at the front door of her flat so as not to seem over-eager. Her guest was, after all, not much more than a glorified private detective, and a contact of Davenport's at that, albeit one who had come with something of a health warning.

'He's quite a unique fellow,' Davenport had said, but refused to elaborate beyond, 'Pay what he asks, if you can afford it, and he'll give you what he says he will. That's all you need to know about him – he's a pro.'

A minute ticked by on the clock above her head, and then two. Unable to sit still any longer Glasby made for the front door, realizing as she did that some noises that she had noticed outside a moment ago were now getting closer.

She opened the door and found herself looking at the biggest man she had ever seen. He was leaning against the wall at the top of the stairs, breathing thunderously. With each intake of air there was a huge ripple of skin, starting at the base of his neck and moving up to his forehead and then back as the air was released again. Glasby had never before thought of her doorway as at all narrow, but the man actually had to enter it on the diagonal to fit through it.

He held out a hand to her which felt as soft as a boneless chicken breast, and smiled. '*You* are Alison Glasby and *I* am John Smith,' he announced, as if there might be some confusion as to which of them was which. 'My father's name was Smith, and his father's too. My mother liked the name John. So they left it up to me to make myself memorable. And' – a shifting of some of the pools of flesh around his jaw and cheekbone heralded a self-satisfied smile – 'I like to think that I have done a very good job.'

Having no idea what to say, Glasby opted for silence. Her over-sized visitor reciprocated, protruding eyes staring straight into hers so that she had to look away. 'Won't you . . . won't you sit down?' she asked, gesturing rather hopelessly at the chairs around her kitchen table, which now seemed very small indeed.

Mr Smith looked thoughtfully at them, and then back at Glasby. 'Nah,' he said, his vowel sounds even rougher in person than on the phone, 'I think I will stand.' And he leaned against the connecting wall between the kitchen and the sitting room, which bowed a little as if in sympathy.

Glasby was struggling not to feel that she had somehow insulted him. By offering such a blatantly inadequate piece of furniture, hadn't she as good as accused him of being fat? Not just a little but hugely overweight, misshapen, grotesque? She blushed, certain that he must be able to read the appalling thoughts that she couldn't manage to keep out of her mind.

But Mr Smith looked at her quite benignly, a smile spreading as before in slow motion across the expanse of his face. 'Bill D., he is what I call good people. So I am happy to conduct my trade with you, because he tells me I should. You want information, and I sell information. Y'understand?'

He paused, apparently wanting an answer. Glasby nodded, ready to explain. 'Yes, of course. You see, I'm interested because of some issues connected with Operation Longhammer, you know the police investigation into corruption in the Metropolitan Police—'

Mr Smith held up a massive arm, making a stop sign in front of her. She obeyed.

'I do not need to know, nor do I want to know, your business. We can go there, if you want, but ah say don't go there, y'know? Because if we go there, then I am going to know your business. And then, pretty soon you'll be thinking that now you must know my business. And believe me, I don't want you to go there, and you *don't* want to go there. Understand?'

Glasby didn't trust herself with more than a nod this time. It seemed to be sufficient.

'So.' The man paused, but apparently only to reorganize his jacket and chest, perhaps to free up some space for his lungs to operate in. There was a swaying of clothes back and forth for a moment which Glasby tried hard not to look at.

'You tell me what you need. I tell you what it costs. You want to buy, you pay, I deliver, we say goodbye and farewell. You don't want to buy, you say so, we say goodbye and farewell. Understand?'

Even in Glasby's still discomfited state, there wasn't much not to understand.

'I need to know something about a man. His name when

he was at Burstone School was David Gold. He would be forty-seven or forty-eight by this time. I think he could be using a different name these days. I want to know what it is, where he lives and works, and some background on who he is and what he does for a living.'

Mr Smith said nothing, but the smile reappeared, a rather more calculating look in his eyes than before.

Glasby continued. 'And I need one other thing. A home address for Henry Dunne. Chief Superintendent Henry Dunne.'

This time the look in Mr Smith's eyes changed, to something like respect.

Glasby never normally found much time for managing her finances, but she had at one point registered for internet banking and by a miracle discovered her user number and password, scribbled on an old bank statement. To her surprise and pleasure there was almost £2,100 in her account, a little more than Mr Smith had asked of her.

She drove up to her local branch, which boasted new longer opening hours of 9.30 a.m. until 5 p.m., which meant that their working day was roughly three hours shorter than hers. Getting Mr Smith's money would have to wait until the next day. It required a trip back across town from her office at lunchtime.

'Cash?' asked the boy behind the bullet-proof glass, sounding concerned and not a little suspicious.

'Yes,' said Glasby defensively. 'I need it . . . for a car. I'm buying a car.'

'We offer a very competitive service in bankers' drafts,' the teller persisted. 'Or have you considered an electronic transfer? Normally people don't want cash these days.'

'I want cash!' Glasby responded, rather more loudly than she had intended. A large Sikh man turned from the window beside her to see what was happening. The woman who had been serving him gave a sympathetic look to her colleague, who clearly had a difficult case to deal with.

'Yes madam,' he replied, sniffily. 'Sign here, here and here.'

She left, sure that she would be appearing on the 'drug dealer of the month' section of the bank's website. For the rest of the afternoon the forty large, bright red notes burned a hole in her trouser pocket, like a guilty secret wanting to be told.

Mr Smith was right where he said he would be, halfway across Westminster Bridge. The fifty-pound notes, which had seemed so large, shrunk as they found their way into his palm. He produced a large envelope from a large pocket in the lining of his extra extra extra large jacket and handed it over to Glasby. She held on to it with both hands. It had just cost her ninety-five per cent of her savings, after all.

'Martin Danielson?' said the receptionist at Tower Properties. 'I don't think he works here, madam. Can anyone else help?'

'I don't know if he's based at this office,' said Glasby impatiently, 'but he's on your board of directors, or something like that. You must have a contact number for him.'

'Mr Brewster-Smith is the chairman of our board, madam. Would you like me to put you through to his office?'

Two thousand pounds had bought her David Gold's current identity, and the information that he was a very wealthy man indeed. A search of the newspaper's records, Google and various company and financial databases had told her very little more. Martin Danielson cropped up very occasionally in stories about some large-scale property transaction or other, in which he was variously described as 'shadowy', 'publicity shy' or just straightforwardly 'secretive'.

According to Mr Smith, there was no doubt at all that Danielson was the man behind Tower Properties, considered second only to the Duke of Westminster's Grosvenor Estate in the value of its holdings in the more exclusive parts of central London. But even his own staff seemed not to have heard of him.

'Maybe he's a consultant?' suggested the still assiduous receptionist. 'Have you tried his mobile number?' Glasby hadn't, for the very good reason that she didn't have it.

As well as what was supposed to be Danielson's office details, Mr Smith had also provided her with two residential addresses. One, a penthouse apartment in a shiny glass building overlooking Lambeth Bridge and the Palace of Westminster, got her no further than an unanswered intercom and an almost equally taciturn porter.

The other, on Bishop's Avenue – much beloved of the tabloid newspapers as 'Millionaire's Row', although in honour of London's property price inflation they probably needed to

change the initial 'M' to a 'B' instead – was predictably pala-
tial, and equally predictably surrounded by high walls and
security apparatus sufficient to deter the most determined
burglar, or journalist.

'Did you say you had an appointment, madam?' came a
voice out of the metal grille to the side of the front gate, in
what sounded like an Israeli accent.

'Yes, with Mr Danielson,' Glasby improvised.

But this wasn't enough even to give Mr Metal Grille pause
for thought. 'I can't help you there,' was the reply. 'Leave
immediately, will you?'

However much Gold/Danielson paid for his peace of mind,
he was getting good value for money. Which, Glasby reflected
ruefully, was more than she could say for her £2,000. So far,
at least.


'Hello, Henry, I hope I'm not disturbing you?'

Dunne knew perfectly well that he recognized the young
woman, but seeing her out of context at his own front door,
at first he couldn't place her. He stood smiling rather blankly
while his mind raced through the possibilities. She looked too
old to be a friend of either of his kids, but he didn't think
that she was a neighbour . . .

'Alison Glasby,' she said, coming to his rescue. 'John –
John Redgrave – mentioned to me once that you lived here.
I do hope that you don't mind me dropping by, just on the
off-chance?'

'Of course, Alison!' Dunne hoped that his embarrassment
wasn't too obvious. He hesitated, feeling obliged now to ask
her in. Slightly ashamed, he realized that he was pleased that
Patsy was out. It wasn't as if he was planning to ravage the
girl on the sitting room sofa, but the way Patsy was nowadays, him inviting a young woman into the house was exactly
the sort of thing that would set her off.

'Um, Henry?' It was Glasby who was looking awkward
now. 'I was just wondering, if you had a few minutes?'

Dunne hastened to answer, feeling like a complete fool.
Whatever was wrong between him and his wife, it shouldn't
get in the way of common courtesy. 'I'm so sorry, Alison.
You just caught me daydreaming, that's all. Do come in.'

He sat her down in the front room and hurried off to make

tea and compose himself. Only on his return journey from the kitchen, bearing a tray laden with tea cups and chocolate biscuits, did his mind turn to where it should have been in the first place. Idiot!

'Alison,' he said firmly, plonking the tray down on the fruit-wood coffee table to emphasize his point. The effect was spoiled a little by some milk slopping out of its jug and on to the plate of biscuits.

'Of course it's a pleasure to see you, but you do under-stand that I can't talk to you about anything to do with Operation Longhammer, don't you? Anything at all, I mean.'

Glasby was at pains to reassure him. 'Actually, there was something I was hoping you might be able to help me a bit with, but it has absolutely nothing to do with Longhammer, I promise you.'

She sounded like she was being truthful, but he reminded himself not to let his guard down anyway. She was a pleasant girl, and – a thought that he would certainly be keeping to himself – by no means bad looking, but she was still a jour-nalist, and one who had caused him a great deal of grief already.

As he busied himself pouring the tea, Glasby was explaining. Apparently she had requested a new focus in her work so as not to be pigeon-holed into crime too much. She told him how she had wanted for some time to cover more genuine human interest issues, like the problems faced by families of those serving in the forces, and that had led her to Anne Bedingfield. From her Glasby had discovered the coincidence of a shared schooling at Burstone between Mrs Bedingfield's tragically deceased husband and Dunne himself.

'So,' she finished, noticing that her host was looking more relaxed again, 'you see, I'm working on an article for next Sunday's edition based on my interview with Mrs Bedingfield, and she just wondered that there might be something that you could add, about Richard's character, perhaps as a boy, that I could use. Just as background, of course, I wouldn't risk causing any embarrassment by using your name.'

He wouldn't have been able to refuse even if he'd wanted to. In fact, it was a genuine pleasure, one of the few moments of escape from all of the problems that he seemed perma-nently bogged down in now. And Alison was a good listener

as well, nodding and making the occasional note as he remi-
nisced about life at Burstone, and Richard – old Bedbug; when
was the last time that he remembered that silly nickname? –
who had been captain of the rugby first XV to Dunne's vice
captain, and head boy with Dunne as his senior prefect.

He noted approvingly that she'd done her research well. If
only some of his men put in the same attention to detail! The
games teacher dying, for example – Richard must have
mentioned it to Anne, and Alison had picked up on it.

'It's a terrible thing to say, but I think we both enjoyed the
excitement at the time. Once the shock was over, I mean,
talking to the local plods, and we had to give evidence to the
coroner as well. Not that there was much that we could say
– it was just one of those accidents that can happen in that
sort of place. It must have been a cruel blow for his family,
of course; Mr Dickson's son was at the school too, you know.
He was in the same form as us, in fact.'

Glasby did her best to maintain the low-key approach that
her cover story demanded. 'What sort of a person was the
teacher?' she asked, as she leant forward to help herself to a
biscuit.

Seeing Dunne hesitating she decided to prompt him a bit
more, interpreting his reticence as a desire not to say anything
bad about someone who had died young. 'I understand from
Mrs Bedingfield that Richard remembered him as quite a bully,
the sort that would pick on a boy if he didn't like him.'

Upon hearing this he became quite animated. 'If that's what
Richard said, he was absolutely on the nail, as usual. The man
was a racist, to be blunt. You're too young to remember the
nineteen-seventies, things really were very different then, especially at an old-fashioned place like Burstone, but even by the
standards of the time Dickson was a violent bully. His son
was in our year and he was just as bad. There was a Jewish
kid that they both picked on terribly, he wasn't particularly a
friend of mine, but it used to make my blood boil, you know?
Even at that age, you know when someone's doing something
that's just plain *wrong*, don't you?'

Glasby smiled in agreement. This was a side of Dunne that
she'd never seen before, and she was finding him rather
admirable. But she wanted to keep the conversation on track,
as much as she could, without arousing his suspicions.

'Were you anywhere nearby when the teacher fell from the mountain, Henry?' She hoped that she had managed to keep her voice casual.

'I was quite near, yes. But the visibility was terrible, though – I didn't really see anything. It was a combination of bad weather and bad organization, I think. Richard was closer, as I remember, but I could be wrong. It's strange to hear you talking about Mr Dickson now, really; I can't say that I've thought about it in thirty years.'

She decided to shift to another angle of attack. 'Do you keep in touch with anyone else from Burstone, or was it just Richard?'

'Well . . . I don't really, to be honest. But there's this funny chap who insists on organizing old boys' reunions, and there was one a little while ago. He made a point of calling me, to ask if I'd say a few words about Richard – it was just after Richard died, you see – so I couldn't really say no, much as I wanted to. Doesn't that sound terrible?'

They both laughed. 'I can't imagine anything worse than having to mix with everyone I went to school with,' Glasby told him. 'I left nine years ago, and no one's tried to do anything like that so far, so I think I'm probably safe.'

She must be only twenty-seven, Dunne thought. How strange, to think that she was twenty years younger than him. He smiled at her, for no particular reason, and let his thoughts drift. There was an easy intimacy between them, he felt, something which bridged the disparity in their ages.

'Actually, I came across another Burstone old boy recently,' Glasby was saying. 'Michael Fisher. It was while I was working on a crime story this time. Was he in your year as well?'

'Fisher?' Dunne was surprised again. 'He was, yes. In fact, he was at the reunion as well. It was the first time that I'd seen him since the late Seventies, and I honestly don't think he looked much different. He was always a little . . .' He hesitated, thinking better of what he'd planned to say. 'What's he done, anyway?'

'Oh,' Glasby responded in what she intended to be an offhand sort of way, looking carefully at Dunne. 'It was more what was done to him. Someone banged him over the head. They killed him, I mean.'

Somehow this wasn't as much of a shock to Dunne as it

might have been. 'I don't like to speak ill of someone who can't answer back, you know, but Fisher . . .' Glasby was smiling at him again, obviously on his wavelength. 'If anyone was going to meet a bad end; you know what I mean, don't you? He was just that *sort*. Where was he living? Did they find who did it?'

Before Glasby could answer Dunne heard a familiar sound at the front door. Once it would have been so welcome, but not now. 'That'll be my wife, I should think.' He started to rise, and as Glasby did the same, waved her back to her seat.

'No, do sit down again, please. I'll let Patsy know that you're here, and introduce you.' He rushed out, feeling guilty without knowing what it was he was supposed to have done wrong. He had little doubt that Patsy would think of something for him.

He wasn't disappointed on that score. She was barely through the door before she started. 'Who's that girl you've got in the front room? I saw that little smile you were giving her! What's going on?'

'Don't be ridiculous!' he hissed at her, glancing over his shoulder to make sure that the door was closed and his guest hopefully out of earshot. 'She's a journalist, from the *Herald* newspaper . . .'

That was as far as he was allowed to get. 'A journalist from the *Herald*! It's not that Glasby girl who's caused all this trouble, is it? I suppose now that John Redgrave's dumped her, you're having a try to get in there, are you?'

'Patsy!' he shouted, forgetting to keep his voice down.

'Don't you "Patsy" me!' she snarled. Her face was no more than a foot or two from his now, the smell of alcohol hanging around her like a cloud. 'If you want to get your hands into some little tramp's knickers, you make sure that you damned well do it!' The last two words were screamed at full volume, and were still echoing round the hallway as she stamped furiously up the stairs and out of sight.

He could hear his wife throw herself on to the bed and as he did, the door to the front room opened. 'Henry, I hope you don't mind, but I really should be going,' Glasby said.

Dunne did his best to smile at her, but the mood that had been created during their pleasant little interlude had been shattered beyond repair. He showed her out and stood at the door, deep in thought, as she walked along the tiled path and out through the gate on to the street.

Once she was safely out of sight Glasby breathed a loud sigh. Poor guy, having such a nightmare for a wife! No wonder he looked petrified to see her! Then, her face resuming its normal businesslike expression, she checked in her handbag. The paper tissue that she had used to wipe the teacup from which Dunne had been drinking was neatly folded and wrapped in clingfilm. She hoped that it would work well enough as a DNA sample.

Although, she thought, Dunne hadn't seemed remotely worried about anything other than Longhammer. And the awful wife, of course. He seemed perfectly at ease talking about the teacher's death and he didn't even seem to be aware that Michael Fisher had been murdered.

Either he was completely innocent, or he was a very good liar indeed. All she had to do was work out which.

It was nearly ten, and Glasby was lying on the lumpy sofa, trying to find a position comfortable enough to allow her to concentrate on the rather complicated novel which she was trying to finish.

She was tired after another twelve-hour day in the office, filled – inevitably – with bicycles and other equally fascinating modes of transport. And there was Davenport's latest wheeze, angling. He'd decided that the *Herald*'s readership would appreciate a guide to how to take up different outdoor activities. Together with Mike Marshall, Glasby was taking a light-hearted look (if you could be light-hearted and grit your teeth at the same time) at what was out there.

She turned a page and as she did so, her phone rang. The caller had withheld their number, but everyone seemed to do that to her nowadays.

'Hello?' She could hear traffic in the background but nothing else. 'Hello, who is it?'

'Listen bitch.' He had a London accent and a voice that reminded her of Vinnie Jones and gangster movies. 'You might think that we're numpties but we ain't. Your little piece on Richard Bedingfield and Burstone School, we saw it on Sunday. This is the last time you get told, so you be a good girl and listen carefully. You are going to write nothing!

Nothing on Longhammer, nothing on Henry Dunne, nothing on Michael bloody Fisher, Burstone School, no questions, no little visits to policemen's houses, no clever little bits in your newspaper, nothing. End of. Last chance for Miss Alison Glasby. Simple as that.'

The line went dead. Glasby was still lying on the sofa and it was a warm evening but she started to shiver. The phone rang again, the number withheld as before. She hesitated, not wanting to answer but too frightened to ignore it.

This time the voice was completely different. 'Alison Glasby?' She recognized the accent; it was the girl who said that she had been Michael Fisher's friend. 'My name is Mia. You say you want to meet me. Is it OK, we will meet tomorrow?'

'Tomorrow?' asked Glasby, wearily. 'Yes, that should be fine.'

*Alison,*
*I know this world is killing you,*
*Oh Alison,*
*My aim is true*
*Elvis Costello*

*From the notebook of Michael Fisher*

# Eleven

The bar was supposed to be right on Trafalgar Square and it shouldn't have been hard to find, but it was. Three-quarters of the square was pretty much taken up by the National Gallery and various embassies, so there was only really the south side for Glasby to look along. After walking back and forth a couple of times she noticed a large man with a ponytail dressed entirely in black, complete with wrap-around dark glasses. He was standing outside a pair of large metal-covered doors. There was nothing at all to indicate what the doors might lead to but she decided to try her luck.

'Excuse me.' From a height, Ponytail looked down at her. His glasses were dark enough that she could hardly see his eyes. He didn't actually deign to say anything but just looked steadily at her.

'Is this the Furnace?'

'Yes,' he replied, which she correctly interpreted to mean: 'Yes, why would someone like you need to know that?'

Glasby, wishing that she had thought to dress in something a bit more elegant than jeans and trainers, was about to explain that she had arranged to meet someone inside, but stopped herself just in time. It was just a bar, for God's sake, and he was just a doorman!

Glasby walked past him and pushed hard against the door, which was so heavy that she could hardly move it. Ponytail did nothing to help her. She managed to open it just wide enough to squeeze through, her bag slipping off her shoulder on the way in.

She found herself at the edge of a large rectangular room with a crowd of people in it, drinking and talking. Towards the middle there were some low leather couches and a few slate-topped tables with chairs round them, but mostly people were standing. Some of those near the door turned in her direction. The looks which she received were not particularly friendly.

Mia had said that she would be sitting at the bar, which was diagonally across from where Glasby stood. Unfortunately for her it ran the full length of the room, and at least thirty people were clustered around it. So far as she could tell, none of them looked particularly Russian and although there were plenty of young women (all of them dressed much more fashionably than her), none of them was on her own.

Feeling more than a little self-conscious, Glasby went up to the bar and started to move parallel to it, hoping that if Mia was there she would identify herself. Two middle-aged men walked past, leaving behind them a young oriental-looking girl who was sitting on a high stool, a bottle of champagne and three empty glasses in front of her. As she drew near, the girl looked straight at Glasby, smiled, and said, 'Hello, Alison.'

Surprised, Glasby replied, 'Oh, hi, are you Mia?' She already knew the answer; the accent was exactly as she had remembered it from their phone conversation. But this girl looked like she came from Thailand or Vietnam, not Russia. 'Are those guys with you?'

Mia laughed, a little birdlike sound. 'No, of course not.' (She put the emphasis on the 'not'). 'They just want to buy me champagne. But when I see you come in I tell them they must go away, because I have important meeting.'

'And they went, just like that?' Mia gave Glasby a smile but said nothing. 'Anyway, how did you recognize me when I came in?'

'Oh, it was easy.' A pause, then that little laugh again. 'Your clothes, you don't look like people who come in here.'

Glasby felt herself flush but tried to force a smile on to her face. Mia's outfit was not even that different from hers: jeans, sandals and a cotton top. Although it was true that the other girl had on heels higher than any Glasby had ever worn, her jeans looked a lot more fitted and her top was a black singlet with pink bows at the shoulders and 'Dollbaby' written across it in large, shiny, pink letters.

It was pretty obvious whose appearance the waiter appreciated more. A polite nod in Glasby's direction was quickly followed by something a lot more friendly aimed at Mia. 'What can I get for you two ladies?' he asked in a broad

Australian accent, continuing to look exclusively at Mia. She gave him a dazzling smile in return, adjusting her legs and leaning back a little on her stool. Standing next to her, Glasby was beginning to feel like an elderly chaperone or lady's companion.

'We don't need nothing,' Mia told him. (Glasby controlled the urge to correct her vocabulary.) 'We have champagne, you see it. Please take two glasses to our table.' And Mia treated the waiter to another smile.

Glasby looked round. So far as she could see, all the chairs and tables were taken up already. But in no more than a few moments one had been found for them. Mia led the way followed by the waiter with their bottle of champagne (its purchasers, having rapidly outlived their usefulness, had thoughtfully disappeared) and two glasses. Along with several other men, he was admiring Mia's bottom. Her jeans, which seemed impossibly tight, had large crystal crowns on the pockets. Glasby had never felt so unattractive in her life.

'How did you meet Michael Fisher?' They were seated at their table sipping champagne, Glasby's poise returning now that she was asking the questions. She also had the chance to get a proper look at Mia, who really was an extraordinary looking girl, tiny even in those heels, and very fine boned. Her wrists and fingers looked thin enough to snap and her voice was just as delicate, high pitched but with a curious lilt which still sounded Slavic to Glasby. She had long, lustrous jet black hair.

How a girl who looked like a Chinese emperor's concubine came to have a Russian accent was a subject that Glasby decided to put off for the time being. She was curious about what the girl was doing in London. Whatever it was, her English was a bit basic, that was clear.

'Michael was customer. He was one of my first.'

'Customer?' Glasby was surprised. 'What was he buying?'

Mia opened her mouth as if to reply but said nothing and laughed instead. Glasby looked at her, perfectly made-up, ultra-feminine and exquisite, and realized that it was a stupid question. Both women reached for their glasses and drank. Then they caught each other's eye and started to laugh.

'Sorry,' said Glasby, at the same time as Mia began her explanation.

She was twenty-two years old and had been in London for four months, travelling on a student visa with a boyfriend. Her home country was Kazakhstan, which Glasby thought must be one of those bits of the former Soviet Union that stretched out along the Silk Road in Central Asia. Presumably that would explain the looks and the accent. After she had found the boyfriend with another girl ('one fat cow') Mia left him, but decided to stay on in London to make some money. A friend had introduced her to an escort agency boss ('she is one crazy Polska woman') and everything had gone along from there.

'Michael, he was' – she paused – 'sort of, *strange*.'

'What do you mean, "strange"?' asked Glasby, as it didn't seem that the girl intended to say more. To her Fisher had appeared seedy and down at heel, not at all the playboy type that she imagined Mia spending her time with.

Another pause. This time Glasby kept quiet, hoping that Mia would fill the silence. Her ploy worked. 'He liked to *watch*.' Mia stopped again, looking embarrassed, and glanced up at Glasby. 'When I first know him he say he wanted to watch me, you know, with other customers.' She stopped again. Her skin colour and make-up made it hard to tell, but Glasby had the impression that the girl was blushing.

'Did you let him?'

'Of course *not*!' replied Mia, sounding indignant. Then she laughed. 'I said *he* strange, not me! He had this website he looked at, you know, you could watch the swingers doing it, and things. He liked it if I look at it with him. It was so funny, seeing fat men going pfff, pfff!' She blew her cheeks out and exhaled loudly several times, moving her body half out of her chair. Her imitation of a man in heat drew several looks from people around them. Both women giggled.

Mia's tone changed. 'You know, Michael was a good guy to me.' He had helped her when she needed to find a flat, to get a phone line and so on, and even when he couldn't afford her any more (she went to a new agency and her prices doubled) she used to see him and sometimes have sex with him still.

'Was he your boyfriend?' asked Glasby.

'No, he was old guy. But he not like those stupid guys who buy our champagne. He was like a customer, but he wasn't crazy. Customers from my new agency, it's expensive, and often they really crazy. One guy, he want me to be like cat, pussycat he says, and I have to jump on him bed going meow meow, you know?'

As she wasn't totally sure whether this was supposed to be funny or not, Glasby thought it best to change the subject. 'Do you know what work Michael did? What did he do for money?'

Mia avoided looking at her, concentrating instead on repairing some damage to a blue-painted fingernail. Her nails extended way beyond the end of her fingers and were cut square across. They were pristine so far as Glasby could see. Eventually she answered, still looking down at the table. 'He say he was painter. But I never see him paint anything. Only the walls in him flat once. And he always write things in his book, he say they were important. He did not have lot of money, just some . . . sometimes, from someone. You know. He *say* he got it from him grandmother. But I don't think so.'

There was another silence which Glasby didn't want to break. It was clear that the girl knew more than she was saying. Glasby had the feeling that it was something important. After a few moments Mia opened her mouth as if to talk.

'Are you doing all right here, ladies?' It was the friendly waiter again. Glasby brushed him away quickly before he had the time to try his luck on her glamorous companion. Mia continued.

'I think he get money sometimes, not from working. I mean, he was not mafia man. But he got money that was not his. Because he use to tell me he had money, and then do like this.' She turned her head sideways on to Glasby, and winked, looking so comically conspiratorial that Glasby couldn't help but to burst out laughing. For the second time, Mia looked a bit indignant. 'That is not how *I* look, it is how *he* looked.' Glasby stopped hastily. Obviously her new source was a bit sensitive about not being taken seriously.

'Was he a generous friend?' she asked.

'I did not like him because of him money. I can make my money myself, you know.' It looked as if Glasby had said the wrong thing again. But the girl carried on before she had time to interrupt her. 'He was generous, you are right. He give me him laptop computer and he show me how to use it. And before they kill him . . .' She tailed off without finishing her sentence.

Glasby felt her hand tighten on the stem of her glass. She forced herself to relax and gave Mia what she hoped was an encouraging smile. It seemed to work.

'I seen him maybe three times just before he dead. Because he was teaching me on the computer, for internet and chat. He keep showing me one big knife he had to use if someone try to do something bad to him. And the last time, I went to his flat and he give me this bag. It has letters in it and some other things. He said if he dead, I must call you. And you will give me lot of money for it.'

Glasby tried not to show her excitement. She leaned back in her chair and took a breath before replying. 'This bag, you said it has letters in it? And what else?'

The girl looked at her suspiciously. 'Why? Will you pay for it? Because you are *dzhornalist*.' She pronounced the word as if it might hurt her if not used with care. 'And I think there are many *dzhornalisti* in London. Maybe someone can pay me more than you.'

This was not what Glasby was hoping to hear. She needed to get control of the situation. If this strange young girl had got hold of evidence that implicated Henry Dunne in a murder, a Fleet Street bidding war would put it out of the *Herald*'s reach – *her* reach – almost before it began. She leaned forward over the table.

'Listen, Mia,' she began, with as much confidence as she could muster. 'Fisher, I mean Michael, was right. If you have what I think you have, my newspaper could pay you for it. I know all about it, I understand what it all means, but no one else does. Nobody will pay you for a load of old letters. If it was so easy to get money for them, Fisher would have sold them while he was still alive.'

Glasby wasn't sure how much of this Mia had understood, but it seemed to make an impact. Her expression changed to one of concentration. Glasby pressed home her advantage.

'The first thing you have to do is to show me what he gave you. That's what he told you to do, isn't it? Then I can talk to my boss, he's called the editor of the newspaper, and then I can give you money. Maybe a lot, really a lot. But first I have to see what you have.'

The suspicious look returned. 'Maybe you will see it, and then you know everything, and you don't pay me. First you have to pay me, then you see it.' Unexpectedly Mia laughed, the same musical little giggle as before. 'You know crazy Polska woman? From my first agency? She teach me, customer always pays first. If you give him what him wants, then he don't want pay you, afterwards.'

Both women smiled this time. 'Mia, it's not really like that. I mean, your agency boss was probably right. But the newspaper can't use your evidence, your letters, just because I've seen them. First I see them, then we would tell our lawyers to make a proper legal agreement with you, with your money in it. Then we test the evidence to see if it's genuine. We can't start using material until then, not in a case like this.'

Strangely, it was the reference to lawyers which seemed to satisfy the girl. She put out a delicate little hand for Glasby to shake and they agreed to rendezvous in two hours.

The meeting place which Mia had specified was mundane enough, a street like many others in west London, lined on either side by Victorian terraced houses long since turned into columns of anonymous apartments. The pavement was decorated with black bin bags and plane trees that had strips of bark missing. Glasby was fortunate to have found a parking space although she felt uneasy about whether some parking warden looking to up his bonus on the late shift might spot her in the residents' only bay. As a result she stayed put behind the wheel with the engine running, keeping a careful lookout for officialdom as well as for her diminutive new informant.

It was this that saved her and Mia, and which led to the deaths of two men who she had never met but who shared her interest in matters concerning Michael Fisher and Henry Dunne.

Glasby being Glasby, she was on time or (as she mentally noted on arrival) forty-five seconds early, to be precise. She sat waiting for twenty minutes or more, anticipation at what she might be about to see gradually being replaced by boredom.

Finally she caught sight of Mia in her wing mirror, although she had to look hard to make sure that it was the same girl who she had met at the bar. Skin tight jeans and heels had been replaced by a track suit and trainers, topped off with an oversized peaked cap. More importantly to Glasby, she was carrying a blue zipped bag on one shoulder.

Glasby stuck her arm out of the car window and waved. Mia acknowledged her but made no move to quicken her stride. Impatience beginning to get the better of her, Glasby let down the hand brake and put the car into gear, holding it steady with the clutch. Then things started to happen fast.

Mia opened the passenger door, threw in the blue bag and followed it on to the seat next to Glasby. As she did so, Glasby caught sight of a thickset man running along the pavement towards them. He was balding and shiny with sweat, strands of dark hair stuck down on to his forehead.

Before Mia had finished pulling the car door closed the man drew level with them. He wrenched the door open and reached inside across Mia's legs, towards the bag. She screamed. Instinctively, Glasby put her foot down on the accelerator. The Punto jumped forward, its door connecting first with the man's arm and then swinging out again, until it bounced off the bumper of the car in front and slammed itself shut.

Now Glasby was sweating too, the car engine protesting as it lurched along in first gear. Mia shouted something that Glasby couldn't understand. In the rear view mirror she could see the man running back away from them and getting into a black saloon car. It was obvious that whoever he was, he didn't intend to let them escape.

'Who is that mafia man? Who is he?'

'I don't know, Mia. I never saw him before! Maybe he followed you!'

She was concentrating too much on controlling the car to look at the girl beside her, moving up through the gears and racing down the side street as fast as she dared.

'God sakes, drive fast! God sakes! They following us!'

The road turned into a much larger dual carriageway. There was a cyclist coming towards her but she cut right in ahead of him. He swerved and swore, sticking a finger up at her. Just in front were some traffic lights. As she got near them she glanced back and saw a large Mercedes with two men inside. It was no more than a couple of hundred metres away and making ground fast. Ahead, the signal turned to orange.

'Don't stop! They catch us if you stop!'

Mia was right; there was nothing for it. Glasby jammed her foot down on the accelerator, passing the lights exactly as they turned red. The Punto shot straight across four lanes of traffic. In the furthest lane, a double-decker bus made ready to pull across the junction. A bright red motorbike had jumped the lights and was already moving from behind the bus towards them. There was just room enough for her to swerve past.

Her pursuers were not so lucky. The driver braked hard as the bike appeared in front of him. The big car skidded sideways, tyres screaming. The sound of metal on metal rang violently loud even inside Glasby's car. She jammed her foot down on the brake and looked round just in time to see a car windscreen turn a full 360 degrees in mid-air and land, somehow unbroken, on the road. Behind it were the crushed remains of the black Mercedes, sandwiched between the bus and a blue delivery van.

'Don't stop, don't stop now!' Glasby had momentarily forgotten her passenger but she turned to her now. The girl was shaking, her eyes wide with fear.

'Don't stop,' she shouted again. 'Please drive us. We are not safe here.'

# English as a Foreign Language

*Cough*
*Enough*
*Bough*
*Through*
*Though*
*Thought*
*Lough*
*Borough*

*From the notebook of Michael Fisher*

# Twelve

The noise from the bathroom had been going on for a long time but Glasby had no time to wonder what Mia might be doing in there; she had asked to use the shower in order to relax after the scare they'd had earlier. Glasby was cross-legged on the carpet in her sitting room, Michael Fisher's blue holdall behind her, working her way through its contents.

She started, naturally enough, with a clipping taken from a newspaper. It felt brittle and dry to her touch. At the top, someone, presumably Fisher – she made a mental note to try to find a sample of his handwriting so that she could check – had written '*Fort William Times*: 19.4.1974'.

Under the headline 'Failings in Safety Precautions May Have Led to Fatal Fall' (which was not exactly snappy and would have had no chance of passing muster at the *Herald*, in Glasby's professional opinion) she read the following:

> A number of parties gave evidence to the Coroner's Enquiry after a fall from Ben Rosimore last weekend led to the death of a games master from England. The teacher, Mr Alan Dickson, was aged 38 and was a former soldier in the Parachute Regiment. He was leading a party of children on a fell walk up to the summit of the Ben.
>
> Among those appearing before James Murdoch, the Inverness-shire County Coroner, was Hamish Fraser, a senior member of the Fort William mountain rescue group, which recovered the body of Mr Dickson later that day from its resting place in the Four Fingers Gully, more than a thousand feet below the summit. Mr Fraser was questioned both as to the weather conditions and the preparedness of the party led by Mr Dickson.
>
> 'There were squalls as we expect at this season of the year,' Mr Fraser told the *Times*. 'They bring the cloud

down. Up above a thousand feet or so, great care is needed until it lifts again.'

Although Mr Fraser did not wish to comment outside the court on whether the school party had been properly trained and equipped, in his evidence to the Coroner he had made it clear that neither the teacher himself, nor the boys whom he had been leading, had boots or clothes suitable for the conditions which they encountered that day.

Three of the boys, all aged fourteen and from Burstone School in Oxfordshire, England, also appeared as witnesses. Although two of them saw the unfortunate master lose his footing, due to the very limited visibility none was able to inform the court as to the precise circumstances that led to his fall.

A verdict of accidental death was reached, upon the advice of the Coroner, Mr Murdoch. In his closing remarks he thanked all those who gave evidence, in particular the three schoolboys, whom he described as 'Brave young men, in the face of a very distressing circumstance.'

Mr Murdoch also praised the work of the mountain rescue group, and appealed for all those visiting the area to take appropriate precautions and educate themselves in advance as to the risks involved.

Clipped to the newspaper cutting was a black and white photograph, showing what looked like the dead body of a man lying face up. His arms had been placed at his side. There was no obvious sign of the injuries that had caused his death, although a hole had been torn in his tartan print shirt, across the left side of the chest. His eyes were open wide, staring out from under a light-coloured thatch of hair.

Glasby's eye was caught by a piece of cloth that had been sealed in a plastic bag. She picked it up and held it up, closer to the light. It was a mixture of dark greens and blues, with a square red pinstripe; a classic tartan which, so far as she could tell, exactly matched that worn by Alan Dickson when he fell to his death. It was about ten centimetres long and a little less across, and roughly made up the shape of an oblong – just like the hole in the games master's shirt.

There were two dark brown stains on the cloth, both about the size of a 2p piece. They could have been anything, including, Glasby thought, blood.

She turned to the remaining contents of the bag, a small bundle of letters. The first was on the headed notepaper of a laboratory, Bioscience UK, who were based in Oxford. It confirmed a DNA match from 'a fragment of brushed cotton material, c. 112 mm x 91 mm at its widest points, and coloured predominantly blue and green with a tartan pattern' and another sample 'which as provided to the laboratory was labelled "taken from Henry Dunne, dated 24 March 2007".'

The remainder of the bundle was a series of notes, all from Richard Bedingfield and addressed to Michael Fisher. There were eight in total. They were undated, except for the occasional mention of a day and a month. Most were headed with the address of the Bedingfield family home, although a couple had been written on the notepaper of the Parachute Regiment, from garrison headquarters in Colchester.

The notes were all brief, written in a strong, confident hand. Most contained a reference to money being given by Bedingfield to Fisher. Only in one was any amount mentioned, the figure of £2,000 being specified.

Hearing a sound from the bathroom Glasby looked up, realizing that the noise of the shower had finally ended. The door opened and Mia emerged, looking more fragile and tinier than ever. Her long black hair was shining wet. She was clad only in a towel, which just about covered her from chest to thighs. Glasby felt her face go bright red.

Patsy had switched the bedroom light off at least twenty minutes ago, and he had thought that she was asleep, so Henry Dunne was surprised to hear his wife speak. 'You know that he was bullied, don't you?' she asked him, her voice quiet and strangely calm.

'What do you mean, bullied? Mattie?' He had no idea what she was referring to.

'Yes, Mattie. At that school, for years. He used to come home with spit all down his blazer, and they pinched his money sometimes, and . . . Well, all sorts of revolting things. You wouldn't believe what animals they had there. It used to make me boil.'

'Why the hell didn't he tell me?' Dunne was sat up in bed now, but his wife was still turned away from him, her head a shadow on the pillow. 'Why didn't *you* tell me, for Christ's sake? I could have done something, you know that!'

'I didn't tell you because he always asked me not to. If I hadn't have promised that, he wouldn't have said anything to me either. I found out, because I was here, at home, when *he* got home. And you didn't, because you were never—'

Dunne sucked in air. 'Why the hell would anyone want to bully Mattie? I mean, he's always had friends, and he's such a great kid. Why, Patsy? Do you know?'

This time his wife was facing him. Her voice dropped even more.

'Oh, Henry, you really don't understand, do you? All those years, poor Mattie was the son of a *pig*, and you wonder why he got bullied? How many of his lovely classmates had fathers, or brothers, that the *pigs* had put away? He hated it, but he always admired you, he still does, he really looks up to you. That's why he didn't want you to know. He hates asking you for help, the boy just hates it . . .'

She turned away again. He could hear her start to cry. His own eyes filled up and tears started to spill down his face.

For what seemed like a long time they both stayed like that, and then Patsy turned back to him, her arms outstretched. They lay tightly together, their tears intermingled, crying very softly in the darkness of their bedroom.

Mia had exchanged the towel for a bath robe of Glasby's which, even with the sleeves turned up, was several sizes too large for her. They were sitting at opposite ends of the purple sofa, Glasby sprawled out, Mia with her legs tucked neatly under her.

The shock that they had been through earlier left neither of them particularly hungry, which was lucky, as there was nothing much to eat in the apartment. They sat sharing a bottle of wine and some digestive biscuits which Glasby had found in a cupboard.

The girl's English was patchy to say the least, but Glasby gradually got used to it, and so long as she was careful to express herself clearly, they found that they could communicate well enough. There was a gap of a few years in their ages and a much bigger gulf in their experiences of life but they found things in common as well: two smart, independent young women determined to make their own way in a world that somehow had never been that easy on them.

'Don't you miss your family and home, Mia? Do they know what you do here, for a living I mean?'

She was rewarded again with that musical little laugh, and, 'No, of course *not*! If they know, they kill me! It is Muslim country, I can never live like this there.'

'Wouldn't life be better there?'

'No! There they tell me I must marry, you know. I am twenty-two-year-old girl now, very old for not married. If I married, I must stay at home, clean house for husband and his mother and family, never go out. In London I have my flat, my friends, I can do anything I want. I love my family, but here I am free!'

Glasby hesitated, not wanting to offend, but too curious to hold back. 'But here, you are a . . . I mean, you have to work . . . Don't you find it difficult, working as an escort, I mean? Having sex with men, even when you don't want to?'

Mia unfolded her legs and stretched them out, her toes pointed. She smiled, admiring herself, delicate and shapely.

'It is work,' she replied, still looking at her feet rather than at Glasby. 'Sometimes is nice, top places, rich guys, often they just like chat you know. This one guy, he book me for four hours. He wants sex, once, then he wants sit in my bath and I talk to him, holding him hand in bath.' She giggled again. 'My bum it hurts! Sitting on bath during many hours, it very hard!'

She smiled at Glasby, and yawned. If this was supposed to be a hint to change the subject it wasn't taken.

'It can't always be that easy, though, surely? What if you've got some guy, a customer I mean, who smells bad, or if he wants to do things . . .' She stopped, embarrassed.

'It is not always easy, you are true,' Mia conceded. 'A lot of girls, they drink much, or they start with drugs, because always they must smile and be happy, always sexy and romantic for customers, and this is not easy. And sometimes, customer say nasty things to girl, or he tries to push her too much, make her do things she don't want. And all girls get nervous, you know, you see guy just first time, have to take clothes off, touch him . . .'

She took another drink from the wine glass in front of her. Glasby did the same, as if in sympathy. 'I don't know how anyone could do it, honestly,' she said, with more feeling and less tact than she'd intended. 'Doing what men tell you to do, just because they have money, it must be just awful.'

It seemed to upset her guest.' Escorts are just girls, not different to you. If you had to, you could do it like me. You went to university?' Glasby nodded. 'I did not have chance to do this. When I was young, they teach me to be dancer, ballet. I was good dancer, but they take me away from my family. They made me independent, when I was very young. My body was very light, but not strong, so always I was hurt, and they make me perform anyway.

'Now, nobody make me do nothing. I never have possibility for good education, never have real job like you, but I have my own money, if I need to work, I work; if I don't want to, I don't. It is not easy, but I am independent girl.'

She had such a proud expression on her face that Glasby laughed, mostly just to share the girl's pleasure.

'You laugh, but is true!' Mia said. 'You have men who tell you what to do?' Glasby, thinking of Ellington, and Davenport, and even Daniels, all of whom seemed to think that they owned her these days, had to admit that she did. This wasn't enough, however; Mia seemed determined to prove her point.

'You have boyfriend?'

Glasby hesitated. 'Well, sort of. On and off, you could say. He's a detective, you know, at Scotland Yard, the police?'

'And if he was useless man, with no job, you still love him?' Glasby didn't know what to say to this – not least because she wasn't sure whether or not she currently could be said to love Redgrave even with his splendid occupation.

Apparently an answer wasn't required of her. 'No, you don't!' said Mia, proving the point for her. 'Your boyfriend, he is useful to you, and my customers, they are useful for me.'

If only it was true, Glasby thought. Here she was, with the clock ticking down fast in her hour of need, and Redgrave was not only not useful, she wasn't totally sure if he was even on the same side as her.

What began as a sigh turned into a yawn. She glanced at

her watch; it was nearly midnight. 'Look, I'm really sorry, Mia. I have to get up to go to work tomorrow, pretty early. Do you mind if . . .'

It was understandable enough that the girl didn't want to go back to Olympia. Whoever it was who had been chasing them earlier, and whatever had happened to them, two things were clear: they meant nothing good to Mia or her, and they knew where the girl lived. Glasby had agreed readily to put her up, and had started making up a bed on the sofa.

Then Mia had surprised her by coming in just as Glasby was getting into bed. Literally speaking Mia was dressed, but the underwear that she had on was not exactly extensive and it was . . . well, a bit see-through. Without asking permission beyond a quick smile in Glasby's direction, she slipped under the duvet and lay down next to her.

Glasby started to get up again. 'I'm sorry, I mean . . . Wasn't the sofa comfortable enough to sleep on? I'll try it myself, you stay here . . .'

Mia said quietly, 'In my country, we sleep in same bed, if we are family or good friends. Is OK if I stay? I hear noises outside, on street, and I think that maybe there will be more mafia guys. I am scared.'

Glasby stopped and sat back down again. In truth, she was frightened herself. She'd been glancing at her phone all evening, expecting to receive more threats of violence, and hadn't dared switch it off in case it might provoke someone into delivering a message to her personally instead. It hadn't made her feel any better when she remembered how easily Mr Smith had found home addresses for two people, both of whom were much better placed than she was to keep themselves hidden.

It was very strange to have someone else in bed with her, let alone another woman – let alone this exotic girl, who was barely even dressed. A borderline insomniac anyway, Glasby resigned herself to a sleepless few hours, as she reached up to switch off the bedside light.

A moment later she felt an arm across her ribs and a hand against her stomach. Five minutes after that she was asleep, wakened only by the alarm the next morning. It was the best night's sleep that she'd managed in weeks.

\*   \*   \*

'OK, Alison. So *if* these letters are real, and *if* the DNA samples are what they say they are – which, given that Fisher was the sort of guy who you wouldn't trust any further than you could throw our friend John Smith, we'd better put a note of caution on – as I say, if all is what it seems, what have you got?'

'It's supporting evidence, isn't it, Bill? Be fair, Fisher said that he could back his story up, and this does. If it's all real, as you say.'

'Supporting, maybe. But what does it prove? Nothing! Mrs Bedingfield has already told you that her husband may well have given Fisher money.'

Glasby snorted. 'Oh, come on, Bill! I know that Bedingfield seems to have been a very moral guy, but two thousand quid, to help out someone he was at school with thirty years ago – you can't be serious!'

'Maybe, and maybe not. As for your forensics; a bit of blood on an old piece of cloth, what does that prove, even matched up with Dunne's DNA – if it *is* his, of course—'

'I can easily check that out, Bill,' she interrupted, triumphantly. 'I took a DNA sample from him myself, at the weekend.'

'Oh, dear God, tell me you didn't say that, Alison! What the hell did you do?'

'I went to visit him, and he invited me in for tea, and when he was out of the room I wiped a tissue around the cup. Why? Do you think it's illegal to do that? Should I ask Jonathan Constance?'

'I don't know if it's illegal and I hope that I never find out! And no, don't talk to Constance about it. He'll be duty bound to brief Ellington, and then you'll be out on your ear and I'll be needing a new assistant. Probably I should tell him about your escapades myself, come to think of it. And then we'll never get the commuting series done.'

Glasby didn't smile, although she knew Davenport well enough to understand that he had no intention of shopping her to Ellington.

'There is one other thing, Bill.'

She told him everything that had happened: the threatening phone call she had received, then her contact with Mia, what the girl had said that Fisher had told her, meeting up with her outside her apartment, the heavies waiting there, the chase . . . 'And the last thing I heard was an almighty clang, it really sounded bad. But I don't know what happened after that.'

He quizzed her for full details of time and place. 'That's right, where Addison Road crosses Kensington High Street. Right by that funny garage.'

'Do you mean the showroom for Bristol Cars? I know where it is. Let me make a call or two; give me twenty minutes, and come back to me, OK?'

The time passed slowly as Glasby waited and worried about what Davenport might find out. The look on his face when she walked back in to his office didn't make her feel any better.

'What happened, Bill?'

'The two men in the car that chased you, Alison, they died, I'm sorry to say. Apparently their car ended up between the bus and a truck coming the other way. One of them went through the side window – he can't have had his seat belt on – and the other, the driver, ended up with the bus more or less on top of him.'

Glasby, who had gone white, sat down quickly.

'Oh God, Bill, that's terrible. Do you know who they were? I didn't do anything, you know, I just kept driving, and they followed me. Do you think that the police know anything about my car? Could anyone have got my registration?'

'Don't worry, Alison. The police think that it was just a stupid bit of driving that got them killed, and from what you've said, they're right. No one seems to have mentioned anything about any other car being involved and I don't think that they will. As for the two men, well I'm afraid that you've not been keeping very salubrious company. Ex-coppers, the pair of them, and with a reputation for rough stuff. They were in Special Branch, which is about as close as this country comes to having a secret police force, with methods to match.'

Glasby, still pale, was back on her feet. 'You know I told you about Fisher's neighbour, the old man, who said that he saw two retired military types hanging around, just before the murder? If you can get photos of these two, we can try to see if he'll identify them! It must have been them!'

'Hold on a moment, Alison. Listen to me, please.' Davenport was standing as well now.

'I just told you, those two men were very serious characters.

Whatever it was that they were up to, they wouldn't have been doing it off their own bat. Someone must have hired them, for sure. They were part of George Pincher's firm – *Inspector* Pincher he was, he's retired now but not so *very* retired, I don't believe. I've already told you, I don't want to have to start looking for another journalist, so listen carefully: calm down, slow down, and take a deep breath. Oh, hello chaps!'

This last was directed at the doorway, where the other three members of Team Davenport were assembled and waiting.

'I do believe that it's time for our editorial conference,' said their leader cheerfully. 'Is everyone's cup brimming over with ideas?'

It didn't matter whether they were or not; apparently Davenport had quite enough to go round.

'First off, someone mentioned Bristol Cars to me a while ago. Jack, Mike, I want a bit of research please. Have a look at famous British sports car makers of the Fifties, Sixties and Seventies. Where are they now? Have they gone out of business? Why? Or if not, who owns them, and what sort of motors are they making? I'll give you a head start: Jensen, MG, TVR, Alvis, Aston Martin – and Bristol, of course, as well.'

He wasn't finished. 'Now ladies, I've something for you. The elderly. There's more of them. OK' – he held his hands up in mock surrender – 'more of *us* than ever. What are young people's attitude to the old nowadays? Are they changing as the population balance shifts, or are we just becoming more of a nuisance to all of you? How many of the old are in work? Would more of them work if they could? Answers on a postcard please!'

All four of them filed out again looking thoughtful, but none more so than Alison Glasby. Davenport followed her with his eyes. The smile had left his face, replaced by a worried expression.

It wasn't even that hard, once she made herself do it. She just picked up her phone, pressed a button, and there he was, sounding much more like his old self, thank God.

'Hi, Alison, it's so nice to hear from you! How are you, keeping yourself out of trouble?'

'Hi, John, it's really nice to talk to you too. And I'm fine thanks. I've had one or two scares lately, to be honest, but I'm OK. Listen' – she lowered her voice, conscious that Hetal was no more than a couple of metres away – 'I was wondering, do you think – I mean, would you like to, well, meet up and talk? I know I said some things, when I was angry I mean, and a bit upset by what you said, but . . .'

He laughed. 'If that was an apology, Ali, then you deserve one from me too. I'm sorry, really I am. It was a misunderstanding really, between you and me, and I said some stupid things too, which you know isn't how I really feel about you. So does that mean that we're friends again?'

'Of course it does. You know how much I think of you, John. And, well, there are some things in particular that I'd really value your advice on . . .'

There was a brief pause. 'I suppose that these "things" might just have something to do with work? Yours, and probably mine as well?'

'Well, yes,' she admitted. 'Yes, they do. But I really want to see you anyway, really I do. Even if you don't want to help me with work, I mean. We can just meet, and talk, and – you know.'

Redgrave laughed again. 'Do you remember on our first date, I had to take you to hospital? Well, if we meet – *when* we meet up, I mean – and you don't talk about work inside the first ten minutes, I'm taking you straight back there!'

Afterwards, Glasby allowed herself a few moments to sit and smile to herself. She hadn't felt as good in ages.

*Dear My Prince,*
  *My Grandmother tell me when I was little girl that England is country of all world most gentlemens. She always say me when I find my English prince I will love Him always and do everything only for make Him happy. When we together in your country this is I will do, obey You and give my life for You, so you understand always that I am girl who wants only you my Man.*
  *Now I must ask you my Prince to help my dear Grandmother. She is everything to me, all family, I tell you this before. Bad man owns our little flat in Voronezh, now he tells her she must buy from him or must go out in two weeks. I am young girl and can find place stay with other people but Grandmother she lives here all her years, she so upset now she makes her very ill.*
  *Little flat costs $12,000, without this I so frighted she will dead.*
  *Can you help your little Vlada my Prince? I never will ask for me but for my Grandmother who is all family of me, I must do everything. Other man, friend Landlord, says he buy flat for me but I no want this, he is not gentlemen as you.*
  *My girlfriend father he say flat is good price, will worth two times after two, three years. Soon I think my very loved Grandmother will dead, she have eighty and one years, then we sell again.*
  *Please dear my Prince, I want no money for me, only for dear Grandmother, I want only to be with you. I dream all days when I will be in your country and you will hold me and love me always, I want be perfect girl for You.*
  *Kisses very much from your little Vlada.*

  *From the notebook of Michael Fisher*

# Thirteen

Glasby looked at her watch; it was just before two. Mia had phoned earlier, the third time that she had called in the last few days. Despite the fact that the girl seemed to be checking up on her, presumably concerned to make sure that Fisher's story – and the reward she was hoping to get for it – hadn't been forgotten, Glasby had been pleased to hear from her.

Mia had felt forced to abandon her flat, concerned that it was no longer safe for her to be there, and was staying with a friend. Glasby tried to tell herself that there was no reason for her to feel guilty about this state of affairs; she hadn't asked the girl to get herself involved, after all. But Mia was young, foreign and all in all rather vulnerable, and it was hard for Glasby not to have a sense of responsibility for the girl's predicament.

Glasby herself had been waking up frequently at night, each time with the sound of the car crash ringing in her ear. Lying in bed afterwards she found herself worrying about whether anything bad had happened to Mia. Possibly she was simply transferring her real fears for herself on to the girl, or maybe their shared escape from danger had created a bond between them.

Whatever the reasons, Glasby was looking forward to seeing her again. She, who had often forgotten to dress up for a date with Redgrave, had cast off her jeans and after several false starts had selected a rather short denim skirt. Kate Hall had persuaded her into the purchase a couple of summers ago but she hadn't worn it since. Coupled with a brightly coloured top and a pair of wedge sandals, Glasby was a long way from her usual look and, checking herself out in the bathroom mirror, she felt distinctly good about it.

Later on she was due to see Redgrave, but for now all her attention was on her young visitor.

If she had dressed up, Mia seemed to have made a move in the opposite direction, in jeans, a shapeless T-shirt and no make-up. It didn't matter; somehow she still managed to look elegant. 'You look nice!' she exclaimed, kissing Glasby on both cheeks and then standing back to admire her. 'Not so serious like before. And you got very long legs, you lucky. Like Nicole Kidman!'

Glasby, who had never before been compared to Ms Kidman, or any other Hollywood star come to that, didn't want to show her pleasure at the unexpected compliment. 'You said that you had something you wanted to show me?' she asked, noticing a laptop bag in Mia's hand.

Mia smiled. 'Yes!' she replied emphatically, sounding very pleased with herself. 'Can we sit down?'

'I'm sorry, of course.' Glasby gestured towards the kitchen table, but her guest was already walking into the living room. She took up her previous place on the sofa and waited for Glasby to join her.

'You tell me that newspaper cannot pay me yet, you must get more proof that Michael was saying truth. I think this could help you.' She lifted the computer bag on to her lap and began to unzip it. 'This is his laptop, he bring it to me, in the bag I give you, with all other things.'

'His laptop?' Glasby repeated, looking puzzled. Something didn't seem right, and she realized what it was. 'Why didn't the police notice, if there was a computer missing from his apartment? Didn't he have a printer, and a modem or a router, things like that? It would have been really obvious that the computer was gone.'

Now it was Mia's turn to look confused. 'He just had laptop, no printer or nothing. He don't use modem for internet. Michael use wireless connection, but it was not his wireless. He used neighbour's connection, from upstairs he say. But neighbour did not know, Michael laugh about this sometimes. Because Michael do naughty things on internet, so he don't want to have his own connection.'

It sounded as if Mr Fisher's moral standing was about to take another downwards step. Seeing as his credibility was an essential part of her getting any sort of story to stand up, this was the last thing that Glasby needed, but she felt obliged nonetheless to enquire as to what these 'naughty things' might have been.

If she was expecting the worse, Fisher, through the medium of Mia, didn't disappoint.

'Michael, he want to be internet scammer. You know, he make up girl's identity, and stories. He asked me to register Russian email addresses for him, and then he pretend to be Russian girl. She called "Vlada Romanova". And he get photos from website of pretty blonde girl, and he register her on dating sites. I think sometimes it was fun for him, he show me letters from men once, and he laughing a lot.'

'What did you think about what he was doing?' asked Glasby, observing the girl closely.

'I tell him it wrong. When I understand what he want to do I say I won't help him more. You know, these mens, they maybe American, or German, and mostly they are old men and lonely, and Michael he very clever, he want to make them fall in love with him, with Vlada Romanova I mean, and then he say he will make up story about why Vlada needs money. Maybe he can say her sister ill, or her ex-boyfriend beat her up and she must move city, things like this. And old mens, they must send her money, because they love her.'

Glasby leant back on the sofa, deflated and depressed. 'How would he get the money? Where could he tell them to send it to?'

'He ask me to help him, because he need address in Russia for men to send money to. But I give him no help, because I think this is bad, so he never tell me too much. I think maybe some other girl she did find address for him to use.'

Glasby bit her lower lip. She stared moodily at her legs, Mia's compliment on her appearance a distant memory now. Her source's credibility was shot for good; if all this was true, Fisher had been not just a blackmailer but a fantasist and a fraudster as well. It was a wonder that he had managed to stay out of prison long enough for him to get himself murdered instead.

Mia wasn't finished, though. 'When I look in laptop bag, I find this. And I think it could help you get more information for newspaper, so you can give me my money.' She was holding a plain, A4-sized piece of paper which was covered in scribbles. Glasby thought that she recognized the handwriting.

'Michael, he write all his passwords here. Because he older man, I think maybe him memory is bad. It has email addresses and I think bank passwords as well.'

Glasby had to force herself to look. The username and password that Mia showed her were in the same format as her own; she and Fisher must have used the same bank. 'I'll try, Mia, but honestly I don't know how much this will help me.'

Mia looked worried. 'Are you scared, because of they two men, mafia guys? You think they can catch you?'

'No, that isn't it. I don't think they were really mafia. They were ex-police, like private detectives. And they died, you know, in the crash, I told you.'

In truth, she wasn't frightened, or at least not enough to make her drop her story. She had been relying on Fisher's claims to break through the impasse she'd found herself in and find a way out for her – and Mark Ellington – from the mess that publishing allegations about Salmon and Shipp had got the *Herald* into. And with the rescue of her faltering career at stake, Glasby was more than prepared to take risks.

It seemed that Glasby's newfound partner was as determined as her. Mia opened her handbag, an ornate white affair with a big brass padlock built into the design. The bag looked like it had cost a lot of money. In it was a small snub-nosed gun.

Glasby's eyes opened wide. 'Is it . . . is it *real*?' she asked, trying to keep her voice steady.

Mia laughed, her usual musical giggle back again. 'Yes, of course it real! I buy it so if we see more mafia mens, I show it and they will run! If you want, I get gun for you as well. You want one?'

Glasby wasn't sure that any gangsters would be quite so easily frightened away. She politely declined the offer.

The girl seemed unfazed. 'OK, I look after you anyway. I protect both of us!'

And, despite Mia's small and fragile stature, there was something in her voice and the expression on her face which made Glasby feel that, if they ever needed protection, she would probably be as good as her word.

\* \* \*

A waiter approached their table but, after catching a look from Redgrave, discreetly withdrew again. He had suggested the venue of their first date, a Chinese restaurant across the Thames from the Houses of Parliament. They had been there for forty-five minutes and had got no further than an introductory gin and tonic.

'We'd better order something, John, or they'll throw us out.'

Glasby reached for the menu which lay unopened on the table in front of her. He leant across and took her hand in his, an unconscious echo of the move which Mick Doherty had tried on during the evening which had begun Glasby and Redgrave's estrangement.

Somehow she hadn't been expecting that Redgrave would still look the same, as though their separation had lasted for years, not just two or three months, but everything about him was exactly as she remembered: wavy brown hair falling across a forehead which was creased from too many hours spent tracking down criminals, his build not unlike hers, tall and lean, with a rather pointed face and sharp brown eyes.

He had looked surprised too, when he saw her. Glasby had been pleased enough at the reaction which her outfit had got from Mia to keep it on, and from the quick glance he took down at her legs, it seemed to produce the same effect on Redgrave.

'You look great!' he had greeted her with, and the evening had taken off from there. It all seemed so natural, like they truly belonged together, and after all the traumas of the last few weeks, it was such a relief for her to be with someone – the only person, it felt to her – with whom she truly could relax.

But Glasby wouldn't have been who she was if there hadn't have been *something* on her mind, something, inevitably, connected with work. 'John,' she began, a little more tentatively than normal, 'do you mind if I ask for your advice?'

He burst out laughing. It was a friendly laugh, but there was a look of resignation on his face too. 'I don't suppose,' he said, 'that this advice you need might just have something to do with your job?'

Their main courses had come and gone and Glasby had just about got Redgrave up to date on all that had happened over the last few weeks. She had diplomatically avoided anything to do with her evening with Doherty, and although she had included Mia and the brush with death that the two of them had, she had decided not to mention Mia's occupation, or her ownership of a gun.

Glasby had also decided to skirt over what story it was that Michael Fisher had been trying to sell to her. Redgrave had great respect for Henry Dunne, and she didn't think that he would be ready to listen to claims that he might have been a murderer. It didn't quite seem fair, asking for his assistance without telling him what she was getting him into, but she couldn't really see any alternative. She would tell him more when it seemed necessary to do so.

'So what did you find on Fisher's computer?' he asked.

'Well, I got into his bank account, and he was certainly getting money from Richard Bedingfield, almost every month. And there were quite a few other sizeable cash deposits. I suppose that they were probably from his scamming activities, cheating men, I mean. I found twelve different email accounts, and loads of correspondence with different men. Some of them certainly posted money to him. Fisher was good at it, from the ones I read, flirting and then making up hard luck stories.'

'So you've found an informant for your newspaper who's an expert at lying for money,' said Redgrave, dryly. 'Was he rich?'

'Not from the bank balances that I saw. As I said, there was a fair amount going in, but he took it out again pretty regularly. Mostly in cash.'

'Probably those foreign girls that his neighbour saw him with didn't come cheap, then?'

'You're probably right, John,' she agreed. 'The problem is—'

'The problem is,' he cut in, 'that you haven't just got one problem. First, you're in exactly the same boat as Henry Dunne; someone's fed you a line on PCs Salmon and Shipp, the Police Federation is all over you, and you're both going to take a fall unless you can come up with something to back up your story.'

He held up his hand to stop her from interrupting. 'And, for some reason that I don't quite get, you have the idea that this Michael Fisher's tale of murder long ago that puts Dunne in the frame, might just crack your problem with Salmon and Shipp. But Fisher is a liar of the worst order, the sort that sends newspaper editors running for cover. Right?'

Glasby winced. It wasn't like Redgrave to be quite so dismissive of her efforts. Maybe it was going to take a bit longer than she would have liked to get their relationship fully back on track.

'There's one thing about Fisher that you didn't mention, John – he's dead. Whatever we both think about his morals, he had a story, and just as he was about to tell me, someone killed him. And your Inspector Mallam doesn't seem to be too interested in who that was.'

'From everything that you've found out,' Redgrave retorted, his voice above its normal level, 'the only surprise is that he lasted out as long as he did. What do you think, was the murderer one of his blackmail victims, Fritz from Düsseldorf looking for Vlada or Gary from Indiana all upset because Natasha had betrayed him? Or could it have been a friend of one of those sinister "foreign girls", hoping that he had a big wad of cash hidden away?'

'Well I notice one possibility that you didn't cover was that a random burglar dropped by on Fisher, persuaded him to open the door, then lost his temper and smashed the place to pieces, stopping only to steal nothing except Fisher's note-book! That being Inspector Mallam's theory. Right?'

Redgrave started to answer, then stopped himself and grinned at her. 'Alison, if I ever say that I didn't miss you, I'll be lying.'

He gave her a fond look. 'You know, there's two things worth saying about Mallam. He's . . .' Redgrave hesitated, then continued, trust in Glasby winning out over his professional loyalties. 'He's basically serving out his time. He's only got another few months until he retires. These days he would never have got as far, being an inspector I mean. I wouldn't be one bit surprised if he just wants to get this one over and put it behind him without anyone asking him any difficult questions.'

'Great,' said Glasby, sarcastically. 'You said two things?'

'Yeah. The other one is this; he's *Inspector* Mallam. Inspector, just what I'm hoping to be. And the last thing that's going to get me promoted from sergeant is to start sticking my nose into someone else's case. Sorry, Alison, but that's the way of the world, you know it is.'

There was a moment's hesitation as they stood at the end of Westminster Bridge, her Punto in a car park over on the left, his silver sports car (which was one of the few things about Redgrave that she'd never liked) in the other direction. He put his hands on her shoulders and drew her in gently for a kiss, but even as he enjoyed the touch of her lips, he could tell that Glasby had made up her mind that the evening should end there.

'Goodnight, John, and thanks.'

Glasby walked away briskly. If she had turned back she would have seen Redgrave still at the spot where they had parted, a slight look of disappointment in his eyes. No one had ever said that a relationship with Alison Glasby was going to be easy, but they'd been estranged for the best part of three months. And now, when he finally had her back again, they'd spent most of the evening talking about the thing that had pushed them away from each other in the first place: her work.

Still, she really was in a pickle this time, and he hadn't needed any reproach from her to know that he'd been out of line the way he'd reacted over that muppet Mick Doherty. He hadn't behaved all that much better when he'd let Mallam persuade him into contacting her, either, interrogating her over Fisher's death. Even putting his personal feelings aside, he owed her now, and if he could help her, he would.

There'd been times over the last few weeks when he'd had his doubts, but the way that he felt about her was clear enough to him now. Redgrave was not a complicated man, and he knew that he loved her. He was sure of that. All he had to do was to work out how to get her back again.

'You know you say I must to become more independent.' It was true, she had said things along those lines to Mia, trying to encourage the girl away from being exploited. This, however, wasn't what Glasby had meant.

It was the afternoon after their last meeting, and they were both in Glasby's apartment again. Mia was still staying away from her own flat, in case any associates of the two heavies who had met their death chasing them might have come by, and Glasby thought that it might be for that reason that she had taken to visiting her. Be that as it may, she was enjoying the other woman's company and Mia seemed happy to make herself at home.

In fact, she had arrived with ingredients for something called plov, a dish from Central Asia made out of lamb and chick-peas. It was taking a long time to cook and was by quite some margin the best-smelling dish to have been prepared in Glasby's kitchen.

Meanwhile Glasby was doing her best to assist Mia down the path to independence. To be precise, she was acting as copywriter for a website through which the girl intended to advertise for customers, without the need to pay an agency.

'This fragrant mystery from the Steppes of Kazakhstan,' she wrote, 'wishes to bring the warmth of her companionship into your life. She will massage your ego as she soothes your cares. Nothing will be too much trouble for her . . .' Sensing the girl's presence behind her, Glasby looked round.

'You must not say I am from Kazakhstan,' Mia told her. 'Only immigration mens knows this, or someone from my country who knows my family can see it. Please say I am Korean girl.'

'I thought you didn't approve of Fisher lying to men?' said Glasby. 'Aren't you doing the same thing?'

'I do not cheat men.' Mia sounded indignant. 'I don't say I am Vlada the blonde Russian girl and really I am old English man! Customer, he pay me, and I give him what he want from me, this isn't cheating him.'

Feeling that she had a point, Glasby apologized quickly. 'OK, Korean it is. What else do I need to say?' She was hoping not to have to go into too many details of what exactly the girl would be offering.

'Oh, you just say I am sexy teenager, student, very friendly, do everything for men be happy.'

Glasby sighed, preparing to take her prose a little more downmarket. An image of Jack Daniels came to her mind. He would probably be good at this sort of thing.

'Alison, sometimes these things just die down.'

Reassuring as this might be, it wasn't Bill Davenport's career

that was on the line. 'Bill, you know that isn't what's going
to happen in this case. Bloody Fish and Chips have got a
lawyer involved . . .'

'Fish and Chips? What does that mean?'

'It's what Mike Marshall called them – Salmon and Shipp,
the two policemen, you know. Mike's a funny guy, he's always
thinking things like that up.'

'Well, with the amount of work which he doesn't get
through, he should have plenty of time for it,' Davenport
replied, tartly. 'That and writing other people's autobiographies, from what I hear. Actually, that reminds me, where
have you got to on "Views of the Elderly"?'

'I'll be ready to talk about it at our team meeting, later.'
Glasby was keen not to have the subject changed on her again.
'Listen, Bill, I know you keep saying that I should just leave
things alone, but I have to do *something*! A lot of what Fisher
said looks true, you know; he ,was being paid off by
Bedingfield, and the blood that was on the dead teacher's shirt
really *was* Henry Dunne's. What I think—'

'Alison! For crying out loud!' Davenport shook his head
emphatically. 'You've spent quite some time building up rela-
tions with the police, which any crime reporter needs. You're
starting to get yourself a bit of a reputation as well – a good
one, I mean. And you want to go after Henry Dunne, to throw
all this away, because of some guy you know was a fraudster, a liar, probably half-crazy . . .'

'And dead,' said Glasby, quietly. 'Someone killed Michael
Fisher, and I am positive that it wasn't just a random burglar.
Someone paid those guys to chase me, and threaten me.
Something's going on, Bill, and someone doesn't want me to
find out what. Doesn't that tell you that I'm doing the right
thing, not letting it go?'

Davenport gazed at his protégé thoughtfully. 'Just be very
careful, Alison, that's all. Please?'

There were a lot of photographs on display in the assistant
commissioner's office. Horses and people featured in roughly
equal number, in both cases accompanied often by a beaming
Horgan, green eyes shining out under a carpet of white hair.
Centre stage was taken by a gold-framed shot of the assistant commissioner receiving the Queen's Police Medal from

Her Majesty, a ceremony which Dunne himself had been present at.

'I said it before, Henry. You must keep the loyalty of your men. However mighty we are, or well-respected or successful, without the men we're worth nothing.'

'Are you saying that I don't have my team's loyalty any more, Alec?' Dunne asked, quietly.

'I'm not saying that, no, Henry. Not yet I'm not. But I'm saying that it's time to start asking yourself that question, and take it from me, you're going to need to be very sure you know the answers. How long d'you need?'

'For what?'

For the first time Horgan looked impatient. The eyes flashed at Dunne, famously a warning sign. 'For what, Henry? For what we're sat here talking about, that's what! Salmon and Shipp, clear them, publicly I mean, or bring 'em in and take them down. Those are your choices, and I'm asking how long you need to decide. Which way are you going to jump?'

Dunne managed to keep his composure. 'I know that you're not trying to put me on the spot, Alec. If I knew the answer to your question I'd tell you, you know I would. How long have I got?'

Horgan looked steadily at a point on the wall above Dunne's head. 'Two, maybe three weeks, maybe longer, maybe not. When the time comes I think that you'll know, and if you don't, it will be my job to tell you.'

He lowered his gaze to meet Dunne's. 'I like you, Henry. You're a good man. I don't have your upbringing or education, but you're a good copper and I respect that in you. I want you to find a way through this, for your sake and the sake of the force. I know that those two fellows are dirty. I know it just the same as you do. The trouble is, where we've got to now, either you bring them down, or they will you.'

George Pincher had a new team on now. It was a rotten business, losing men, it always was, but he was a professional and the job went on.

'My lads will be up to the mark, sir, don't you worry about that,' he told his boss, with more confidence than he really felt. Getting unplanned replacements in a hurry wasn't easy and the truth was that Pincher's new recruits were men who he didn't know well. He wasn't really sure how much he trusted them.

But there was no point in telling any of this to the man who paid the bills. 'That young girl, Fisher's tart, she's in and out of Glasby's place the whole time now. We'll hold our positions for the time being, but the boys, they'll be ready to make a move, if they get the word, like.'

# Mia's Recipe for Plov

*Ingredients:*

*1lb lamb, chopped into bite size pieces*

*1lb carrots, chopped into small cubes (about ?")*

*2 onions, chopped*

*5 tbsps of vegetable oil*

*1 tbsp of caraway seeds*

*1 can chick peas*

*1 head of garlic, left whole*

*2 cups of basmati rice, washed thoroughly*

*Salt (2 teaspoons), pepper*

*Fry the meat until it's brown and a bit crispy*

*Add the onion, fry until it's soft*

*Add carrots, chickpeas, caraway seeds and salt and pepper*

*Cover with boiling water*

*Put lid on, simmer for 10 minutes*

*Add rice and garlic*

*Cover with boiling water ?" above the level of the rice*

*Boil fast until the water evaporates down to the surface of the rice*

*Cover with lid, turn heat to low, cook for 15 minutes*

*Remove garlic and stir well*

*Eat with chopped tomatoes and onions or some other salad*

*From the notebook of Michael Fisher*

# Fourteen

'Hi, Alison, are you feeling happy today?'

It was always nice to hear John's voice, but to Glasby he sounded more cheerful than was warranted. It was a Tuesday morning, the Tube train that she had been on had broken down leaving her stuck in an unventilated tunnel for twenty minutes, and the only reprieve that she was going to get from pursuing Davenport's latest annoying idea for an interesting feature would be when he moved on to the next, equally irritating, piece.

Her response was a little less enthusiastic than Redgrave had been expecting, judging from the rather more cautious tone of his voice. 'I was just wondering if I could invite you for dinner this evening? Unless you've something else planned?'

Barring the occasional visit from her new friend Mia, Glasby's social life was practically Saharan in its aridity, so Redgrave was on pretty safe ground. And not even Glasby in a bad mood could find fault either with his manners or with the warmth of his invitation. She accepted happily enough, and the rest of the day weighed a bit less heavily on her shoulders as a result.

The first thing she saw as the waiter led her to the table was Redgrave. The next was her friend Kate Hall, followed immediately afterwards by Kate's fiancé (a word which Glasby took no pleasure in associating with him), Simon. 'What . . . ?' she started to ask, and then realized.

'Happy Birthday!' they all cried, rising from the table and taking it in turns to embrace her, first Kate, then Simon (whose beard she found even worse to touch than it was to look at) and finally John, who allowed himself to plant a kiss firmly on her lips.

'I thought that you mustn't want people at your office to know, or something,' said John smilingly. 'That's why I didn't say anything earlier.'

'I just forgot,' she said, feeling a bit lame.

'Forgot?' Simon echoed, as the other three laughed. 'I know you're another year older, but it's a bit early to start losing your marbles so you don't even remember your own birthday, isn't it?' He burst out laughing at his own joke, joined by Kate and Redgrave too, until he noticed that Glasby was not looking as happy as she might have done.

'Let's sit down, anyway,' he said, an arm around Glasby's shoulders. 'Poor thing, you look exhausted. It's not been the easiest of times for you, has it?'

Glasby tried to smile at him but to her surprise and embarrassment felt tears beginning to well up instead. She swallowed hard and sat down quickly, hoping that no one would notice.

Simon's attention had been drawn by a copy of an Etruscan fresco which was painted on to the wall behind them. He was taking the opportunity to give Kate the benefit of his knowledge of the period. Redgrave opened his mouth to say something to Glasby, then saw her quickly hold her napkin to her eyes.

He took her arm. 'Oh, Alison, sweetheart, are you OK?'

She nodded, unable to speak, more tears falling now.

'Do you want to go the ladies' room for a moment? I'll talk to Simon and Kate, don't worry. I'm sorry, darling, we just wanted to help you let your hair down a bit. Go on, they won't notice.'

Glasby got up and walked rapidly to the back of the restaurant. Thankfully there was no one else in the bathroom. She wiped her face with a tissue taken from a metal container on the tiled work surface next to the basin. If she had known that tonight was supposed to be a special occasion, she would have put some mascara and other make-up on, but now Glasby was glad that she hadn't.

Pink-eyed, she looked at herself critically in the mirror. She was twenty-seven years old now. She had few friends, her parents hadn't got round to sending a card on their daughter's birthday, and her job was taking far more out of her than it ever seemed likely to give back.

'Don't be pathetic.' She spoke aloud and as she did so

straightened her shoulders and forced a smile on to her face. She thought about Redgrave, a man who clearly cared for her deeply, *her* man, and the smile became broader and more genuine.

Back at their table, Simon was still in full flow. 'Of course, Romulus himself is said to have followed Etruscan rituals, after the founding of Rome—' He broke off on seeing her return. 'Ah, the birthday girl!' he exclaimed. Redgrave was looking anxiously at her.

Glasby smiled, first to him and then the others. 'Yes, the birthday girl,' she replied. 'And without my friends, I wouldn't even have known it!'

Leaning over to Redgrave she kissed him on the cheek. She accepted a glass of champagne and told herself that tonight was going to be fun, even if it was only for the sake of her friends. After two or three drinks, Simon would probably start to become bearable.

'I never would have thought it,' Kate was telling her. 'I mean, all that "I do" stuff, and "honour and obey", it isn't really you and me, is it? But whenever you tell someone you're getting married, they're always so thrilled, you know, you can't help but get caught up in it yourself. And as for Simon, you're just an old romantic softie, aren't you, dear?'

The object of Kate's affections smiled back at her through his beard. Glasby had slightly underestimated the amount of alcohol needed to make his company enjoyable, but two glasses of champagne and an unknown amount of white wine later, she was feeling quite warmly towards him.

'Well, as the poet said, "The joys of marriage are the heaven on earth". Even for us chaps, eh, John?'

Glasby lifted her wine glass again; it was going to be necessary to keep her blood alcohol level well topped up.

Redgrave smiled broadly back at Simon. 'Oh, you're spot on there, mate.' Glasby thought he must be drunk; she had never heard him call anyone 'mate' before.

'In fact,' Redgrave continued, 'I want to make a toast. My mum and dad have been together over thirty years now. And now you two, you're going to be hitched soon. And' – he looked fondly at Glasby – 'if I get lucky, maybe it'll be our turn after that. To marriage!'

All four of them brought their glasses together as they repeated his words, self-consciously so in Glasby's case. To Glasby's surprise Redgrave winked at her. He had never said anything about them getting married before, and she assumed that it was the drink which was talking.

'Oh, Ali, that'd be fantastic, if you and John tied the knot as well! Imagine, we could plan the whole day, and choose our dresses together.' Glasby gave her friend the most benign look that she could manage and retreated back to her wine glass.

Kate's experience as a junior school teacher meant that she recognized a sulk on the way when she saw one. She changed the subject to something that she was sure would cheer Glasby up. 'So how's your job going, Ali? John was saying before you arrived that you've been having a tough time.'

Glasby took a deep breath. 'You know, Kate, I really don't know what to say. I was given some wrong information about a story and that seems to have got the paper into trouble, legal trouble I mean, and Bill Davenport – you remember him?'

Kate nodded, having listened patiently on many previous occasions to stories about the great man.

Redgrave and Simon were deep in conversation, presumably about football, which despite the fact that they'd known each other from university was in fact one of the few things that they had in common. Glasby leaned forward so that she could speak more quietly.

'They've brought him back on to the paper, because my boss . . .' She hesitated. 'My boss is ill, so Bill has taken over as head of my group, and he's just a *nightmare* now, you wouldn't believe it! I've spent the whole summer writing all this stuff about cycling, and hobbies, and this interminable series on old people and how society sees them, what he insists on calling "the generation game".'

Kate interrupted her. 'Oh yes, I saw one of those pieces, one of the other members of staff brought it into school the other day. It was about all the talents that older people have, and how they still want to play their part. I used it in a citizenship class, actually.' Noticing the look on Glasby's face she added hastily, 'Of course, it's not the type of thing that you really want to be doing, is it?'

Glasby sighed. 'Honestly, Kate, I don't know what I want

any more. I feel like that Greek bloke, rolling rocks uphill the whole time.'

The blokey football talk must have run its course; Simon leant over, looking self-satisfied as ever. 'Sisyphus,' he pronounced. 'King of Corinth. He insulted the gods, and was condemned to push a rock up a hill forever. A terrible fate. And who have you insulted, fair Alison?'

Glasby gave no answer, but drained her glass and then immediately reached for more from the bottle. Next to her, Redgrave was starting to look anxious again.

Both of them were lying on the carpet, propped up against two cushions taken from the sofa, sipping mint tea. Lying around them was the detritus from a birthday that hadn't been forgotten after all, cards from Kate and Simon and Redgrave, and from Lester and one from her parents too, which she had found in the mail when they got back to Glasby's flat.

There was a small eau de nil coloured paper carrier bag as well, in which Redgrave's gift to her had been nestling, a solid silver bangle from Tiffany's which was now gleaming on her wrist. It was a wonderful present, the best that she'd ever had so Glasby had told him, and she had meant it, too.

'It's really getting to you, this Longhammer stuff, isn't it?' asked Redgrave, sympathetically. Glasby said nothing, but after a moment nodded her head, almost a gesture of defeat. Most of the alcohol that she had consumed earlier had worn off now, and her head felt strangely clear.

'Look, I wasn't going to talk about it now, what with it being your birthday and everything. But in case it helps, I did have a word with one of the lads who's in Paul Mallam's firm. You know, about the Fisher case.'

Glasby nodded again, this time impatiently. She didn't need reminding who Inspector Mallam was.

'This is so off the record, I can't tell you. I mean, my job would be on the line, you know what I mean? But what I heard was, Mallam ballsed the Fisher thing right up, and then some. There's no witnesses that saw anything useful, as you know. And Mallam didn't get the scene properly secured, there were ambulance blokes and a couple of neighbours that wandered in, and loads of plods – I mean, uniformed guys – as well. So the forensics are basically useless.'

Glasby shook her head in disbelief.

'Mallam's not a bad guy,' Redgrave continued, 'and like I told you, he's coming up to retirement anyway, so no one wants to pin anything on him. But barring a major stroke of luck, there's no way in the world that he's ever going to find who killed Fisher, and he knows it. That's why he lost interest in you so fast, and where the random burglar theory came from, just to cover his blushes up. Unless Hercule Poirot or Sherlock Holmes feels like taking up the case for us, that's the end of that one, I'd say.'

He stretched his arms above his head, and made to rise. 'Work tomorrow, darling, and for you too. I suppose it's time I was going. Unless . . .'

She turned to him. 'John, thank you so much for this evening. I just can't tell you how much I missed you after . . . well, after we had our argument. Please, don't you want to stay with me tonight?'

They kissed, first gently and then more deeply, arms finding their way under and around each other, pulling them together. 'Did you miss me?' she asked. 'Really?' They were the last words that either of them said for quite some time; his answer, although unspoken, was as clear and as unequivocal as she had hoped for.

Later, quite a lot later, Glasby was lying in her bed listening to the sound of Redgrave's breathing. She felt safe with him beside her, and calm, but her brain still wasn't quite ready for sleep. Sherlock Holmes, he'd said, or Poirot. Well, there were some pretty good female detectives around as well. And they weren't all works of fiction, either.

George Pincher's telephone rang. It was after midnight, but late at night was often when interesting things starting happening, in his world. In one corner of the living room a television was showing a repeat of a 1970s sitcom, the sound turned down low so as not to wake his wife, who was sleeping upstairs. He reached for the remote control, hit the mute button and picked up his phone.

'You'll never guess, boss!' Pincher sighed. The two men who had died chasing Glasby had been his A team. In his day on the job, retired coppers used to jump at the sort of work he was offering now. These days, what with fat pensions and a hugely expanded security industry handing out decent salaries to anyone with a few years' experience under their belt, he had to take what he could get. These two weren't total chumps, but they weren't going to win any prizes either.

'Try me,' he said.

The man on the other end of the phone sounded triumphant. 'Glasby turned up back at her gaffe, an hour or so ago, right? And she was a bit all over the shop, know what I mean, like she'd 'ad a few. And she had this fellow with her, all right? And here's the good bit – I managed to cop a peep at 'im. It's only bloody John Redgrave – you know, he's CID, a sergeant in the murder squad he is now. Well in there with her, he was, she was all over him, know what I mean?'

'Did they see you?' asked Pincher, as patiently as he could manage.

'See me? I don't think so! Only had eyes for each other, they did, know what I mean? And that's it, that's what I'm telling you. Fifteen minutes ago, he pulls the curtains, lights out, and no sign of him leaving. Like I say, he's well in there, if you ask me.'

Pincher sighed again. 'Stay another hour. If anything happens, call me. If not, you can call it a day then.'

'An hour? You sure, guv? It's getting late you know, and I ain't even had my dinner.'

There was a brief silence at the other end of the line. Then, 'You know what I hate?' Pincher didn't wait for a response. 'An argument, that's what. Even my milkman doesn't start any arguments with me. It gets right up my shirt, if someone starts getting narky with me. You got that?'

The man hastened to tell him that he did, but realized soon enough that he was talking to no one. Pincher had rung off.

Meanwhile Pincher himself sat for several minutes, deep in thought, stroking two sore spots either side of the bridge of his nose where his glasses had been rubbing, as the sitcom came silently to an end to be replaced by equally soundless advertisements for insurance websites and other financial services.

After a while he stood up and made his way heavily up the stairs and to bed.

\*    \*    \*

'I'm sorry, sir. Could I come in?'

Dunne had only half registered the knock at his office door. When Longhammer was in full swing he would have been lucky to have five minutes in the day undisturbed but with the operation effectively suspended now, he had more time for reflection than was good for him.

He looked up. It was Matthews, one of the young detective constables under Mick Doherty. He was a man who obviously liked a challenge: not content with being black and a graduate, two categories which while not as rare as they had been in the Metropolitan Police certainly both qualified for minority status, he had also volunteered for Longhammer as his first posting as a detective.

A stint investigating internal corruption was not exactly guaranteed to enhance your career in the Met, a thought which Dunne had found increasing difficulty in banishing from his mind recently.

'Come in and sit down, Keith.' Dunne had formed a good impression of Matthews, a serious-minded and diligent man.

Matthews settled himself across the desk from his superior. 'I'm sorry,' he said again. 'You know how much I believe in Longhammer, what it stands for, and the direction you've taken it in.'

Dunne nodded, waiting for the inevitable 'but'.

'I want to stay with it, sir, but . . .' He hesitated. Dunne remained silent. 'But some of the lads are saying . . .'

The man clearly needed a bit of assistance, and deserved it too, in Dunne's view.

'Keith, you've done what, nearly a year with us? You're a good man, that's how I see it, and you've your career to think of. There's no reason at all why you shouldn't be looking for a transfer now, and you'll have my full support. If that's what you want?'

Apparently that wasn't quite it. Matthews still looked like a man struggling to unburden himself of a guilty secret. Dunne got up, walked across his office and closed the door.

'You look like you came here to say something, Keith. Don't make me guess what it is. Just spit it out, whatever you want to. Is it something personal, or work?'

The young detective smiled. 'Thanks, sir. It's not personal, not like that, anyway. It's the sarge, sir, Sergeant Doherty.

He told some of the lads that Longhammer's gone belly up, that it's finished. Of course we've all been wondering for a while, but now he's told us, and . . .'

'And?'

Matthews took a deep breath. 'And what I heard was, he said that you gave those stories to that journalist, the woman on the *Herald*, and that's what backfired on us. He said that you would be disciplined, that the assistant commissioner was on your case now, and that when you went down, it would damage the rest of us. My wife's pregnant now, and I was thinking I'd be in with a chance of getting a promotion in a year or two, and . . .' He tailed off again, looking miserable.

Dunne tried not to show how shocked he was. Scotland Yard was just as full of gossip as any other office, and with Longhammer currently falling to pieces as it was, canteen talk of this sort was inevitable. But if Mick Doherty really had been stirring things up like this, that was the last thing that he would have expected.

He interrupted Matthews in the middle of yet another apology.

'You've said enough, Keith. Here's my advice. Have a good think, and talk it over with your wife, about where you see yourself going next. You're absolutely right, you've a good chance of becoming a sergeant in the next year or so, so your next posting is very important. Once you've worked out what you want, we'll talk again, and we'll decide together how you can best get it.'

After giving Matthews a few minutes to get clear, Dunne went in search of Doherty and an explanation. He gave his deputy the gist of what Matthews had said, without mentioning him by name. Doherty's eyes narrowed.

'It was probably one of the young lads you were talking to, boss,' he suggested. 'They haven't been round the block like you and me. They get things arse over tip, sometimes, you know what this place is like. A's talking to B in the canteen, he tells him that he's got a bad throat and a headache, C overhears them, next thing you know, the whole place says that there's an outbreak of the bubonic plague.'

The two men looked at each other warily. They had fifteen years of shared experience, much of it spent working as close colleagues. Doherty was probably right; it was understandable that Matthews would be nervous – Christ, Dunne was nervous himself, nowadays – and rumours did indeed spread around the Met in much the way that he had described.

But his team, the Godsquad, they weren't any old coppers, they had been hand picked, every one of them. Many of them had worked together before, and they had all understood that Longhammer would not be an easy assignment or one that would gain them any popularity among their colleagues. The only surprising thing was that Longhammer had gone on as long, and been as successful, as it had.

'Mick,' he said, eventually. 'Who do you think leaked those two names to Glasby, Shipp and Salmon?'

'I couldn't say, boss. You know she had a thing going with John Redgrave. I hear they're back together again.'

Dunne hadn't heard this news, and, remembering the strangely intense encounter that he had shared with Glasby, had a momentary pang of what could only have been jealousy. He told himself firmly that he was pleased for her.

'Redgrave's on the murder squad, not Longhammer. Even if he wanted to, how would he know who our targets were?'

Doherty acknowledged the strength of this with an inclination of his head. 'Glasby knows plenty of coppers,' he mused. 'She knows you, boss. And me. Doesn't she?'

It seemed to Dunne that Doherty was avoiding his eye, although as he thought things through later that day on his way home, he decided that he was probably being more suspicious than was necessary.

'Do you think I should get a different sofa?' she asked. They were sitting at opposite ends, Glasby with her feet curled under her, Redgrave reclining, his legs outstretched.

'Why?'

'Well, it's hideous. I mean, purple! Right?'

'Mmmm,' he agreed. 'Hideous. You're right.'

'And it's damned uncomfortable. Right?'

Again he agreed.

'So, why wouldn't I get rid of it?'

'You could. Or you could leave it here, and just not sit on it.'

'Don't be silly! Why would I want to do that?' She pulled a face at him.

He sat up. 'My sofa's nice and comfortable, and it isn't

purple. If you moved in with me, you wouldn't need to sit on this one any more, would you?'

Glasby threw a cushion at him. At the same time, her doorbell rang. Surprised, she went to the entry-phone. She wasn't expecting anyone, and the state of her social life didn't make for many guests, impromptu or otherwise. Except . . .

'Mia, hi!' she said, and waited as the girl climbed up the stairs. Today Mia was dressed casually, albeit in a style that Glasby would not have dreamt of trying to emulate, in a bright red skirt that came not very far down her thighs, a T-shirt which was tight enough to leave little to be imagined and a pair of pale blue wedge-heeled sandals which added significantly to her height. Her early training in classical dance must have been a real advantage when it came to avoiding a broken ankle, thought Glasby.

'I come to see that you OK, and also, can I please use your computer, for look at some websites? So I can see designs to tell my webmaster he must use for my independent site.'

'Yes, of course. I'm fine thanks. But maybe you can leave the websites until a bit later. John Redgrave is here. You know, I mentioned him to you . . .'

Mia looked concerned. 'Your boyfriend?' she whispered. 'He is the policeman? I'm sorry, I better must go. You busy with him, sorry.'

Glasby tried to reassure her. 'Don't worry, Mia. We were just chatting, we're not busy. He's very friendly, you know, and he won't start asking you questions. I mentioned you to him already, he knows that you're my friend.'

The girl still looked ill at ease but she seemed reassured enough to stay. They went through into the sitting room together. Redgrave stood up. He towered over Mia. She held out a delicate hand for him to shake. Her nails were painted to match the colour of her shoes.

'Hello, Mia. Alison's told me a bit about you. *Priyatno poznakomitsa. Kak dela?*' He gave her a very friendly smile.

She looked surprised, as did Glasby. '*Spasebo, horosho,*' she replied. 'You know how to speak Russian?'

'Oh, I learned a bit when I was at school. I can still manage "How are you, pleased to meet you". I used to know enough to count to a hundred, and how to ask a girl for her telephone number.' He laughed. Mia joined in with her usual little giggle. Glasby didn't.

'Do please sit down.' Redgrave motioned her to where he had been sitting and went to fetch himself an upright chair from the kitchen, which he placed opposite the sofa. Glasby sat down as well, trying to banish the thought that he had just given himself a perfect view of Mia's legs.

'What are you doing in London, Mia?' asked Redgrave, again treating her to a broad smile.

Glasby found herself hoping that Mia wouldn't offer him another giggle. In fact, she looked uncomfortable, possibly worrying about her residence status or the legality of her professional activities.

'I am study English,' she said, avoiding his eye.

'John only deals with very serious crime, Mia. He works as a special detective, in the murder squad.'

'Murder?' Mia relaxed again. 'Isn't it bad that you always looking at bodies? My friend, her boyfriend was security guard in striptease club. All night he looked at naked girls, very pretty. After some time, he no interested in sex at all. My friend, she say him, he must change job or she going to leave him.'

'What happened?' asked Redgrave. 'What did he do?'

'He left her,' said Mia, dolefully, then burst into laughter, joined by Redgrave and, a few moments too late to be convincing, by Glasby as well.

More pleasantries followed, the conversation conducted almost exclusively between Mia and Redgrave, with Glasby having to try harder and harder not to look out of sorts. When they had got to the point of discovering a shared liking for sports cars of exactly the type Redgrave drove, she decided it was time to intervene.

'Mia was a friend of Michael Fisher's, you know,' she said to Redgrave, seizing advantage of a momentary break in their conversation. Then, turning to Mia, 'John has promised to help find out who killed him.'

She leant back, feeling a guilty pleasure in the fact that they were both now looking thoroughly awkward.

Redgrave broke the silence first. 'Well, it's not my case, Fisher – I mean, *Mr* Fisher's murder. I'm very sorry that your friend was killed, Mia, and if there's anything I can do to help Alison and you, of course I'm always pleased if I can help.'

'Thank you, John,' Mia replied. 'I am helping Alison too.

I give her things that Michael give to me, and she will write big story about them. That's right, isn't it, Alison? About soldier and very important policeman. Michael he knows things about important mens, and maybe this is why they must kill him. And perhaps they try to kill us too.'

This time it was Glasby's turn to look uncomfortable. She managed to change the subject and they began to chat again, this time as more of a threesome. But after another five minutes or so when Mia stood up to leave, neither Glasby nor Redgrave tried too hard to persuade her to stay.

As soon as the door had closed the argument started. Glasby went first: ' . . . And not only were you flirting, you were even doing it in Russian, for God's sake. Right in front of me!'

'Well, of course it was in front of you. You introduced me to her. We were in your flat!' he countered. 'How could I not be talking to her in front of you?'

'So are you always that friendly with people you get introduced to? Or is it only when it's a glamorous young woman with a skirt that barely covers her underwear?'

Redgrave defended himself again. 'What do you want me to do, be rude to your friends? How often do you introduce me to anyone, anyway? I've never even met your family! You know I think that we should meet each other's parents.'

Sensing he was on to safer ground, he pushed forwards. 'And by the way, what is this story that Fisher's girl – who doesn't seem much like a student to me, by the way – is helping you with? And who is this important policeman? You don't seem to have got around to mentioning that to me. Or have you told Paul Mallam about it?'

'John! Don't start turning this into one of your interrogations again! I haven't said anything to Paul Mallam. You told me yourself, he doesn't even want to know, remember?'

They glared at each other for a moment, then Redgrave relaxed and reached out for her hand. 'I'm sorry, Alison. Forget what I said about Mallam. But if you want me to help you, you're going to have to tell me what's going on. Right?'

She said nothing, then made up her mind. 'It all started when Fisher contacted me. I think he tried me because he knew that I had an interest in Henry Dunne . . .'

\*    \*    \*

This time there was nothing said that George Pincher took exception to.

'Yeah, it was her all right, Fisher's tart. I recognized her from the photos you gave me. Nice looking bird, looks like you'd need a few bob if you wanted to spend some time with her, if you get my drift.'

'So the tart and Redgrave were both at Glasby's place, that's what you're saying?'

'That's the one, guv. Him first and then the girl joined them. Forty-five minutes later she's off out again, 'ops into a taxi that's going past. He's still in there as we speak, and so's our little Miss Glasby.'

As before, Pincher sat in silence for a while after the call had ended, but this time he seemed to reach a decision quickly.

Moments later he was on the phone again. 'It's George here, sir . . . Well yes, I have got some news, as it goes. We've got Glasby, in her flat, with the CID sergeant boyfriend who I told you about, remember, and Fisher's Russian girl. I think that we're going to need to make our move, sir. I do.'

*www.BlackCatInvestigations.co.uk*
*www.privatedetectivesuk.co.uk*
*www.ukprivateinvestigator.co.uk*
*www.findadetective.co.uk*
*www.nohiding.com*
*www.nig.co.uk*
*www.answers.uk.com*
*www.theabi.org.uk*
*www.privatedetectivescorporation.co.uk*
*www.metropolitaninvestigations.com*
*www.suspected.co.uk*
*www.salgadoinvestigations.com*
*www.andersonchance.com*
*www.aepd.co.uk*
*www.teaminvestigations.co.uk*
*www.detectivesuk.com*

*From the notebook of Michael Fisher*

# Fifteen

Redgrave had left some while before to play squash and go out drinking with a couple of his colleagues. Glasby just sat, folded up in the same position as before on the sofa. Every now and again she focused on the layer of dust covering the two framed posters which were hanging on the wall opposite her. They needed cleaning, as did the rest of the flat. Once she turned and looked at the bookshelves, as if to confirm that they too wanted her attention, but she made no move to do anything about it.

Redgrave's parting words were still ringing in her ears: 'Think, Alison, for God's sake think! You're really getting in deep here – and for what?'

And that is what she was doing, trying to get clear in her own mind what exactly she had found out, and what she could do about it.

Eventually, as if she hoped that it might help her to reach a decision, she got up from the sofa and sat at the kitchen table instead. 'OK, Alison, it's time to get real,' she said out loud.

The most important thing that she needed to work out remained the identity of her informant on Longhammer. It was also, remembering her conversation about her confidentiality obligations with Jonathan Constance, the *Herald*'s lawyer, the one issue that she had still not felt able to tell Redgrave about. Although whoever had been emailing her information had not only ultimately got it wrong but had run for cover too, leaving her exposed, he or she was still her source. Almost certainly they were a serving police officer too. Whoever it was, she had a duty to protect them.

No way could she even give any hint to Redgrave of how her informant had communicated with her by email. He would be bound to pass anything on to Dunne, after which a full-scale investigation would begin to find out who was behind the leak. The police, who could potentially seize computers and look for IP addresses, might well make headway with this, but she couldn't. All she knew was that her source knew how to set up an email account (not the hardest thing to do) and was well enough informed that they were probably part of Longhammer, or senior enough to be kept informed of Dunne's likely targets.

In other words, she was still looking at a complete dead end, or more accurately, a set of buffers into which the *Herald* was about to crash, leaving only the wreckage of her career and an expensive law suit from Messrs Salmon and Shipp.

Beyond that, she had Michael Fisher and his story, which had sounded less and less probable as she'd recounted it to Redgrave. True, some aspects of what he had told her seemed to be corroborated. It was likely that Dunne's blood really was on the teacher's shirt, and equally probable that Bedingfield had, for whatever reason, been buying Fisher's silence. But she was an awful long way from proving that Dunne, or anyone else, had been a schoolboy murderer.

And even if she could manage this, even if Dunne did have a dreadful secret in his past, would she still be any nearer to extricating herself from the mess that her Longhammer stories had created? She sat morosely, head propped up on her right hand, seeing herself fired from the *Herald* – Jack Daniels' smirk following her on her ignominious final walk down the corridor and out to the lift – and back on a local paper, if she was fortunate, for a second-rate career. Covering meetings of the Borough Council, and traffic accidents.

Thinking of Council meetings reminded her that Mr Bushell, the organizer of the Burstone School Old Boys, had mentioned to her that the games master's son was leader of the local council in Burstone. Possibly, just possibly, he would have something to add, either concerning his father's death, or maybe something that had passed between Fisher and Henry Dunne at the school reunion.

A couple of minutes on the internet yielded a telephone number for Gary Dickson. It being Sunday evening, her luck would need to be in for his phone to be answered. It wasn't. Another dead end to add to her collection.

Back at the kitchen table, she tried hard not to feel utterly defeated without much success. So far her investigation had brought with it three deaths: Michael Fisher, and the two ex-coppers who had died chasing her. Redgrave had had nothing much new to say about Fisher's murder, but when he found out about her connection with the car crash, he had looked very serious indeed.

'Alison, this isn't a game, you know. Those lads, they were George Pincher's men, they always were. What Bill Davenport told you was spot on. No way is Pincher a man who you want to be messing with. He gets involved in some very serious business. If he's mixed up in things, someone has hired him, and they'll expect results.'

A shiver went down to the base of her spine from the back of her head, as she sat hunched over the pine tabletop. The best that could be said was that no one had made any threats against her lately, but in Glasby's current mood, she interpreted even that as a sign of failure. She sat up, shook herself to try to relieve the tension in her shoulders, and looked at her watch.

It was past seven, long after the increasingly anachronistic laws on Sunday trading hours would have forced the large supermarket up the road to close for the day. Glasby decided to go down to the Indian shop next door and find herself something for dinner.

As she turned from shutting the street door behind her she saw a long dark-blue Jaguar saloon which had stopped across the pavement from her. There was a man with a bushy moustache in the driver's seat. An older man was standing next to the passenger door nearest her, which was wide open. He was wearing wire-framed glasses and a beige trench coat which the September weather didn't really call for.

As she looked at him a gust of wind caught his hair. It had been combed across his head to cover a thinning patch on the top of his skull. Strands of hair blew a good ten centimetres upwards. Glasby suppressed a smile and moved away. The man quickly took a pace in her direction and placed his right hand on her arm to detain her. Startled, she stopped and looked round at him.

For a moment neither of them spoke. She could see his bloodshot eyes through the lenses of his glasses.

He broke the silence. 'Hello, Alison. You don't know me

but you've heard my name before. I'm George Pincher. There's someone who would like to meet you, and we're going to take you to him.'

The grip on her arm tightened as Glasby started to pull herself free. His left hand, which up until now had been in the pocket of his raincoat, moved towards her. She looked at it and saw to her horror a shiny metal object. It was a gun, much smaller than the one that Mia had shown her but very real, and it was pointed straight at her from a distance of not more than a few centimetres.

It was easy after that for Pincher to usher her into the car, her legs unsteady and body limp from fear. Not until they had been driving for five minutes or more did Glasby stop feeling the sensation of her heart beating against her ribs. Having planned to go no further than the shop a few metres down the street she was dressed only in jeans and T-shirt and barring a few coins had neither her phone nor anything else in her pockets.

Neither George Pincher nor his driver spoke to Glasby during the journey. It was only after they had turned off a main road and had driven through three or four side streets that she began to notice her surroundings. She thought that they must be in the Borough, an area south of the Thames and not far from her flat that had once been covered in light industrial buildings but now, not least because it was home to the Tate Modern art gallery, was rapidly becoming fashionable and being redeveloped.

The car drew up in a deserted road at what looked like a rear entrance to an old brick-built warehouse. Pincher slid out from the Jaguar's leather bench seat and placed his hand firmly back on her arm. He drew Glasby out with him and half guided, half pushed her through a heavy metal door which he pulled closed behind them.

The room which they were in was windowless but brilliantly lit with fluorescent bulbs. It was empty of furniture except for a battered metal desk that stood against one wall. Two dirty mugs stood on the desktop, either side of a telephone. Pincher stepped towards her, his arms outstretched. He had a large gold signet ring on one hand. To Glasby's relief the gun was nowhere in sight. Her heart was throbbing loudly again.

Pincher spoke with authority, the voice of a man used to dealing with people who were frightened and intimidated.

'I'm going to search you now, Alison, just to make sure that you don't have any recording devices on you. Hold your arms away from your sides, please.' He felt her, carefully but professionally, through her clothes. Finding nothing of concern, he moved away from her again.

Glasby steeled herself to try to take the initiative. Sounding as calm as she could manage, she said, 'Do you think that I am the only person who knows about you and your bosses, Mr Pincher?'

He gave her a humourless smile but didn't respond. She tried again. 'If you know anything about the work I've been doing on this story you must know that there's a whole team of us involved. We know about you, and we know that you're working for Henry Dunne and Martin Danielson – or should I be calling him David Gold?'

Pincher sounded surprised. 'Henry Dunne? What makes you think . . . ?'

The speaker on the telephone crackled, and then a voice came from it: 'Bring Miss Glasby through to me please, George.'

Again there was the watery smile, and again the hand wrapped around her elbow. Glasby allowed herself to be led along a dimly-lit corridor. They turned a corner to the left. The light disappeared altogether except for a small crack visible under a door ahead of them. As they approached, the door opened and a man stood, visible at first only in silhouette.

He took a pace backwards and spoke courteously. 'Thank you, George, I'll call you when Miss Glasby is ready to go home.' Then he held out a hand to her. 'Alison, my name is Martin. Martin Danielson. Please do come in.'

He showed her into the room and on to a dark green leather sofa which stood facing a large mahogany desk. The door behind her closed. She could hear Pincher's footsteps echoing down the empty corridor away from them.

Danielson was a small man, Glasby's height or a little less, and slightly built. If she hadn't have known that he was a contemporary of Dunne and Fisher she would have thought him younger; his dark brown hair was closely cropped but full and unmarked with grey, as was his neatly trimmed beard. He wore an expensive looking mid-blue suit with white shirt and tie but had no jewellery or other obvious signs of wealth. He sat down at the other end of the sofa. 'Thank you for coming to meet me,' he began, but got no further. 'You're thanking me!' Glasby threw at him. 'You didn't exactly give me much choice, did you?'

Danielson smiled. His teeth were bright enough against his darkly tanned skin for Glasby to think that he might have had them whitened. He didn't look like the sort of man who would hire gun-toting thugs.

'Alison – I can call you Alison, I hope? – I am certainly aware that I owe you an apology. Sometimes, the methods that have to be used are not entirely as one would like them to be. I want to be very clear that at no time would you have been hurt. Nor did I intend that you would be in any danger, but I do accept that you may have been given cause for concern. I am very sorry for that.'

He smiled again and this time she relaxed and chose to smile back, nodding her head in acceptance of his apology. His formal politeness made it hard for her not to be disarmed.

'If at any point you wish to leave, please do tell me, and I will make arrangements for you to be driven home. But I know that you have been trying to talk to me, and I would like to speak to you as well. Is that acceptable, Alison?'

'Does that mean that I'm allowed to ask you some questions, Martin?'

Danielson gave her his broad smile again and nodded. 'You may, Alison, on the condition that everything which may be said in this room is off the record and not in any sense for publication. Please feel free to ask away.'

Glasby decided to be blunt. 'Did you have Michael Fisher killed?'

Again Danielson smiled, this time rather more ruefully. 'Alison, your approach is very direct. I suppose that in your profession that is to be commended. I have been following your stories, you know; although Burstone School is a very long way behind me, Henry Dunne is one of the few pleasant memories it left me with, and I have enjoyed reading of his successes.'

The smile disappeared. She waited to see if it was going

to be necessary to repeat her question. 'No, Alison, I did not. I did not have Michael Fisher murdered, and I do not know who killed him. From what I learned of what he made of his life I was not surprised by his death. But you knew a little about him, so I suppose that you understand what I mean by that.'

Although he sounded credible enough, Glasby had no way of knowing whether or not she could believe him.

Reading her mind, Danielson added, 'Of course, you don't know to what extent you can trust me, I understand that. I will do my best to help you in that respect, but let me ask you a question first. Why do you think I might have wanted Fisher dead?'

Glasby had no hesitation. 'I think you know the answer to that. Because he knew the truth about your games teacher's death, and because he was threatening to tell me about it. Is that why you have been hiding behind a false name, Martin? Why don't you want anyone to know that you are really David Gold?'

Again she was treated to Danielson's smile. 'Alison, I have a great deal of respect for you and how you go about your work, but why on earth would one think that there was any truth in this wild story, or indeed anything that Michael Fisher would say? The man was a confidence trickster, a fantasist, really he was no better than a common blackmailer. This is my information about him and I think it must be yours too.'

Glasby looked Danielson in the eye. 'You did say that you would answer questions as well as ask them.' He nodded. Satisfied, she continued. 'Two of your men spent some time following me, and someone else. The same two men were seen outside Fisher's flat. That doesn't mean that they killed him, or that you told them to do it if they did, but if I'm going to give you answers I want to know what they had been instructed to do, and why. OK?'

'It is,' replied Danielson. 'What you say is absolutely fair, and understood. Please, if you answer my query I will then tell you everything that I can, just as you ask.'

She told him of her attempts to corroborate Fisher's story, including the payments made him by Bedingfield, her conversation with Henry Dunne, and the DNA that connected Dunne with the teacher's death. She was careful to refer to Mia only as a friend of Fisher's, giving no name or any further details about the girl.

When Glasby had finished she settled back on the sofa, observing Danielson closely. He made no reply at first.

Then he took a breath and began to speak. 'Alison, first of all I want to say that I am very impressed, with your determination and with the quality of your research. I also notice that you have, even under these rather pressured circumstances, the presence of mind not to mention the name of Miss Svetlana Alieva – I believe that she has been using the professional name "Mia" – which is very proper of you.' Danielson stopped again as if to collect his thoughts.

'You already know enough of my life at Burstone School to understand that it has few positive associations for me. I have already mentioned Dunne to you as one of the exceptions, but Richard Bedingfield was head and shoulders above him, and all of the rest of us.'

For the first time the man sounded genuinely emotional. 'Bedingfield was a decent, honourable boy and it is very distressing to hear that a creature like Fisher could have got his claws into him.' He paused again.

'No one was responsible for Mr Dickson's death except possibly the man himself. I am not a supporter of capital punishment so I will not say that he deserved to die. The weather was appalling, the man had lost control of his temper and the most that Bedingfield did was to defend himself and me. I don't remember Dunne being anywhere nearby when it happened, and I really can't think how his blood would come to be on the teacher's shirt. But nothing more occurred other than an accident caused by bad weather, unfortunate circumstances and the man's own stupidity and ignorance. And, incidentally, I am far from convinced that Fisher would have been near enough to see if it had.'

Danielson was still looking upset but Glasby was determined to keep on with her questioning. 'But Fisher knew something, didn't he? Why were you having him watched, and Mia, and me?'

'Alison, you are aware that I am a particularly private man. And I am very fortunate that I am able to use others to help me protect my privacy. Mr Pincher is a very able person, in this regard. But he is a professional, a former senior police officer as you know, not a gangster. It came to his attention that Fisher had hired a private detective to try to find me. The detective was persuaded instead to pass on to Mr Pincher what was on Fisher's mind. It seemed that he was planning to threaten to embarrass me with a story from my past, the same story which you are now aware of, in the hope that I would reward him financially for his silence. Mr Pincher took certain steps to monitor Fisher's movements and actions, from then on.

'And yes, before you ask me, you will have received certain communications on my behalf. I'm sure that I am not the first person to say that you are a very persistent woman, Alison. It was not enough for you to receive a request from your editor, or rather more direct messages from Pincher and his men. Even the regrettable car accident has not been enough to put you off following up on this.'

Glasby swung round to face Danielson directly. 'These communications – do you know what you have done? You've scared the life out of Mia and me. I could lose my job because you've found someone who knows how to lean on my editor. And those two thugs, they tried to steal something by force out of Mia's hands when she was in my car and they nearly got me killed as well as themselves. Is that what your privacy costs? What gives you the right to that, Martin? What are you hiding from, anyway?'

Danielson stood, and for one bizarre moment it seemed that he was going to walk behind the sofa to address her, as if he was Mark Ellington. But he simply steadied himself for a moment and moved across to lean against the desk.

'You already have my apology, so I won't repeat it. But I accept that you are in a position – that I have put you in a position – whereby you have the right to ask those questions. I'll tell you who I'm hiding from: David Gold, the person I used to be.'

His voice was higher in pitch now and he sounded younger, almost like a schoolboy. 'I hated David Gold. They made me hate him, that bully Dickson and his vicious, hate-filled, anti-Semite of a son, those people, that school. They were the worst, him and his son, but it wasn't only them. The whole place was set up for it – they *approved* of it, as if being humili-ated was some sort of rite of passage that a teenager should go through. David Gold was a coward. He spent his whole time frightened, scared of being attacked, beaten and degraded. He was ashamed that he wasn't like them, ashamed to be Jewish, he was ashamed of his parents, he was weak and ashamed of himself. How could you not despise a boy like that?'

Glasby looked at the floor, not knowing what to say. 'Burstone School made Henry Dunne, it made Richard Bedingfield, it made that evil thug Dickson and it made David Gold. But *I* made Martin Danielson. And that, Alison, is more than I've ever said to anyone on this subject before, and I think that it is quite enough.'

He reached over to a button on the desk. In a few moments she heard Pincher approaching.

As the Jaguar pulled away Glasby decided to try her luck on Pincher. 'Those two men of yours, the ones who died in the car crash, how can you be sure that they didn't kill Fisher?'

Pincher gave her a quizzical look. 'Haven't you already covered that one with the boss? My lads, they were pros, the best. That pond life Fisher, he was going on about having evidence on the boss. They let themselves into his place, all right. Maybe they didn't get round to waiting for his invitation first, I'll grant you that. And they did a bit of eavesdropping on Fisher and his bird, and you 'n' all, but that's as far as it went. First thing they knew that he'd been topped was when they saw all the plods outside, next morning, like.'

Before they reached her home Pincher pulled an envelope from inside his trench coat and handed it to her. 'This is from the boss. And you don't need to hire John Smith no more. He's a good lad, Smithy, but he'll be a bit heavy on your pocket, if you know what I mean. If you need to know something, you can ask me. When you're home, you'll find my number on your phone. You can reach me on that. And one more thing, we had a tracker on your car, but it's off now. All being well, me and the boys are off your case, and the tart 'n' all, the little Russian girl or whatever she is. The boss wanted me to tell you that.'

Glasby made herself wait until she had climbed the stairs and was safely inside her own front door before she opened the envelope. She was hoping that it would contain some evidence connected with Fisher's death, or possibly a written statement that she could use in a story, so when she found a large bundle of banknotes she was both surprised and disappointed.

It wasn't until she had counted the money out that she understood. Two thousand pounds, the price that she had paid John Smith to track Danielson down. She was being re-imbursed, but not paid off. Martin Danielson was a man who carried out his business with a certain style.

# MARCH

**RB £1200**
*Vlada R.*
*Stefan Krűger, E800,*
*Randolf Schmidt, E200*
*Dave Beck, $500*
*Polina*
*Enrique Gomez, $700*

# APRIL

*Polina – Enrique Gomez, $250*
*Dave Beck – X*
*Stefan Krüger – X, finished*
*Tania – Dave Beck, $200*
*Folkes – √*
*Dickson – √*
*Aspinall – ?*
*Gold – ???*
*Dunne – X*
**Sunday Herald,** *Alison Glasby – Longhammer??*

*From the notebook of Michael Fisher*

# Sixteen

She still hadn't made it as far as the Indian shop but the last thing that Glasby felt now was hungry. She wanted to talk to someone. Redgrave would probably still be out with his mates from work, and anyway she wasn't sure how much she could tell him about what had happened to her that evening.

Until recently the natural person for her to call would have been Davenport. But since he had replaced the Leer as her boss, Bill had been acting like a completely different person. He had taken almost no interest in her problems; his only concern seemed to be to push his own stupid, old-fashioned ideas into the paper, with no thought for whether it was what she wanted to be working on at all. And once or twice he had dropped little remarks to her about the need for professional standards in journalism, which was not something that she could remember him being particularly preoccupied by in his own work.

It was if he had set out to prove that you couldn't be a friend and a boss at the same time.

Danielson had more or less killed off her last hopes of making anything of Fisher's tales about the death of the teacher, but despite that, Glasby was strangely elated after her dramatic encounter with George Pincher and his enigmatic paymaster. She certainly felt nothing like going to sleep.

If she really had reached the point of abandoning any chance of turning Fisher's allegations into a story which the *Herald* could run, there was one person who she certainly did need to tell about it . . .

Mia sounded pleased as ever to hear from her, any awkwardness from her visit earlier that day seemingly forgotten. 'But I can't speak to you now, I busy, can I come to your home for visit you? I am close to you flat, can see you in forty-five minutes, OK?'

The flat hadn't got any cleaner while Glasby had been away from it, of course, and neither had the job of dealing with it become any more appealing, but she thought that it would be a constructive way to burn off some surplus energy. There was enough time before Mia would arrive to at least make some impression on the grime that surrounded her. Fishing around in the rarely visited territory of the cupboard under the sink, Glasby found a half full aerosol of furniture polish. She set to work, with a cloth that was hardly any cleaner than the surfaces it would be used on.

A physical outlet for her bottled-up stress was indeed exactly what Glasby required. The sitting room was gleaming – by its usual standards, at any rate – and the hoover was going full blast when she heard the door bell. She looked at the clock; a full hour had gone past since she had spoken to Mia.

Her visitor had with her a small Louis Vuitton wheeled suitcase and matching handbag. She was back in jeans this time, the same pair that she had worn on their first meeting Glasby thought, and despite the casual wear looked utterly gorgeous. Smiling a greeting to her, Glasby pushed out of her mind the thought that she was glad that Redgrave would not be returning that night.

Pointing at the overnight case Mia said, 'Is it OK if I stay here tonight, Alison? Your boyfriend not here? I bring T-shirt to sleep in this time, because I know you a little embarrassed last time.' She gave her usual little giggle. 'You English, you so funny people.'

'Oh, well, yes of course.' Glasby was trying hard not to be a strangely prudish English person, not helped by the pink glow she could feel moving up the back of her neck and into her cheeks. 'Listen, Mia, I've got some news. Some more information about what Michael Fisher told you, important information.'

This time Mia laughed with excitement as well as pleasure; she literally jumped up into the air and embraced Glasby. 'Great! Now you can write story, and we both will make lots of money!' she exclaimed. Glasby cursed herself – what she intended to say had come out completely wrong.

'Let's sit down, and I'll tell you what has happened.' She led the younger woman through to the sitting room and did her best to explain. It was more complicated than had occurred to her: the teacher who was a bully; the three boys, one now dead, another a senior policeman, the third a billionaire who she had just that evening succeeded in tracking down, both of them saying nothing that helped to back up Fisher's claims in any way.

Glasby wasn't sure how much of it Mia had understood, and decided that she needed to be brutally clear in her conclusion. 'So you see, really we just have what Fisher said, against what they both say now. There are two of them, and they are both important men as well. And Fisher, well, I know he was a friend of yours, but you told me yourself what a liar he was, and I found all these emails on his computer where he was trying to make money out of cheating people.'

She shook her head for emphasis. 'The newspaper isn't going to be able to publish our story at all. I'm sorry, Mia, I really am.'

Glasby looked anxiously at the girl, who was looking concerned and possibly still a little puzzled. 'Alison, what you saying? You looked at Michael computer, and the other things, but you saying you not going to write story? What about my money you promise? You promise me that!'

It was the first time she had seen Mia looking upset. Her face was so expressive in its disappointment, almost a caricature of an unhappy child, that Glasby had to fight the urge to hold her hand as she delivered the final let-down.

'I'm sorry, Mia. Legally there is no way that the *Herald* can cover Michael's story. And without the story, they won't pay for the information.' Her high spirits of earlier were completely deflated by now.

Then she thought of the one piece of good news which the evening had brought her. 'Those men who chased us, and they threatened me as well, they were working for the billionaire. He promised that we are safe now. So you can go back to your flat now, it's safe.'

Even this had come out wrong; Glasby added quickly, 'I don't mean you have to go tonight of course. You're welcome to stay here.'

But her guest had already leapt up off the sofa and stood, tiny and trembling with anger, in front of her. 'You go see this rich man, and he pay you! That is why you say we safe. Mia, she is stupid girl, stupid foreign *tart*, that is what you think! You promise me that I can trust you. First I get scared then I was nearly killed. Now you take billionaire's money, and you say I get nothing!'

She literally stamped her foot in her rage, nearly treading on Glasby as she did so. Glasby noticed that she was still wearing the powder blue sandals of earlier. Before she could think what to say in reply, Mia had turned on her heel and had stormed out through the door, pulling her beautiful suitcase behind her.

Jack Daniels' chirpy face was not what Glasby would have chosen to help her get over the stresses that her weekend had held, but this was what the fates offered her on a Monday morning in early autumn that was much brighter than her mood.

'We're back in business, Ali!' he proclaimed, reclining in his chair with his feet up on the desk, as befitted a man in control of great events. She noticed that a large piece of chewing gum was stuck to one of his shoes, but decided that it was unnecessarily kind to point it out to him.

'What do you mean, Jack?' she asked, cautiously.

'The Jackie and Senty show, of course. Fasten your seatbelts, ladies, we're rolling again!'

Looking round, Glasby saw that Hetal was standing nearby, listening in. She really needed to tell the girl not to smile like that at Daniels. Encouragement was the last thing that he needed.

'You've managed to salvage something from the wreckage, then?' she enquired, acidly.

'The comeback kid, that's me,' he informed them. 'Listen and wonder: Nemo and I have cracked it. Only a joint story – no pun intended, Ali! – Senty and the Gunarathnas, shared values, the importance of the family, the works. They've just done the photoshoot and it went like a dream. Another *Herald* exclusive. High five, girls!'

An old-fashioned look from Glasby was sufficient to keep Hetal from slapping hands with Daniels; he lowered his arm and, gratifyingly for her, looked a bit sheepish.

But not for long. 'How did you persuade Mr and Mrs Gunarathna to do it, Jack?' asked Hetal, as Mike Marshall left his desk and wandered over to join them.

'Oh, it wasn't too hard,' replied Daniels. 'Nemo and I scripted it perfectly. Senty called them last week. He turned on the waterworks – you know, he loved his son, the boy was wrong but what could any father do but forgive him? He told them how much he respected what they had done – we even got him to thank them for saving the boy from getting in with an even worse crowd. It was downhill racing all the way from there.'

'What about the son?' asked Marshall. 'Isn't he a doctor? He should recognize a bedside manner when he hears one.'

'Bedside is about right,' replied the man who put the bump into bumptious. 'That part of the production was courtesy of yours truly. The delicious Mrs Mayback joined the party this morning, with just enough décolletage to stay the right side of classy.'

At this point Daniels leered in Hetal's direction. Glasby felt her hands tighten, wishing that they were in closer proximity to his neck.

'So the good Dr G was getting an eyeful of Kelly Mayback's charms, while Senty worked his magic on the old folks. Result: two happy families, a great set of pics are winging their way up to Ellington as we speak, one purring editor – Jackie D, at your service!'

On a better day Glasby might have managed to maintain a dignified silence, but not today. 'Are there no limits to your cynicism, Jack?' she asked, hoping that she sounded cutting but achieving not much more than pomposity.

Marshall saved her. 'I think you're being a bit hard on Jack, Ali. He's achieved a lot, but it's still early in his career. Of course there are limits to how cynical he can be at this stage, but he's pushing them back, day by day.'

Glasby could have kissed him.

Wonder of wonders, she managed to persuade her boss to have a conversation that didn't centre on commuting, hobbies or the generation gap. Even though Martin Danielson had made it clear that everything which he had told her was off the record, she thought that it would be within the bounds of journalistic ethics for her to brief Davenport, in strict confidence, so that she could take his advice.

The account Glasby gave him of her encounter with the

billionaire and his security staff was more or less verbatim. The only thing she omitted to mention was George Pincher's gun, mainly because she didn't feel like describing how terrified she had been when he had pointed it at her.

Davenport was impressed. 'That's quite a story, Alison. From anyone else, I might even be asking myself whether a bit of embroidery had gone into it, but you . . . You have quite a way of going about things, young lady.'

Impressed, maybe, but realistic too. 'That really is it, though, I guess you agree? On the one hand, you've got the words of a highly respected police officer and a super-rich businessman. On the other you've got Fisher: seedy, nutty, deceitful – and dead. End of story, I'd say.'

Glasby thought of Mia. But however badly she wanted to disagree with Davenport, she couldn't.

'I know, Bill. I've worked this one as hard as I possibly could. But someone killed Fisher, and I still don't know who or why. And I'm still in just as much trouble over Fish and Chips as I ever was.'

Davenport looked at her strangely. 'Fish and Chips? What on earth does that mean?'

'I told you before, Bill! Those policemen who we named as being investigated by Longhammer. Salmon and Shipp, remember? The ones who are suing Mark Ellington. And me.'

'Yes, of course.' Davenport really hadn't been concentrating when she'd talked to him before, that was clear. He looked a bit abashed. 'Well, if you've managed to get George Pincher on the side of the angels now, why don't you ask him? I can't imagine that his boss is going to want him mixed up in an investigation into who killed Michael Fisher. But you know what they say, "set a thief to catch a thief".'

'What do you mean?' asked Glasby, surprised.

'Well, you're on the trail of two dirty coppers. And not wanting to cast any aspersions about ex-Inspector Pincher, that happens to be a subject that he knows a great deal about. I'm not sure that I understand why you think that he's under an obligation to you . . . ?'

He paused, but barring an embarrassed clearing of the throat Glasby gave him no reply.

'Well, whatever it is, if he's offering to help you, why don't you see what he can do? With Danielson's money and George

Pincher behind you, the name "Alison Glasby" might just open a few doors.

'By the way,' Davenport added, 'you haven't heard from Thomas Lear, have you?'

Glasby was surprised. 'No,' she replied, wondering if this was going to be another attempt at getting some more details out of her of the day when Lear had lost control. 'Why?'

Davenport pulled a strange face. 'His wife called earlier. Apparently Thomas checked himself out of the hospital, and he hadn't shown up at home yet. She wanted to know if he had made contact with anyone here.'

'He certainly hasn't called me,' replied Glasby. 'Not that there's any reason why he would. I wonder who his friends are, at the *Herald*?'

Neither of them knew the answer to that one.

Glasby had been looking at a blank computer screen for the last ten minutes. It was something that Davenport had said . . . something – her name, that was it!

She shook the mouse impatiently to clear the screensaver and went to her Favourites folder. Hotmail, sign in; here it was. She typed in the email address that had burnt itself on to her memory: long.hammer@hotmail.co.uk.

Then she stopped. She didn't know how many tries at a password hotmail would allow before it locked her out, but she had an idea that it might be as few as three. If that happened, whoever was the owner of the email account would find out next time he tried to get into it. She had no idea what effect, if any, that might have, but it could hardly leave her in a worse mess than she was now.

Typing very carefully and deliberately, she made her first attempt: g-l-a-s-b-y. The *Herald*'s internet connection was slow as ever; the screen went blank for a good few seconds before returning to the log-in screen. She cursed; written in red was the message 'The e-mail address or password is incorrect. Please try again.'

Glasby did as bidden, this time trying her first and last names, separated by a full stop. The same message returned.

The air conditioning on the twenty-sixth floor worked perfectly well, but she could feel a trickle of sweat running down the back of her neck. Her secret informant's password might have been in capitals, it might be her first name only and not her last – or for all she knew it might have been his lottery numbers, or his mother's date of birth.

More careful than ever not to make a mistake, she threw the dice for a third and potentially last time: alisonglasby. For another agonizing second or two her screen went white while the gods of the internet wheel of fortune considered her fate. Then she saw in front of her the cheery greeting 'Hi, Long Hammer!'

There was an empty feeling in Glasby's stomach. Her fingers were trembling so much that she had to try a second time before she could grip the mouse properly. There were six unread emails in the inbox.

Again, she had a wait while her computer decided that it felt like working, but this time there was only disappointment at the end of it. Not only were all the unread emails from her – how many times had she written pleading for him to get back in touch? – but so was every other email in the inbox, nearly fifty in all. Her name had opened the door, just as Davenport had suggested, but all it had led to was an empty room.

She tried the other folders, hoping for a clue, anything, that might lead her to Mr Hammer's identity. 'Junk' was empty. 'Drafts' likewise. And in 'Sent' there were three pages of emails, all addressed to her – except two!

Glasby exhaled, not just air but what felt like several tons of pressure escaping from deep inside her.

The doorman was surprised enough to see Glasby leave that he actually checked his watch as she passed through the glass security barrier in the atrium of the *Herald*'s building. It really was only five thirty, and yet there she was, having managed to beat the rush of shift workers and clock-watchers to the exit, a good couple of hours before her normal departure time.

He should have known better. Her day's work was far from over; in fact the most important parts were yet to come. She had some calls to make, but not the sort which she wanted to do from her office.

First, however, she had to negotiate London's public transport system, which was state of the art, totally twenty-first century and fit for a world-class city. That was all true, if you looked at the advertisements heralding the Olympic Games, which were due to take place in 2012. Maybe by then the Tube would live up to its publicity, but unfortunately Glasby couldn't wait that long.

In the meantime, she was trapped in one corner of the slowly moving carriage as it shuddered and lurched its way along the almost certainly nineteenth-century tracks, a rucksack with smiley faces sewn on to it jammed against her to her left and two gum-chewing teenagers in front of her. Every now again a man with an old-fashioned broadsheet newspaper threatened to clip her ears with it.

None of this spoiled her mood, however, or even made much of an impression on her thoughts. She fairly bounced up out of the station at Stockwell and charged home, buoyed up with what lay ahead.

Her first call was straightforward enough, and a pleasure too. 'You were right, John,' she told him. 'About that story of Fisher's, I mean.' She filled him in on some of what Danielson had told her, being careful not to mention Pincher, or any details of how he had made contact with her.

'Anyway, I was wondering if you wanted to come round tomorrow?' She had been tempted to ask him over sooner, just to make sure that there were no lingering bad feelings from the little scene they'd had over Mia, but had decided that the evening ahead might need to be devoted to more serious matters. They arranged to meet after work. There was talk of them going to see a film, something Glasby hadn't done all summer.

Next it was time for George Pincher. She explained to him the background on Salmon and Shipp, gaining as she did the clear impression that Pincher knew at least as much as her about the situation. 'So what I need,' she concluded, 'is something that will make the story we ran hold up. It has to be evidence of some sort that they have been involved in things that they shouldn't have done. Someone who will speak out, or a document, anything like that.'

'Evidence,' echoed Pincher. 'Evidence . . . That's always the tricky part, if you know what I mean.'

He was proving to be a bit less positive than she had been hoping for. 'I thought that I might try John Smith,' she suggested, hoping that it might get Mr Pincher's competitive juices flowing.

'John Smith,' he echoed again. 'No, I don't think so. You'll find that Georgie Salmon and Bill Shipp, they won't quite be his cup of cocoa. If you know what I mean.'

She wasn't sure that she did, except that it didn't sound very encouraging.

'Mind you,' he mused, as if to himself. 'Mind you, old Georgie Salmon, he never was straightest bit of spaghetti in the packet. Nor the tastiest, I must be honest with you. The boss, he does feel that we owe you one . . . Leave it with me, love, why don't you? We'll see if Georgie or his mate have thought to leave us with any *evidence* for you, shall we?'

Now it was time for the big one. Glasby decided to change her phone setting so that her number was withheld. Possibly he wouldn't take the call if he knew who it was coming from.

She had already decided what to say, so as soon as he answered she went right ahead. 'Mick, Mick Doherty? It's Alison Glasby. We need to talk about Longhammer, and an email account that you've been using.'

Glasby had braced herself for a fight but Doherty just seemed to be in shock, he answered her questions so meekly. Yes, it was him who had been sending information to her. No, nobody else knew about it. As for his motivation, Doherty said that he just liked her and wanted to help her, and Longhammer too.

'But up until the last time all the information that you gave me was about people who were firmly in the frame. Why did you send me Salmon's and Shipp's names? You must have known that Dunne wasn't ready to charge them with anything.'

'Well, it was after that misunderstanding you and me had, that evening, and I admit I thought it might put you on the spot a bit. But I never meant more than that – I was still trying to help you, that's the honest truth. I never thought that there would be any real problems, not for you, nor the boss.'

He was sounding thoroughly shifty now, in Glasby's opinion. It smelled nasty, like a bit of revenge on her for turning him down. But she didn't think that there was much to be done about it now.

'If I knew anything more I'd pass it on to you in a heart-beat, honest I would. I'd have told the boss before now as well. I want to bring them bastards in as much as you do. Mick Doherty's a straight shooter, you can ask anyone that.'

His voice was trembling a bit at these last few words, but Glasby still didn't expect what came next. Before she could say anything, he was in tears, and she was only glad that she wasn't with him in person; she could imagine the man down on his knees begging her to help him, something which, considering how badly he'd behaved towards her, might have been appealing a while ago but certainly wasn't now.

'I know I'll be out on my ear now,' he wailed. 'Seventeen years I've been on the job, and that'll be it. Goodbye Mick, and good riddance. That's if they don't put me away. You'll have the last laugh, you will, when I'm serving time.'

She hoped that he could hear her over the sobbing that all too clearly was still going on. 'Mick, listen to me. You are my source, and I have a duty not to reveal your identity to anyone.'

It didn't seem as if he had heard, of if he had, he wasn't listening. 'Henry's a top man, he's different class, that's what he is. He took me and made me what I am, and I've gone and ruined it for him! He'll never look me in the eye again, how could he?'

Glasby tried again, more firmly this time. 'Mick! You have to listen, or there's no point in me talking to you. I've already said it once, I won't be telling Henry Dunne or anyone else one single thing about you. Do you understand?'

She never did find out whether Doherty really had got the point of what she was saying, but the sobs gradually turned themselves into rather more subdued sniffles. Then he cleared his throat noisily to allow himself to speak. 'How did you find out it was me?' he asked, dolefully.

'You forwarded two of my emails to your home email account, Mick. Why did you do that, anyway?'

'I wanted to print them out, to think about what to answer you. And I didn't want to open up the hotmail address, not when I was at work at the Yard.'

'Well, the problem was,' she told him, possibly a bit more cheerfully than she should have done, 'that you left the account setting so that it automatically saved sent messages. If you'd have just changed that option, I never would have found out that it was you.'

*Bar called Retox, in Soho*
*Name of Café – Rasputin Restaurant, High Street*
*Acton*
*S&M Café, 4–6 Essex Road, N1*
*Grate Expectations – Gloucester Road*

*From the notebook of Michael Fisher*

# Seventeen

Dunne hardly ever went to the canteen these days. When he did, all too often what he saw were conversations that ended quickly as heads turned his way. Occasionally an unfriendly smirk would be aimed in his direction, but he preferred even that to the sympathetic looks, sometimes bordering on pity, that some kinder souls offered him.

When he needed coffee, ever more often than probably was good for him, he tended to make an excuse to ask someone in the team outside his office to pick something up for him, if they happened to be passing that way. And they, understanding the situation all too well, would quickly find themselves doing just that, so as to oblige without embarrassing him by seeming to make a special trip.

This evening he still had a smallish mountain of the usual dreary paperwork without which no one in the Met seemed to be able to function these days. None of his boys were still around, which was itself a sign of the times for the Godsquad. Even Doherty, who usually seemed to practically live for the job, was not at his desk. There being no alternative, Dunne took the walk down the corridor to the familiar swing doors.

'Henry!' Well, it was neither a dirty glare nor a pitying smile but it was no more welcome than either. Jack Logan, Inspector Jack as he loved to be called, was all bonhomie and handlebar moustache.

'Jack. How are you, and how are Penny and the girls?'

'It's been a long time, hasn't it? Too long, Henry, too long. And what are we doing, standing here in the doorway like a couple of floozies trying to stay out of the rain? Come on over and sit down. Unless you've time for a proper drink, somewhere away from this hellhole?'

'Thanks, Jack, but it'll have to be another time. I'm knee-deep in paperwork, and Horgan has already given me a rollocking for being behind schedule. You know what it's like.'

'Don't I just? Don't we all! Never mind, come and join me for a quiet chat over a coffee, then. It's time we had a bit of a jaw-jaw, isn't it?'

It was all too obvious which direction the conversation would head in. With a dryness in his throat that no amount of coffee was going to cure, Dunne sat down with Inspector Jack and prepared for the worst.

'How's your family, anyway, Henry? Penny tells me that Patsy's on fine form. The two of them, putting the world to right – it's a wonder that the big lad upstairs ever bothered inventing us men really, don't you think? I mean, the ladies, they'd sort us all out in a bat of an eyelid, if we just gave them the chance, eh?'

Dunne wasn't sure how much of this elephants' ballet he could bear. Inspector Jack was considered by many to be a very effective copper, albeit not wholly up with the more modern strands of thought that were encouraged by senior management nowadays, but no one had ever described him as subtle.

'I suppose you're referring to their chat the other day, Jack? About my Mattie?'

Logan did a very poor impersonation of a man who was not quite sure what he was supposed to be thinking of, but who then gradually worked it out. 'Oh!' he exclaimed. 'Of course, Henry. Your Mattie! It had totally slipped my mind!'

'Of course, Jack,' said Dunne, not bothering to make the effort to sound convincing. 'But that was what Penny and Patsy discussed. My Mattie, in your nick.'

'He's a great lad, Henry. Truly, he's one for you to be proud of. Any dad would take pride in a boy like that. A bit of a student jape, that's all it was. A few years ago they were chucking flour around, or running the prof's trousers up the flagpole. And now they're shouting about the war, as if no one ever thought about that one before. Not to say that they mightn't be right, mind you . . .'

There didn't seem anything for Dunne to say, so he just sipped his coffee and waited.

'I mean, look at Senty Mayback's kid! The father's a million-aire, the boy must have girls throwing themselves all over him, and what does he do but get himself mixed up in drugs? You and me, Henry, we're both family men. You know and I know the sacrifices that all good coppers have to make to the job, we've been there and we've both done it. The wife and kids miss out, that can't be denied and it can't be avoided either. So thank God, when sometimes we can make it up to them a bit, eh?'

Again, Dunne waited. This time Logan caught his eye, but chose not to receive the message that he saw there.

'And talking of family men, there's Bill Shipp. Now if he's dirty, he'll go down, and you'll have mine and everyone's thanks for putting him where he belongs. But I know Bill a bit, he worked for me a while back, and I happen to know that he's feeling pretty sore at the moment. You've got him stuck in no man's land, if you like, and that can't be right. Can you see if you can get him out of there, Henry? Just as a favour to me, if you like.'

Dunne rose to go. 'It's a pleasure to see you, Jack. As it always is. And please be sure to give my best to Penny. As for Bill Shipp, that'll be a pleasure too, to put him just where he belongs. I couldn't have put it better myself. If that's the favour you're looking for, I'll be right on to it now. Maybe that paperwork can wait for a bit, after all.'

He turned to leave, then changed his mind. Returning to the table, he gave a broad smile to Jack Logan, picked up his cup, and left. There was no point in wasting perfectly good coffee, after all.

Davenport looked up rather guiltily and quickly pushed some papers over the copy of the *Racing Post* which he had been studying. It had tickled his fancy, and given his ego a stroke too, when Ellington had turned to him, not much more than a year after he'd been pushed out of the *Herald*. But several weeks later, the pleasure of running a team of more or less enthusiastic young journalists was beginning to pall.

The real problem, of course, was Glasby. He'd been feeling more than a little guilty about her. To say that she was a management challenge would have been putting it politely; she was as nimble as a mountain goat when she felt like it, and as stubborn when she didn't.

But Davenport knew that he sometimes underestimated how

young and inexperienced Glasby really was. She'd had very little support or guidance from Lear, who'd obviously had other things on his mind, or Ellington, whose editorial skills seemed to consist of having gone to the right school and knowing how to point a shotgun at a pheasant. Now Glasby had got herself into even deeper waters and Davenport was worried that he had been encouraging her to swim still further, first introducing her to John Smith – a professional, but very definitely a man for adult consumption only – and now sending her back to see George Pincher, of all people.

If it turned out that the girl needed a lifebelt throwing in, he'd better make sure that he was alert enough to be on hand when the moment came.

'Hello, Alison, what's happening?' She'd been walking around as if the building was resting on her shoulders lately. At least she looked a bit more purposeful today.

'I just wanted to tell you, Bill. You remember that it all started with me getting anonymous leaks from Longhammer, and then I got a tip-off about Salmon and Shipp?'

'Yes, Fish and Chips. I remember. I'm not totally past it, you know.' That came out a bit more acerbic than he'd intended. He needed to tone it down, unless he wanted to turn into an old man with a temper.

'I know, Bill!' She seemed to take it in good spirits. You could never be entirely sure, with Alison. Sometimes she could be very moody. 'Anyway, what I was going to say was, I found out where the leak came from. Who had been sending me the emails, I mean.'

'That's fantastic, Alison. Well done! How did you do it?'

'Well, it was something that you said, actually, Bill. It just got me to thinking along the right lines, and everything clicked into place. I can't really say more than that – you do understand, don't you?'

No one could ever accuse her of not taking her responsibilities seriously, that was for sure. But better that than skedaddling off to a second job the moment his back was turned, like Marshall, that little pal of hers. 'Of course I understand, Alison. More importantly, are you any closer to getting anything on Mr Fish and Mr Chips?'

Her face clouded over. 'I wish I was, Bill. No, the advice that you gave me is my best bet, I think. I've talked to George

Pincher, just as you suggested. He was very friendly, and I think he'll help if he can.'

This time it was Davenport's turn to look worried. 'Alison, just watch your step with that man, will you? If it suits him to help you, he will. And just as quickly, he'll eat you up and dump you by the wayside. Look, keep me in touch, that's all that I mean. You've had a difficult time, I know, and I . . . well, I've been trying to play this role as best I can. Old dogs can learn new tricks, it's not true what they say, but it takes us a bit longer to adjust. I've neglected you – maybe I haven't been as good a friend as I would have liked. When you need me, you know how to find me, OK?'

She was a strange girl, she really was. As tough as you like when you had no right to expect it of her, and now after one kind word, there she was, in tears, right in his office where everyone would see. What sort of a boss would they take him for?

'Get out of the bloody way, you stupid old witch!'

If the elderly cyclist had heard Mick Doherty curse her, she gave no sign of it as she wobbled across the side road where he had been queuing, and continued slowly and illegally on her way along the pavement. He sat impatiently for another three or four minutes waiting for the traffic in front of him, gradually edging his way forward so as to create a gap for himself.

The driver of a red van to his left slowed to make a phone call. Doherty took his chance and pushed out in front of him, forcing the van driver to brake. He pulled over to his right a few metres further on, turning in to the entrance of a multi-storey car park.

His hand shook a little as he reached out of his window to take a ticket from the machine at the entrance but he drove steadily enough, circling upwards through the car park until he reached the ninth and last storey. Although the lower floors had been mostly full, there were few other cars here.

Doherty parked neatly between the white lines and got out, locking the doors behind him. He walked past the sign which pointed pedestrians to the exit that would take them to the shopping centre below, and leaned against the perimeter wall. A stain made by rainwater that had run down the wall merged with another that smelled of urine at the ground by his feet.

A woman walked past him to the entrance tugging a small girl behind her. The child sounded unhappy about something. Neither of them paid any attention to Doherty. After they had gone he pulled himself up to a sitting position on the top of the wall. It had been designed to be too far off the ground to make this easy, but Doherty was determined and it presented him with no real difficulty.

For five minutes or more he stayed where he was on the wall, as if he was waiting for someone. No one came; in fact nobody else at all walked past. From time to time he swung his heels rhythmically back and forth. He might have been playing out the beat to a favourite song; if so, the tune remained in his head only, because his lips didn't move.

He clasped his fists in front of him and bent his head forward a little, looking more like a rugby player preparing to take a kick than someone at prayer. This time he seemed to say something; it might have been a woman's name.

Then all of a sudden Doherty threw his head forward, pushed up with his hips and back with his shoulders, and let the momentum take him over the wall. He fell down nine floors until he hit the concrete below, where he died almost instantly.

His body landed next to an entrance intended for deliveries to an ugly brown glass office building which stood just a few metres from the car park, but the offices were between tenants and so the entrance was unused. A keen-eyed security man might have spotted the body on one of the cameras which ringed the building, but the guard on duty was watching television and saw nothing.

As a result it wasn't until nearly an hour later that a shopper taking a short cut had the unpleasant experience of being the first person to discover Mick Doherty. She was a stout woman in her sixties and laden with bags of groceries from the nearby supermarket.

By this time it was obvious even at a quick glance, which was all she could bring herself to give, that Doherty was dead. A pool of blood more than a metre across was centred on the back of his head.

Her children had bought her a mobile phone the previous Christmas and she put her shopping down, well away from the body on which she had turned her back, and searched for it in her handbag. Not being sure of what number to dial she called her son who worked nearby. Although it seemed much longer to her, the first police car pulled up less than five minutes later.

When the phone call came Glasby was diligently working away on a piece that she and Hetal had to complete by Thursday. It was about different people's approaches to retirement. She had been out that morning to a large DIY store over in east London, interviewing two of their staff who were both aged over sixty-five. One said that he didn't need the money but came into work because he enjoyed the company and to keep himself busy; the other had completely the opposite attitude. Between them they would make a good addition to what was planned as a full-page piece in next Sunday's paper.

John Redgrave sounded nothing at all like his normal self. 'Alison, there's something I need to tell you. It's Mick Doherty. He's dead. I'm afraid that he killed himself this morning.'

Afterwards Glasby wasn't sure how long she spent just sitting at her desk, her arms crossed, rocking backwards and forwards as if she was trying to sooth a baby to sleep. She could feel a pounding in her head that was growing stronger; it was starting to make her feel dizzy.

Forcing herself to her feet, Glasby staggered as fast as she could to the entrance to the lift lobby and hurled herself through the door to the ladies' bathroom, narrowly avoiding someone who she didn't recognize as she did so. Without even managing to get the door to the cubicle bolted behind her she bent over the toilet bowl and repeatedly threw up.

Eventually her head cleared and after washing her mouth and eyes with cold water, Glasby was able to walk back to her desk, her face drained of blood but otherwise looking more or less normal. Like Thomas Lear before her, she was thankful that no one seemed to have noticed her unusual behaviour.

There was no way that Glasby could concentrate on work or anything else, though. She felt terrible. There was nothing, she tried to convince herself, *nothing* that she had said to Doherty that would have driven him to suicide. But kill himself was what he had done, the very next morning after he had broken down in tears, under her interrogation . . .

Her head started to throb again. She picked up the phone. 'Bill, it's Alison.'

'Hello, Alison, are you still out at your interviews?'

'No, I'm at my desk, but something's happened, and I'm not feeling at all good. Something happened to someone I know, not really a friend, but someone I knew, I just found out that he killed himself.'

'Oh, Alison, I'm so sorry. Who was it – not someone close to you, I hope?'

'It was Doherty – Mick Doherty.'

'Mick Doherty? You mean the policeman, Henry Dunne's deputy on Longhammer?'

'That's right, yes. He threw himself from the top of a multi-storey car park. Did you know him?'

Davenport sounded as if he was thinking. 'Well, I met him a couple of times, quite a while ago. How well did you know him?'

Glasby really didn't want to start going into any details of her dealings with Mick Doherty. 'Bill, I'm sorry, but I was calling to say that I just need to get some air. Is it OK if I just go out for an hour or two? I'll get that piece with Hetal done in time, don't worry about that.'

Davenport agreed, of course. He thought for a while longer after they had finished speaking, then put aside the newspaper which he had been reading and reached for the phone.

'What have you been up to, Alison?' he said to himself, as he waited for his call to be answered. Davenport had not far off fifty years of experience under his belt, and he thought that he had a pretty good idea now of the answer to his question.

Less than an hour later Glasby was standing in front of Davenport, shaking her head in despair.

'I keep trying to tell myself that it wasn't my fault, Bill. But it's so awful, it's just terrible, I talked to Mick yesterday evening on the phone, and he was really unhappy and worried. I mean, if I'd have only said something, done things right, maybe he wouldn't . . .'

She trailed off, looking close to tears. Davenport got up quickly, walked around the table which was still serving as his temporary desk, and put his arms around her shoulders.

'Sit down, Alison, come on.' He guided Glasby into a chair and stood beside her, one arm still around her. After a moment or two, satisfied that she was calmer, he pulled up another chair and sat facing her as she stared down at the floor.

'Now listen, Alison. You told me yesterday that you'd found out who had been leaking information from Longhammer to you anonymously. It was Doherty, wasn't it? He was your source. Now I understand that you felt you shouldn't tell anyone about it, but I'm your boss, and – well, we're a bit past those sort of concerns now, aren't we?'

Glasby didn't reply, but looked up and nodded.

'Well, the long and the short of it is that I took a punt that must be what it was. I made a couple of calls, and this is what I found out. Mick Doherty was going through a divorce, a messy one from the sounds of it. I've spent too many years covering murder cases not to have to speak ill of the dead sometimes, and I think it's fair to say that Doherty was not a particularly nice man. When they called his wife, she laughed, said "Good" and put the phone down.'

Glasby's eyes opened wider at this and she drew in a breath, but still said nothing. Davenport, seeing that his words had made an impact, continued.

'When any copper dies like that, especially someone working on an internal corruption inquiry like Doherty, the first thing they do is to make sure that it really was suicide. I gather that they're looking at the tapes from the car park's security cameras now. But apparently he left some sort of a note. It mentioned the wife and child – he had a young boy, but there was a restraining order, you know, so he wasn't able to see the kid at all. The point is, Alison, that none of this is anything to do with you. The man's life was a mess, and he just got sick of living it.'

Glasby looked at Davenport, her eyes swollen and pink from crying. 'Thanks, Bill,' she said, then let her head drop again. He waited until she was ready to talk.

She shook herself as if to clear her brain. 'I still feel terrible about it. You're right, of course – it turned out that he was my source. It was that remark that you made to me, about my name being a key. I got into the email account that Doherty had used when he sent information to me, and the password was my name, and then I could see it was him.'

'We make a good team, don't we?' Davenport said. 'I say something clever and you work out what on earth it was that I meant!' He laughed, and even Glasby raised a watery smile.

'I called Doherty after work yesterday. I was so desperate to see whether there was anything more on Salmon and Shipp that he could tell me – it was him who caused all this mess in the first place, when he gave me their names. All my other Longhammer stories came from him, you know, and they were all on the nail. It was just this one . . . To be honest, I think he did it deliberately.'

Davenport was surprised. 'What do you mean? Why would he give you a bum steer on purpose, after all the good stuff that you got from him before?'

Regretting having said this, Glasby changed the subject. 'Anyway, it was obvious that he didn't know anything else that could help. He got really worked up – he even started crying, Bill. But I made it really clear that I wasn't going to tell the police or anyone else about him. I did, Bill, I'm sure I did!'

Typically, Glasby refused Davenport's suggestion that she go home and rest, or even spend an hour or two in the pub with him to help put it behind her. Instead she went back to considering the work experiences of the over sixty-fives.

Davenport returned to his newspaper.

It was early evening, but Glasby was still at her desk when Henry Dunne reached her. He spoke quietly but she recognized his voice immediately, even before he said his name.

'Hello, Henry.' She hoped that she sounded calm, but felt anything but. Had the police traced the call that she'd made to Doherty the night before? Would they be quizzing her on what had passed between them? Maybe they had even found out about the long.hammer email address?

'You heard the news about Mick Doherty's suicide, I know. John Redgrave told you earlier, didn't he?'

'That's right, yes. It's terrible, Henry. It *was* suicide, then?'

'Oh yes, I'm afraid that there's no doubt about it at all. It was all caught on the car park's cameras, I've seen it myself. There was no one else involved – Mick just threw himself off the top. They say that he died instantaneously.'

'I'm so sorry, Henry. You and he . . . you'd known him for a long time, hadn't you?'

There was a pause at the other end of the line. 'You're right, it was a very long time. That's why I'm calling you, Alison, to be honest. I – look, I know that this is a difficult subject for you, but I just want to ask you: was Mick your informant? Was it him who was giving you all that information on the progress of our enquiries, on Longhammer I mean?'

Glasby thought fast. 'Henry, I'm sorry, there's no way that I can answer that question. The *Herald* would never allow me to reveal the identity of my sources.'

Dunne groaned. He really sounded in pain. 'I'm not trying to erode the freedom of the press, Alison. That really isn't what I'm about. This isn't even an official request. It's just that, I just want to know that it wasn't Mick. I don't care who it was, just so long as it wasn't him. Please, just tell me that, that's all I meant.'

Glasby swore to herself. 'I don't know what to say, Henry.'

And in truth she didn't. Of all the awful things to have to tell someone! Why couldn't this be happening to someone else?

'I didn't even know myself who it was, until recently. What else can I say?'

Dunne answered with great deliberation. 'You can tell me this, Alison. Tell me that Mick Doherty wasn't leaking information to you.'

'I can't say that. I'm really sorry, Henry, but I just can't say that.'

She could hear his breathing but he said nothing, the sense of his bitterness at Doherty's betrayal more eloquent than any words.

It felt like her head was going to explode; it would have been a relief if it had done exactly that. Not even Glasby could carry on with the article which she owed to Davenport now. Unable to face any more misery she fled home, only remembering when she got there that she was supposed to be meeting Redgrave for a relaxing night out.

## Everything

*If you see me walking down the street,*
*Please look away,*
*Don't catch my eye,*
*You know we must be discreet,*
*Though you know I'd really like to meet,*
*It can't be today,*
*We both know why,*
*And yet the feeling's so sweet . . .*
*Oh I'd live with you in another world,*
*Oh I'd live with you not another girl,*
*Oh I'd live with you . . .*
*But instead I find myself walking,*
*To the place where sirens sing,*
*Step inside, please step inside sir,*
*We specialize in everything*

*From the notebook of Michael Fisher*

# Eighteen

'Low ebb.'

'Pardon, Alison?' asked Hetal.

She hadn't realized that she'd spoken aloud. Having barely managed to get any sleep, Glasby had left home while it was still dark outside in the hope of escaping her thoughts by immersing herself in her job. It hadn't worked. The same things just kept going round and round like water down a plughole, interrupted only by those words that had got stuck in her head: 'low ebb'.

Since she had climbed aboard the train that had taken her into this house of horrors, four people had died. Michael Fisher had been murdered, the two ex-policemen working for George Pincher had died by accident and now Mick Doherty had killed himself. As if that wasn't enough misery for her to take responsibility for, she had put Mia in danger, been the instrument of Doherty's betrayal of Henry Dunne, and left the *Herald* and its editor facing a potentially huge damages claim from Salmon and Shipp.

Then there was Thomas Lear's nervous collapse; not even in her present despondent state of mind could Glasby find a reason why that would have been her fault, but neither could she understand why on earth it had to be her who had been the one to witness it.

In the meantime she had found herself dealing with people like George Pincher and John Smith, men for whom deceit, fear and violence were just part of their day's work. And Martin Danielson, a man so traumatized by the hurt that Burstone School had done to him that he had killed off his childhood self and hidden himself away behind a wall of secrets and money.

And then it occurred to her. There was still one person who she hadn't made contact with, one piece of the puzzle which she hadn't finished trying to slot into place.

Glasby grabbed some papers from her desk drawer and rifled through them. Plucking one from the pile she drew her finger down a list of names until she found the one that she was looking for. She checked a note that she'd made from one of the other papers, then waited, drumming her fingers as impatiently as ever, until the web page she was looking for was on her screen.

She called John Redgrave. 'Sorry again about last night. Listen, I know that you can't meddle in other people's work, but there's just one thing that I really need you to help me with. Please, John . . .'

Having reluctantly accepted that Redgrave wasn't going to be able to give her any assistance until the next morning, Glasby spent the rest of the day in a much better mood. Like Davenport she found Hetal nothing but a pleasure to work with. She was developing impressively fast, too. On her own initiative she had made contact with an Indian seniors' group, with the result that they would be able to contrast the viewpoints of different cultures on the issue of whether the over sixty-fives should stay in the workforce.

'"The only way is up", that's it, Alison,' she said, as they pulled together the last pieces ready to present their article to Davenport in the morning.

'What do you mean, Hetal?'

She laughed. 'Oh, my father is a Labour Party man, he loves Mr Brown and Mr Blair. When Labour was first elected, when I was a kid, father was always singing that song, but those words, "the only way is up", they were the only ones that he knew. That's how you should be thinking, instead of your low ebb, isn't that right?'

As if to prove her right, when Glasby was walking to the Tube station, just before the point where her signal went as the escalator took her underground, George Pincher called her.

'I might just have something for you, love. Where would you like to meet?'

The walk from Stockwell station to Glasby's flat normally took her between ten and fifteen minutes, and if it wasn't raining or too cold, it made for a healthy and reasonably enjoyable end to her day's labours.

On the other hand, being picked up by a chauffeur was a very acceptable alternative, made that little bit more pleasant by the jealous looks of the crowds of less fortunate commuters who were milling around the many bus stops which lined the street outside the Underground station.

'Your boys Georgie and Bill, they're dirty all right,' Pincher told her. She settled into the dark blue leather and dark brown wood interior of the Jaguar as it pulled off in the direction of her home. 'But even my milkman knew that, know what I mean?'

'Did you find out anything that I can use, though?' asked Glasby anxiously, any momentary enjoyment of her luxurious surroundings fading away quickly.

'Well, I have, and I haven't, as you might say,' was the not particularly helpful answer. It seemed that Mr Pincher intended to savour the experience of passing on information for a little while longer.

'What I need is real evidence, Mr Pincher.'

'Oh, you can call me George, Alison. We're all on the same side now, after all.'

He gave a hearty chuckle. Glasby did a not very good job of joining in. Pincher sat a little more upright.

'Here's how it is. Old Georgie Salmon and his mate Bill Shipp, they've got themselves this little place, a walk-up is what they call it. Two floors above a shop on Leytonstone High Road. It's near where David Beckham was raised, if I'm not mistaken, but it's not what my milkman would call a well-to-do sort of an area. I don't suppose that there's much in the way of running costs, mind you, just a bit of electricity and rent, a few adverts in some of the more downmarket publications that carry these things. You know what I mean, don't you?'

Glasby forced herself to stay quiet. This sounded promising, but there was going to have to be more, something really concrete that even Ellington would agree could be used against the two policemen.

'Now you asked me for documents, and I'm going to have to disappoint you there, I am.' Pincher shook his head theatrically in shame. 'Georgie and Bill, they're not mugs, so they've taken the liberty of putting their little enterprise into a lady's name. Not that she's exactly what you'd call a lady – more of a maid, as it goes. You know, she answers the phones, takes the money, front of house, that's what she is. Carole Hawkins, if the council tax records are to be believed, which they probably aren't.

'It's a perfect little set-up. In fact, there's just one ingredient missing: the girls. Now there's no shortage of such young ladies in London, if you know where to find them, but most of them have one thing in common: they expect to be paid. And like I said, I don't think that Georgie and Bill were aiming too much at the top end of the market, not in Leytonstone, so probably profit margins were a bit squeezed.'

He looked at Glasby, who by now was shifting impatiently from side to side on the richly upholstered seat. They had almost reached her flat. He handed her an envelope.

'There's the address. There's always two girls working there, seven days a week. They're from one of them eastern countries, the new ones. Not Poland – the Balkan sea, up north, that would be it.'

'The Baltics, you mean?' asked Glasby.

'I expect you're right,' said Pincher, agreeably. 'You usually seem to be, don't you? In the envelope you'll find the address, and mugshots of our friends Mr Shipp and Mr Salmon. Those boys turn up round there every now and again – collecting the money, I expect. Good luck, and look after yourself.'

As the Jaguar glided away into the evening rush-hour traffic, Glasby stood outside the street door of her flat, hand on her forehead. It wasn't even worth asking whether the *Herald* would publish more unsupported allegations against the two policemen. Somehow, she had to find a way of getting some real evidence. How on earth was she going to do it?

As the escalator brought Glasby up on to the concourse of Euston Station she saw the familiar figure of Redgrave, smiling down at her. They embraced.

'You did remember to bring your police ID card, John?' she asked.

He rolled his eyes. 'I'm having a good day today, you know. Not only have I got my warrant card, I've even remembered my trousers and my underpants too. Do you want to check?'

She laughed, but only for a moment. 'I'm sorry, John, I know that you're a professional. This is so important, though. It really could be a breakthrough.'

'Well, we'll find out soon enough, won't we? It took enough shouting down the phone to convince Mr Whiteside to see me. Let's hope that he hasn't forgotten and wandered off out somewhere. Didn't you say that he had a bicycle in his hallway?'

'He did, yes. I can't quite see him riding it all that much, though. He'd need a man with a red flag walking in front of him, to clear the way.'

'That's not what the man with the red flag was there for,' objected Redgrave, as they walked towards the apartment block that had been home to Michael Fisher. 'The first car drivers had to have them, so that they didn't go too fast, that's what they were for.'

'The way that certain sports car owners whiz around town, maybe it's time that they brought him back.' She nudged Redgrave with her elbow, but he chose not to understand that this was intended as a slur on his driving.

They were greeted at Mr Whiteside's front door by the inevitable sound of televised applause. Forewarned by Glasby, Redgrave thumped vigorously on the toughened glass panel until the applause ceased, followed some time later by a blurred form dressed in dark clothing which slowly became closer and more distinct. Glasby pointed out with a gesture the window overlooking the stairwell, through which Whiteside had spied on Fisher's comings and goings.

Mr Whiteside wasn't looking any younger than the last time that Glasby had seen him. He tilted an over-sized ear in Redgrave's direction, meaning that the top of his head was pointed straight at Glasby, close enough for her to count the occasional hairs that stood out from its polished surface.

'Is it you?' he bellowed at Redgrave, who looked as if he wasn't quite sure how to answer. 'You what was shouting at me down the phone?'

'That's right, Mr Whiteside. May we come in?'

Without answering and without addressing so much as a look or a word at Glasby, who he seemed not to recognize at all, the elderly man shuffled back to his chair. Redgrave sat in the other, leaving Glasby standing, having been consigned to the role of assistant – which, as she had to remind herself, was part of the game plan. She positioned herself at an angle to Mr Whiteside against a wall, next to a large framed print of an almond-eyed gypsy girl who was looking coquettishly up through her eyelashes at the viewer, while carelessly exhibiting one breast.

'Thanks for seeing me, Mr Whiteside,' shouted Redgrave, leaning towards him.

'Why?' the old man replied. 'What do you want now?'

Seeing that the pleasantries seemed to be over, Redgrave took from inside his jacket an A5-sized photograph over which he had placed a clear plastic case. 'Have you seen this man?' he asked Whiteside. 'He's a largely built man, very big indeed. Did you ever see him visiting Michael Fisher?'

'Fisher?' was the response, as if they might have been talking about someone other than his murdered next-door neighbour. 'He had plenty of visitors, he did, all them girls, foreign strumpets . . . 'Ere, let me see it.'

He grabbed the picture and held it with a surprisingly steady grasp, moving it towards and away from his face as if testing his focal length. Glasby held her breath.

'Oh yes, you're right 'n' all, he was a very big man. He stands about six foot four, maybe even more. He's built like a rugby player he is, and he's older than you. He had a nasty temper on him, you wouldn't want to get 'im wrong. He come round here several times, and I seen him once, kicking at Fisher's door and swearing away.'

Glasby turned to face the gypsy girl in case Mr Whiteside looked her way and saw her smile of triumph. They had him!

Redgrave was continuing. 'So you definitely saw this man visiting Michael Fisher's flat on at least four or five occasions, including the one not long before Fisher's death, when he didn't gain access and kicked at the door? And you put him at six foot four or more, and at least seventeen or eighteen stone. Thank you, Mr Whiteside, that's most helpful. My assistant or I will get back in contact.'

Back outside Glasby threw her arms around Redgrave and kissed him on the lips. 'Thank you so much, John! I love you!'

Startled, he smiled and kissed her back. 'That's OK. Just make sure that you find a way of getting that information to Mallam, remember? Aren't you even going to give me some stick for calling you my assistant?'

'No, that's fine. It was part of the plan, and it fitted our roles perfectly.' She grinned at him. 'Just don't ever even think of doing it again. That's all.'

Glasby's phone buzzed while they were walking back to the Underground to tell her that she had a message. She looked at it as Redgrave waited, then burst out laughing and showed it to him.

The text read 'Sorry I angry, u good girl I trust u'. It was followed by a video close-up of Mia miming a kiss through deep red lips, which she then blew along her fingers – the nails matched the lips, of course – and saying 'I love you' (or, more probably, 'I luv u').

Redgrave was impressed. 'Wow!' he said, eyes wide. 'How much do I have to pay to get one of them?'

Glasby thumped him on the arm. 'Don't start trying to make me jealous again!'

He was indignant. 'Jealous? Look, your little girlfriend is sex on a stick, but if I wanted a girl like that, do you think that I'd be with you?'

If that was supposed to mollify her it most certainly did not. One look was enough to tell him that.

'Ali, that came out all wrong, I'm sorry. You know that I think that you're beautiful. Inside and out. I'm just not interested in anyone else, I had most of the summer to work that one out. You're witty, and smart, and determined, and very attractive, you've got a great figure . . . Look, I'm getting embarrassed now. Can I just say that, if you ever want someone to ask you to marry you, just let me know and I will?'

Glasby could feel tears pricking at her eyelids. She turned away from Redgrave, not wanting him to see. A balding man who was rushing past while looking at his blackberry bumped straight into her and gave her a bad-tempered glare before continuing on his way.

Redgrave reached out a hand to steady her, and they kissed again.

'Alison!' Davenport cried theatrically. 'Just the person I wanted to see! This time, I think we've cracked it.' He started looking for something on his desk, which was covered in papers (not all of them the *Racing Post*) and dirty coffee mugs. It looked as if the cleaners had given up on his office as a lost cause.

Glasby didn't want to be sidetracked like this before she

had even begun. 'Bill . . .' she began, but was interrupted by a cry of victory from the other side of the table. Davenport shoved a piece of paper under her nose.

'Since you are the conscience of our little group, Alison, I wanted you to give this the once-over before it finds its way to Papa Ellington. Just think of it – young Daniels' life work, his fate in your hands.'

He gave her a cheery smile. Apparently Davenport was a bit more aware of the rivalry between Jack Daniels and herself than Glasby had realized.

'What do you want me to do, Bill?'

'Well, this is a mock-up of how the Senty story could work. You know what a fiasco it was last time round. It's a very different kettle of fish now, but you never know what an extra pair of eyes might see, especially someone as clear-headed as you.'

He looked at his watch. 'We've got half an hour, so can you get it back to me before then?'

Although she was gratified at the responsibility that had been given her, Glasby was equally determined to push her own agenda.

'No problem, Bill,' she said. 'But actually I was coming to see you about something completely different. I think I've made a breakthrough at last. And I wanted to ask for your advice. And help.'

Davenport looked at her. 'A breakthrough? Well, I'm glad to hear it. OK, it's a deal. I asked first, but once you've scratched my back and we've got Mr Mayback firmly on his way to immortality on the *Herald*'s front page, we'll sit down and I'll scratch yours, for as long as you want. Now, scoot!'

If Glasby had been able to find fault she would, but the Mayback story, if you liked that sort of thing, read well.

### SENTY'S FAMILY TROUBLES

Veteran television personality Senty Mayback, presenter of Channel 5 hit reality show 'Family Business', spoke today for the first time of his own family misfortunes. Ex-student son Ryan Mayback, 21, has been charged with involvement in a drugs smuggling ring.

'Ryan will always be my little boy,' said Senty, who

is reputed to be Britain's highest-earning TV entertainer. 'But he's a man now and he must take whatever is coming to him. He knows that he made a stupid mistake and he'll have to pay the price.'

Speaking exclusively to the *Herald* last night from his Berkshire mansion, seen on 'Family Business' each week as the location for the 'Powwow', Senty expressed his gratitude to the elderly Sri Lankan couple who were ultimately responsible for his son's arrest.

### Drugs Found at the Home

Retired doctor Sanath Gunarathna, 77, and his wife Amitha, 68, discovered a parcel of drugs addressed to a former occupant of their Leicester home. They alerted police, who swooped when Ryan Mayback arrived to collect the drugs.

'Some may be surprised but I feel nothing but gratitude to these people for what they did,' Senty commented. 'Not only are they public-spirited folk like myself, they could well have saved Ryan from getting himself involved in something much more serious.'

### Shared Family Values

Keen to express his thanks personally, Senty and his vivacious wife of eighteen months, Kelly, travelled secretly a few days ago to the home of Dr and Mrs Gunarathna, where they also met the couple's son, Dr Srinath Gunarathna, a consultant haematologist at nearby De Montfort University Hospital.

'We got on famously together,' said Senty. 'Shared family values, that's what we found. We had a right royal laugh, and I don't mind telling you that there were a few tears shed too.'

### Pain

'What Ryan did has caused Kelly and myself a lot of pain,' Senty admitted. 'It's not always been easy on him, having such a famous old dad. But when times are tough, families pull together, and that is what Ryan, Kelly and I will do.'

Ryan Mayback has been charged with possession of controlled substances with intent to supply, and is

currently free on police bail. It is not yet known if others
will also face criminal charges.

Accompanying the piece were several photographs of the two
families, Senty's famous beaming smile competing with his
young wife's rather obvious charms for the camera's attention. The old couple looked rather bewildered; their son, who
was a little on the portly side, was positioned next to Kelly
Mayback and seemed pretty enthusiastic about that fact.

Glasby did her best to find something wrong but wasn't
able to come up with much. 'Constance', she jotted down,
'contempt?' and 'It was the values that we share, family values,
that brought us together'. Then, after a moment's hesitation,
she wrote 'by-lines?', and headed back to find Davenport.

'So what have you got, Alison? Are we going to find
ourselves on the dreaded spike again?'

'It's certainly improved from before, Bill,' she offered carefully. 'I assume that you're happy with the overall style? And
I wanted to flag up whether it had been run past Jonathan
Constance, in case there was any question of us being criti-
cized for prejudicing Ryan's trial when it eventually happens?'

'After what happened last time, I haven't let young Daniels
brush his teeth in the morning without checking in with old
Rumpole first,' said Davenport cheerfully. 'No, Jonathan
chucked us a couple of "herewiths" and a "heretofore" just
to prove that he was earning his corn, but this time we have
Mr Constance on our side. Anything else?'

'Not much, no. I did a bit of a rework on one of the Senty
quotes.' She pushed a piece of paper across the table to
Davenport.

'Hmmm. "It was the values that we share, family values,
that brought us together." Yes, that works better. We just need
to take out "together" from the sentence before. Let Daniels
know, will you?'

'No problem,' said Glasby, who indeed would have paid a
fairly sizeable sum for the pleasure of telling Daniels that she
had been asked to correct some of his work. 'And, there was
one other thing . . . What by-lines will go on the piece, Bill?'

Davenport was amused. 'What do you have in mind,
Alison?' he asked, a twinkle in his eye.

She did her best to look casual, not very successfully. 'Well,

I was thinking, that several of us have been involved – at different points of the story, I mean. Hetal Singh, for example, and you. Oh, and me too.'

'And Daniels, as well,' he offered, after pretending to think it through for a few moments. 'I suppose that he's played a part in it, hasn't he?'

Glasby gave no reply to this.

'Well, here's what I was thinking. We can't all get a mention, so what will go to Ellington is "By Bill Davenport, with additional reporting from the Herald's entertainment team." I can't say fairer than that, can I?'

She restrained herself from punching the air. So much for 'Jackie D' then! But Glasby couldn't resist getting a final shot in at Daniels while she had the chance. 'At least we're not espousing an anti-immigrant pro-drug-smuggler line any more.'

Davenport grinned broadly. 'At least we're not doing that,' he echoed. 'Now, let's get this little baby safely to bed, and then you can come and tell your old uncle Bill whatever it was you wanted to see me about.'

Davenport had been thinking that once they had the Senty Mayback piece in the frame, he might just get home a little early. One look at Glasby's face was enough to disillusion him of that.

You couldn't fault the girl for hard work and commitment. There was a time when he'd have been right up there with her – leading the way, even. But advancing years had taught him – well, he liked to think of it as keeping things in proportion, the art of giving everything the weight that it deserved in your life, no less than that but no more either.

Davenport had been flattered when Ellington asked him back to help the *Herald* out. The money wasn't important, really. He'd never bothered about it as a younger man and he certainly wasn't going to start now. But doing up the cottage, charging round the countryside on his bike and keeping up multiple flirtations with ladies of a certain age – none of it was really enough to compensate for the daily demands of life in a busy newspaper office. The truth was, he'd jumped at the chance of a new challenge.

Three months on there was still no word of poor old Thomas

Lear returning or of Ellington doing anything about finding a replacement, and the pleasure of managing his little group was wearing thin on Davenport. He, who had never worked on features in his life, was fast running out of ideas. As for the kids, Hetal was a baby, Marshall was lazy, Daniels would be OK if it wasn't for his ego having to be kept under control, and Glasby – it was more obvious than ever that she didn't see herself as part of a team working on soft features.

And neither did Davenport fancy himself carrying on for much longer as Glasby's boss, not if he wanted to enjoy a long and healthy life. He was starting to understand some of the stresses that had driven Lear over the edge. But he had to admit that he hadn't supported the girl much lately. Seeing how vulnerable she'd been after Doherty's suicide had reminded him of that. Whatever it was she wanted now, he would do his best by her. He owed her that.

And here she was, barrelling into his room with a bounce in her step and a gleam in her eye.

## The real commandments

*I AM THE LORD YOUR GOD*
*YOU SHALL HAVE NO OTHER GODS BUT ME*
*YOU SHALL NOT WORSHIP FALSE IMAGES*
*YOU SHALL NOT TAKE THE LORD'S NAME IN*
*VAIN*
*REMEMBER THE SABBATH AND KEEP IT*
*HOLY*
*Honour your parents, don't kill, steal, lie, commit*
*adultery or covet anything*

*From the notebook of Michael Fisher*

# Nineteen

'Now then,' said Davenport, 'what's this breakthrough? Have you spoken to George Pincher yet? Has he got you anything that we can use on Fish and Chips?'

Mindful of the trouble that her story had caused her so far, Glasby didn't feel ready yet to brief him on the information that Pincher had given her about Salmon and Shipp's illegal activities. She still had only the ghost of an idea as to what she was going to do with it.

'It's the Michael Fisher murder, that's what I wanted to talk to you about,' she replied, avoiding answering his questions. 'I think it really is a breakthrough. The police just don't seem to be taking it seriously. Look.'

She passed him a print-out of a page from the South Oxfordshire District Council website, which was headed 'Your local representatives'. The first photograph was of a large man in his middle age, with the battered features of a rugby player under a full head of straw-coloured hair. There was a pen portrait to accompany the picture:

### Gary Dickson: Leader of the Council

Gary Dickson, 47, has lived in Burstone for practically all of his life, attending first King Edward VI school in the town and then Witney Technical College. He now has a successful farming supplies business which he runs from premises in Oxford Road.

First elected as a Councillor in 1996, he became Leader of the Conservative Group and of the District Council in 2004, having served as Chair to numerous different committees. Gary has now been chosen by his party as the prospective parliamentary candidate for Oxfordshire South West at the next general election.

Davenport smelled trouble. 'That's all very interesting, Alison. I suppose that this upstanding gent went to the same school as our friends Henry Dunne and Michael Fisher, deceased?'

Glasby nodded.

'And other than that, what does Mr Dickson have to do with the cost of chickens in Bulgaria?'

'Sorry? Bulgaria?'

'It's just an expression. Young Daniels taught it to me. He's a witty lad, once you get to know him.' He just couldn't resist – the look on Glasby's face was priceless. 'What I meant is, what relevance does Mr Dickson have to the untimely death of his former school-mate?'

'That's what I'm going to ask him. I'll tell you what I know. He was the games teacher's son, but I'm sure you worked that one out.'

Davenport inclined his head, not wanting to disabuse her. In truth, he had forgotten most of the details of Fisher's story, including the teacher's name.

'As you can see, Gary Dickson is making a career as a politician now. If his electorate heard what I have, about what he and his father were like when he was a teenager, I think his career might come to an early end.'

'Oh, come on, Alison. Even politicians were children once. Who cares what the boy did all those years ago?'

'Bill, listen. Dickson was described to me by more than one person as a racist thug. Henry Dunne called him a violent bully, in fact. His school nickname was "Sicko", for God's sake. Martin Danielson is a pretty impressive character, you know, and this guy brutalized him, so much so that Danielson changed his name after he left school, to try to start a completely new life under a different identity. Would you fancy a man like that as your MP?'

'Well, if you put it like that, I probably wouldn't. But then I've never voted Tory in my life anyway, so my views probably don't really count. And from what you've said about him, I can't see Martin Danielson going public with any of it. More to the point, what's it all got to do with who murdered Michael Fisher?'

At least Davenport seemed a bit more interested than he had been before, but there were times when Glasby had to be careful not to appear irritated. He didn't seem to be as quick on the uptake as when they had worked together before. Maybe age was catching up on him at last? He was close to seventy now, after all.

She spoke slowly and deliberately, as if to someone whose first language might not be English.

'Think of everything that we know about Fisher, Bill. He's sneaky, a blackmailer, the sort of man who is always out for the main chance. For years he had a nice little thing going with Richard Bedingfield. The widow told me that Bedingfield would have been paying Fisher just out of the goodness in his heart, but I don't really buy that. Probably I'll never be able to work out what it was – they're both dead now, after all – but somehow Fisher must have convinced him that he had something on him.'

She stopped to check that her audience was fully engaged and, satisfied, continued.

'Then Bedingfield dies. Fisher's got some supplemental income coming in, internet scamming and who knows what else, but it isn't enough to keep up the style of living that he likes. He casts around. He's too scared to approach Henry Dunne. He tries to find Danielson – David Gold, as Fisher knew him – but he can't get close; even after he's invested in a private detective, all it does is to alert George Pincher to Fisher's interest in his boss. But at the same time, Fisher has been keeping tabs on another of his old chums, Gary "Sicko" Dickson.'

Now Davenport got to his feet, looking younger and more energetic than before. 'I think I'm beginning to get your point,' he said. 'But isn't this an awful stretch? I mean, have the police even placed this Dickson at the scene? How do you know that they ever so much as saw each other?'

Glasby allowed herself a second or two just to soak up the moment, then rose to join him.

'The *police* have got nothing. *And* they messed up the forensics too. But I have. First, Fisher and Dickson were both at the Burstone School Old Boys' reunion. That took place just a few weeks after Bedingfield died, by the way, cutting off Fisher's most reliable income stream when he did. I've got the attendance list for the reunion here.'

She brandished the print-out which Mr Bushell had given

to her, on which she had highlighted the names that were of interest.

'And in the weeks between then and Fisher's death, I've got a witness who can identify Dickson as visiting Fisher at least five times. He's a memorable character, you know; he weighs eighteen stone, he's well over six foot tall and he has bright blond hair. So here's how I read it: Fisher had never been to one of the reunions before, but he turns up hoping that he would see Dickson, or maybe learn something about David Gold's whereabouts. He gets his hooks into him—'

'What do you think he had on Dickson?'

'That I don't know,' admitted Glasby. 'Maybe something on his politics, something that Fisher picked up from years ago and stored away. He was like that. Hey – you know what?'

Davenport couldn't stop himself from smiling. When the girl got going, she reminded him so much of a younger Bill Davenport, there were times when he felt like hugging her. Somehow, he didn't think that she would understand, though, if he did.

'The notebook!' Her eyes were positively flashing now.

'You mean Fisher's notebook? The one that he showed you?'

'Yes! It's the only thing that the police noted as missing from his flat. Whatever it was he had on Dickson, Fisher had written it down in his notebook. Or he told Dickson that he had, anyway. When I met Fisher he kept boasting about all the amazing things he had covered in it. Dickson had a nasty temper – my witness, the neighbour, saw him booting out at Fisher's front door and swearing. Fisher wound him up, pushed him too far; Dickson beat Fisher's head in, took his notebook and made his escape.'

Davenport held his palms up. 'OK, Alison, hold your horses, just for the moment. Let's say that this Gary Dickson is everything you think he is: a bully, a racist, a bad-tempered thug. And let's say that he knew Michael Fisher, and your witness can place him at Fisher's apartment. So what?'

'What do you mean, "so what"?' She didn't like the sound of this. Was Davenport going to back out again, after he had at last promised that he would help her?

'Come on, Alison, use your loaf. They were at school together, they met again at a reunion, they kept in touch for

a bit. There's not a word of what you said that makes Gary
Dickson a murderer. And even if he was, how on earth are
you thinking that you could prove it?'

If Jack Daniels had had the same expression on his face
that Glasby now had on hers, she would have called it 'unbear-
ably smug' – or worse.

'That's exactly where I'm hoping that you can help, Bill.
Like you promised me you would. Remember?'

'Oh, hello Henry, how are you?'

For a moment Dunne couldn't place the woman, which was
beginning to be a bad habit with him. She seemed a few years
older than Patsy, but with much the same look: blood red lips,
dirty blonde tousled hair, her skin worn and dry from too
much alcohol and, from the smell of her, nicotine.

'You remember Penny, don't you, dear?'

It was the first time for a while that Dunne had been grateful
for his wife's assistance, and the first time that she had called
him 'dear' for as long as he could remember. Apparently they
were still capable of functioning as a couple, in public at
least.

Anyway, he'd worked it out now, not just who she was but
what she had been doing in his house as well. It was Penny
Logan, come to do a bit of Inspector Jack's legwork for him.
With Patsy, of course, who'd been on exactly the same mission
for him – whether he wanted it or not.

Penny flashed a smile at him. 'Well, I was just going anyway.
Thanks so much for that lovely cake, Patsy. And next time
you must come to me, after tennis one day. Bye Henry, darling.
Jack sends his best to you both.'

With that she closed the door, leaving a small cloud of
perfume behind her.

Dunne started to take his coat off, then caught a look in
his wife's eye. She looked different, more determined, as if
she had been lost for a while but had now worked out the
way forward.

'Henry, I want to talk. Come and sit down with me, please,
in the front room. The kids are both out.'

This didn't sound good. Feeling like he had just been selected
for the part of King Charles I on his way to get his head cut
off at the Banqueting House, Dunne followed his wife as he

had been bidden, noticing as he did the curious absence of alcohol on her breath.

Patsy waited until they were both seated with the coffee table between them before beginning. She was in the same chair that Glasby had once occupied.

'Things haven't been good between us for a long time, Henry, have they?' She was speaking quietly, a quietness that seemed to be born from confidence. It was the way that Dunne liked to think of his wife, the way that things used to be.

He smiled sadly at her, supposing that she was planning to leave him. 'No, Patsy, you're right. Things haven't been good. What should we do?'

'It's not a recent thing, either. It's been years, when you think about it, not months.'

This did surprise him. He hadn't been aware that she had been feeling like that for so long. 'Years?' he asked, indignantly. 'But . . .'

Her voice was even quieter now, but no less distinct. 'When did you last make love to me? *Really* make love? Henry?'

He hung his head, wounded and, for a reason that he couldn't understand, ashamed.

'Do you—' he began, but again she interrupted.

'I don't know yet. Chloe has only just started her AS year. I was planning for us to stay together until she finished her A levels. But – well, they're your kids too, you should know this. Chloe came to me yesterday – you weren't at home, of course – and she told me that if I wanted to separate from you, that I should do it. She said that she didn't want us to stay together for her sake.'

Again Dunne opened his mouth as if to say something, but she waved him away like a cat with an unruly kitten.

'Hear me out, Richard. Penny and I have sorted things out. Mattie will get an official police caution. He's due to go back to the station tomorrow, to have his bail renewed, and Jack is going to administer the caution to him then. That means that Mattie won't get a police record, and he can take up his place at medical school next week.'

Dunne stiffened. 'And what have you offered up to Penny in exchange? Have the two of you decided that I'll be dropping charges against Bill Shipp? I suppose that you know that's what Jack Logan asked me to do?'

'Henry, really, listen to yourself. What on earth has Bill Shipp got to do with Mattie? Or Jack Logan, if it comes to that? All that Jack wanted was for you to stroke him a bit, just to make him feel appreciated! Have you totally forgotten your manners? Hasn't anyone ever done you a favour before?'

Dunne made no reply to this. There wasn't really anything for him to say.

'And that's just it, really. You are so full of that precious job of yours, you've forgotten that the rest of the world doesn't always feel the same way. I wonder if you even remember we exist, some of the time.'

'Oh, come on, Patsy! If you just want another argument, I mean—'

'We've had quite enough arguments, you and I. More than enough to last the rest of our lives. Look, Henry, you've been a good husband, and a good dad as well. You've put bread on our table, and we're blessed with two beautiful children – I won't be able to call them children, will I, not for much longer? You're a decent man, you don't want to live like this and neither do I. Look at me, and what do you see? A stupid old drunken sot, a nag. We were never going to turn out like this, you and me, were we?'

Patsy's eyes were shining but there were no tears on her face. Looking at his wife, waiting to be told that he had lost her, Dunne felt that he had never loved her more.

'It's our twentieth anniversary next month, Henry. I've stopped drinking now. I'm going to spend our anniversary sober, with you or without you. I'm asking you to make a decision by then. It will be your family, or your job. That's all.'

It was beyond Glasby how Mia could walk up a flight of stairs in shoes like that, without so much as a wobble. 'Do you have to practice?' she asked, looking in awe at the platform-soled creations that the girl was balancing on so effortlessly.

'Of course *not*,' was the reply, followed by her trademark giggle. 'When they make me learn ballet, I must walk up stairs like that on only my toes. Up, down, up. If I do it wrong, the teacher she hit me. I hate her, really I hate her!'

'I'm not surprised,' replied Glasby. 'Well anyway, do come in. You look absolutely gorgeous.'

This was no more than the girl deserved, in a dark purple knee-length skirt and jacket, with eyes and nails to match.

'Thank you,' said Mia, with the air of someone who was used to receiving compliments so often that she could afford to treat them like the Queen receiving a bunch of flowers on a walkabout, taking them and then putting them to one side almost at the same time. 'I so happy to see you again. I really want show you my website, it almost ready now. It has your words on it!'

Glasby hadn't ever looked at that sort of a website before and she wasn't at all sure that she wanted to start now, but Mia seemed so excited about showing it off to her that she didn't feel that she could say no.

The home page read, in large pink letters, 'Alicia 4 U', which Glasby was rather sure was not her work. Under it was a picture of Mia (or Alicia, as she was now going to be known) wearing substantially less than she was now, giving the camera what was presumably intended as a seductive pout but which to Glasby's eye looked more like a young child on the verge of a tantrum.

Mia clicked on the nearest link, which was labelled 'About Me'. There were more photographs, this time featuring even fewer clothes. In one of them Glasby thought that she recognized the underwear which the girl had worn on the night that they had spent together at her flat, but she didn't want to ask.

The text next to the photographs was hers:

### Alluring Alicia

Alicia is a fragrant beauty who has wafted her way to our shores from far away Korea. She is in London to study but while she is here she also would love to make the acquaintance of truly distinguished gentlemen of quality.

Her sparkling conversation will excite you just as much as her tantalizing looks. The cares of your day will slip away, with just one glance from her mysterious brown eyes.

Alicia has the poise of a dancer, the looks of a movie star, charms that would have graced the most exotic of harems. Gentlemen, prepare yourselves for a beauty that once encountered, can never be forgotten!

'You can see more pictures as well, here.' Mia moved towards the mouse again, but Glasby, who felt as if she had seen enough already, walked firmly away.

'Do you think I look good?'

'You always look stunning, Mia,' Glasby replied, with feeling. 'And the site is fantastic. Are you pleased with it?'

'Yes.' She sounded uncharacteristically hesitant. 'Only, in "About Me", you did not say my age, and kilograms and height.'

'Well, I suppose that I didn't know them,' said Glasby, defensively. 'I'm sure that whoever is doing the website can add them in. Under my piece, or next to some of the photographs, maybe.'

'You are true, I tell webmaster he must do that. Your piece, the words they are all saying nice things about me?'

'Oh yes, definitely.' Glasby wasn't really convinced that any of Mia's potential customers would stop to read them, once they saw the photographs. 'And they're all true, you know. Well, except for the bit about Korea, and where I said that you're a student.'

'No, this is true,' said Mia, looking pleased with herself. 'I decided that soon I going to be old, and then I cannot do this work. I want to be clever girl, have good job like you. So I start study English. I work hard with English for one year, then I want go to university.'

'That's fantastic, Mia!' cried Glasby. 'What do you want to study at university?'

'I don't decide yet. In my country, I very good in mathematics. I win prize. Maybe I do business, maybe accountancy. I don't know.'

'Well, whatever you decide, I'm sure that you will succeed at it. And if I can help you, I will, of course.'

'Thank you,' said Mia, looking pleased. 'How is your policeman boyfriend?'

'He's fine, thank you.' The reference to Redgrave made Glasby feel a bit awkward. She hoped that it hadn't been too obvious how jealous she had been, the time when they had all met.

Apparently it had. 'It not necessary, you to worry about this man, Alison,' said the girl. 'I know you not happy when he meet me, but he not interested in me. John is man who cares only about you.'

Glasby's smile was broad, but still not enough to hide her blushes. 'Why do you say that, Mia?' she asked.

'Because I know,' was the straightforward reply. 'Many mens look at me, it is my job, I know how men look at girl when they want her. John, he was nice to me, but he look only for you. He really loves you.'

'Thank you, Mia.' It was one of the nicest compliments that Glasby had ever had.

'Don't you want to have another boyfriend yourself?' she asked.

'With this job? Is impossible to be escort and have boyfriend. I choose this work and I must put it first, before I can have relationship. After I study, I get other job, then I can have boyfriend.'

'Even then, it's not always easy,' reflected Glasby rather sadly. Then she brightened up again. 'Listen, Mia, I know that things didn't turn out as we hoped, with Michael Fisher's story. But if you're interested, there's something else. If you want to try it, I think that the *Herald* would pay you a lot of money. And this time, I'm almost certain that we can bring it off.'

Mia looked at her from the side of her face. 'Will be dangerous?' she asked. 'More mafia men?'

Glasby hesitated. 'Look, honestly I don't know. If we plan it properly I think it will be fine. I'll tell you one thing, though. If we can make it work, it's going to be big. For both of us.'

*GHOST STATIONS – disused Tube stations*
*City Road*
*Bull and Bush*
*South Kentish Town*
*King William Street*
*Trafalgar Square*
*Broadcasting House*
*Wood Lane*
*British Museum*
*Down Street – Churchill ran WWII from here*
*York Road*
*Brompton Road*
*Aldwych*
*St Mary's*
*Mark Lane*
*Tower of London*
*South Acton*
*Lord's*
*Swiss Cottage*
*Marlborough Road*
*Uxbridge Road*
*Grove Road*

*From the notebook of Michael Fisher*

# Twenty

There is no denying that Burstone, like many Cotswold towns, has much to offer to visitors.

The long main road, which sweeps downwards and over a picturesque old bridge to a tributary of the River Thames, is lined with buildings from the fifteenth, sixteenth and seventeenth century, almost all of them made from the characteristic golden-hued local stone. Burstone is not a large place and the surrounding countryside is in clear sight, sheep wandering across gentle folds of green, a quintessentially English view.

All of this was lost on Glasby, whose only concern was to find a parking space. Those few that had been left in operation, after successively stricter measures designed to discourage dependence on the motor car, were solidly in use, however. It was not until she reached almost the bottom of the hill that she found a sign to a gravel-lined car park tucked away at the end of a side street.

A sign there demanded that she pay and display, but Glasby had not thought to bring any coins with her. With typical urban arrogance she decided against walking back to get some change from one of the many shops that she had passed, reasoning that Burstone was rather unlikely to have effective enforcement measures in place.

With a last check that her shirt and jacket were straight Glasby left her car and walked back the way that she had come, up the main street, which like many others in the county was accurately if unimaginatively named Oxford Road. She glanced occasionally into shop windows as she passed them; almost all were selling antiques, ranging from the customary mahogany and rosewood Georgian and Victorian furniture to sports accessories and gardening tools. They all looked expensive to her.

A car pulled in front of her into a street on her left. As she waited for it to go by she noticed the name: 'School Road', and looking up she saw it. King Edward VI School Burstone was a collection of mostly very ancient buildings, with the exception of an unfortunate addition from the 1950s that fronted on to the road.

Although she didn't have time to waste, Glasby allowed herself a few moments to stand and stare at the establishment which, for better or worse, had trained the minds of a number of those in whose lives she had become entangled. A bell started to ring. At first she assumed that it was a recording but the rhythm was irregular and stuttering; she envisaged an aged servant, perhaps dressed in waistcoat and breeches, straining on a heavy rope. It was not an uplifting sound.

The shops started to thin out, to be replaced by offices and private houses, some on the street and some set back a little. Her heart beat a little faster, and not just because of the un-accustomed exercise she had just been putting it through. Number 168 was in view.

There was a small brass plaque mounted on the nearer of a pair of stone gateposts which read 'G. Dickson, Farming Supplies'. Through the posts lay a small cobbled courtyard, on the far side of which stood a magnificent Victorian house built from the same honey-coloured stone as the rest of the town. It was sheltered from the road by a high wall, along-side which were a variety of rhododendrons and other large shrubs.

The front door to the house was ahead of her up a large stone step on which stood a boot scraper; to the right, as Glasby had expected, was a sign marked 'Office', with an arrow that indicated a single-storey redbrick structure which had been built on to the side of the house at some point in the last thirty or forty years.

There were two desks visible through the glass panel in the doorway to the office building, but only one of them was occupied. A broad-chested man with blond hair and cheeks that looked reddened from the wind glanced up in her direc-tion and waved her inside. She pushed her way in through the door.

The chair in which Gary Dickson was sitting looked small. As he stood up to greet her she understood why. Even as he leaned forward across the desk, her head was below the level of his shoulders. His build was proportionate to his height.

Dickson was instantly recognizable from the photograph that she had seen on the District Council website, with his squashed-in nose, brilliant blue eyes framed by a pair of misshapen ears, and a jaw like a heavyweight boxer's. Glasby had no doubt at all that Mr Whiteside would be able to identify him if needs be, and quite possibly some of Michael Fisher's other former neighbours as well.

'Can I help you?' Dickson asked, politely. 'Is it the supplies business you were wanting? Or else my Council surgery is on a Tuesday morning, in the Congregation Hall.' His voice was incongruously quiet, with the trace of a West-Country accent, the warm vowels and rounded 'R's sounding pleasing to Glasby.

'It wasn't the local Council's business that I wanted to discuss with you, Mr Dickson,' she replied. 'My name is Alison Glasby. I'm a journalist, from the *Sunday Herald*.'

His eyes narrowed but he held her gaze. 'Alison Glasby,' he repeated slowly. 'I've seen your name, I think. You wrote some articles a while back, didn't you, about Henry Dunne's work? Is that what you're here for?'

Glasby decided to ignore the last question. 'That's right, that was me, Mr Dickson. Thank you for remembering my name. I hope that you enjoyed the articles?'

Dickson continued to look thoughtfully at her, and took his time again before responding. 'I see most of the Sunday newspapers, that's normal in my line of business, although I don't follow every story, I must admit. But I did find it was interesting, following Henry Dunne's investigations. I suppose that you know that he was a Burstone scholar?'

'That's right, yes. You and he were contemporaries at the school, weren't you? You knew each other there.' She thought that Dickson was starting to look more relaxed.

'Oh, that was a while ago. We're not getting any younger, any of us! Won't you sit down, anyway?'

Glasby lowered herself carefully into the seat opposite Dickson, being sure to sit as upright as possible. She refused his offer of tea or coffee.

'So did Henry Dunne mention my name to you?' he asked, looking rather more carefully at her again.

'You did come up in conversation when he and I last chatted, yes. Have you stayed in touch with him?'

'I can't say that I have, no.' The large man leaned back as much as his chair would allow him. 'Actually, he was at the reunion a little while back, in the spring – the Burstone Old Boys, I mean. I saw him there. But that's the first time that I can remember, probably since we were kids. Of course one sees his name in the press, as you know. I imagine that he does a fine job.'

'I'm sure you're right,' Glasby replied. 'And do you keep up with any of the other Burstone Old Boys?'

Dickson picked up a biro from the desk in front of him and turned it in his fingers. He looked at the pen as if with interest.

'I'm afraid I don't, no. My political duties, and the business, they don't leave me a lot of time for socializing, Miss, um . . . Miss Glasby. Although the chap that organizes the reunion, Bushell, he sends a newsletter around.'

He looked back up at Glasby. 'I can probably find you Bushell's contact details, if you're interested? Or was there something else?'

She smiled at him, hoping that she looked more confident than she felt.

'There was another Burstone boy who I came across recently, Mr Dickson. Another one from your year at the school. Michael Fisher. I met him, not long before he was murdered.'

*Got him!* You could tell by the way that Dickson looked away from her. He was twitching in his chair as if he'd just been electrocuted. The only problem was, neither of those things would show up on the recording. Glasby had to keep him talking now, if her plan was going to work.

Dickson managed to do a good job of composing himself. 'Michael Fisher . . . I remember him, of course, but I didn't know that he'd been murdered. What a shame!'

It was interesting, she thought, that it didn't occur to him to ask her what had happened. But that still wasn't nearly enough.

'I covered the story in the *Herald*, but as you say, you could easily have missed it. Did you see Mr Fisher at the reunion, too?'

The biro was back in his hand, looking not much bigger than a matchstick. It was taking up all of his attention again.

'I think that Fisher might have been there, yes. Why do you ask?'

Now he was looking at her again, a challenge flashing in his eyes. She forced herself to stay calm.

'But you haven't been in touch with him otherwise? As you said earlier?'

Dickson pushed his chair back and to one side; one of its legs banged into the bottom of the desk. 'I'm going to have to ask you to leave now,' he said, but made no move to rise.

She ignored him. 'The reason I asked, is that several witnesses saw you at Mr Fisher's flat, quite a few times, including immediately before his murder. You were seen there, Mr Dickson. And Fisher told people that he was meeting up with you. I expect he promised not to do that, but that was the problem with him, he was such a liar. He was beaten to death, really brutally beaten. But you already know that, don't you, Mr Dickson?'

His eyes were wide now, and all trace of his previously pleasant manner had disappeared. But he still remained firmly in his chair, leaning over to his right now, away from Glasby.

'I don't know what you mean,' he growled, 'and I don't know what game it is that you're playing. You'd better have a good explanation for all this.'

'Oh, I have an explanation,' she threw back at him. 'Fisher approached you at the reunion. He would have been after money. He did that, you know, he blackmailed people, and he cheated them, too. What did he do, offer to tell you who killed your dad? Was that it, or was it blackmail? Did he name his price and then keep raising it? Was he asking for more and more, and then more still? Some people might say that he deserved to die – was that what you thought?'

For a moment they both just looked at each other. Then Dickson threw his head forward, his face contorted with rage, his body braced against the arms of the chair as if to force himself to stay seated.

'That slimy little bastard! Oh yes, he said he knew which one of them killed my dad. All he needed was five thousand, just to get the evidence, so the police would have it. Then it was ten, and twenty, and then he started talking about polit-ics . . . He kept waving this bloody notebook at me. But when I looked at it, it was all full of rubbish!'

Glasby thought that she probably had enough, but she still wanted more. A clear confession would put the situation beyond doubt. All the Ellingtons in the world wouldn't be able to find fault with that!

'Politics,' she repeated, as if thinking aloud. 'Fisher threatened you with exposure, did he? What was it, racism from your schooldays, and bullying?' She caught a look in his eyes. 'Oh no, it was something worse, wasn't it? Maybe something a bit more recent. Did he find you on the membership list of some crackpot fascist group, perhaps?'

Dickson said nothing.

'So it was blackmail,' she told him. 'All those years of local politics, building your position up, always waiting for your chance, and there you were, at last, just about to get into Parliament. And there was Fisher, threatening to bring it all crashing down. You were a racist, weren't you, like your dad? It would have strangled your career at birth, wouldn't it? And Fisher knew it. Did he laugh at you? Was that what made you lose your temper?'

Still there was no response. 'Not that it matters, really, not now. Once they find that you're the prime suspect for a particularly violent murder, how long do you think it will take for your party to dump you?'

Dickson gave Glasby a strange half-smile and a knowing look. Then he leant over even further to his right and suddenly stood, looming over her. Clutched in his right hand was a shotgun. Glasby had never seen one close-up before, but there was no doubting what it was, two dark grey metal cylinders pointing at her chest.

Now Dickson was speaking softly again and politely, almost regretfully. 'It would be an accident, that's all. No one would know anything. Just an accident, they do happen in the country, you know.'

He shook his head as if in sorrow. Glasby tried to get to her feet, but her knees felt too weak to support her. She could feel waves of blood flowing gently around her skull, forwards and back again. It was strangely calming. Her eyes started to lose their focus as if she needed to sleep.

A voice came from just outside, amplified through a loud-hailer. 'Armed police! You are surrounded! Gary Dickson, throw down your weapon. Walk slowly outside, with your arms in the air. *Now!*'

There was an explosion. It was the loudest thing that Glasby had ever heard. Something hit her, square in the middle of her face.

The man stood in the doorway listening to footsteps coming towards him down a flight of stairs. There was no sign on the door but he had checked the number twice so he was sure that he was in the right place. He was hunched up inside a dark blue bomber jacket as if against the cold, although it was a pleasant enough afternoon.

The door was opened by a woman who could have been any age from late thirties to early fifties. She was wearing a dark-brown tracksuit and training shoes, greying hair tied back in a loose pony tail.

'I have come because of your advertisement,' he began, but the woman was already waving him inside.

'Come in, love,' she said over her shoulder to him as she climbed back up the steps. 'Follow me.'

She was waiting for him at the top of the stairs. 'I'm Carole, love,' she told him. 'Foreign, are you?'

Without waiting for an answer she showed him into a small room to her left. The curtains were drawn. Inside were two upright chairs and a low table on which some dog-eared magazines had been left, as if it was a particularly down-at-heel dentist's waiting room. A pornographic film was playing on an old-fashioned television which stood in one corner.

'Sit down, love,' the woman invited him. 'We've one girl free at the moment, she's so delightful.' She disappeared, pulling the door closed behind her.

The man did as he had been instructed, his face pale under the electric light in the room. A couple of minutes later there was a sound outside the door.

A girl pushed it open, dressed in a black negligee and a pair of plastic high-heeled shoes.

She smiled uncertainly at the man but said nothing. He made no move to get up. Two large bruises were turning yellow near the top of her left leg. She looked young, probably still a teenager, a little overweight but not unattractive. Her eyes were tired.

The young girl left and the grey-haired woman returned. 'All right, love?' she asked, mechanically. 'How long?'

The man handed over two twenty-pound notes and followed the girl up a second flight of stairs. Once the door was safely closed behind them he pulled a small piece of paper out from his jacket, on which a telephone number was written. He started to talk to her quietly, in Russian.

A few minutes later he left, zipping up the blue jacket as he walked back down the stairs. The woman watched him go from her vantage point across the landing. As he reached the doorway he could hear a phone ringing, and her greeting as she answered it: 'Hello, love.'

'Alison! Alison!'

Glasby blinked several times and tried to focus. Davenport was leaning over her, both of his hands on her shoulders. From what she could see of his face it looked as if he was shouting. She felt as if he was standing at the wrong end of a very long telescope. There was a buzzing in her ears that was much louder than his voice.

He had produced a white handkerchief and was dabbing at her face, somewhere between her eyes. When his hand moved away again the handkerchief was covered in red. She supposed that she must be bleeding.

He was saying something more, but Glasby wasn't sure what it was. She tried to move her head a little. The buzzing sound immediately got louder and her eyes went out of focus again, so she stayed still.

Gradually her vision started to clear. Davenport was nowhere in sight. There was something made from dull grey metal in front of her, two long and thin tubes which were joined together. It was splashed with red, the same sort of red as the blood on the handkerchief.

She stared at it for a few seconds. It was lying on a table or desk, just in front of her. There was more blood, all around it. Some of it was dripping off the desk towards her feet. A bit further back from her, something else was lying there, something much larger that seemed almost human in shape, something . . .

There were hands on her shoulders again. It was Davenport. This time she could hear him.

'The ambulance will be here any second,' he told her. 'I spotted it coming just down the road.'

She tried to smile at him to show that she was all right but her face seemed to be frozen in place.

'Alison, are you OK? Can you speak?' he asked.

She nodded very slowly. 'Did the recording work properly?' she asked.

'I've brought you your tea, dear,' said Lisbeth, taking Glasby by surprise as she appeared in the doorway. 'Oh, those cats, they're so spoilt. Shoo, away with you!'

Two furry black faces peered up at her from inside a nest which they had constructed in the duvet next to Glasby, but neither Lord Jim nor Lady Penelope seemed to have any intention of moving.

'I must have dropped off,' said Glasby, stretching her arms out in front of her. 'This is very kind of you, Lisbeth.'

'Oh, nonsense. Bill told me that you were quite the heroine of the day. And if we left it up to him, you'd both starve, wouldn't you? How's your head feeling now?'

She busied herself unpacking her picnic basket. Something started to smell very good. Glasby, who hadn't had much of an appetite, decided that she was hungry.

'Eat up, now,' Lisbeth told her, handing her a bowl of what looked like home-made chicken soup. 'You'll need plenty of this. I'm just going to change the water in those flowers.'

Glasby had managed to persuade the hospital in Oxford that there was no need for her to stay in for the night and Davenport had driven her back to London. He had flat-out refused to take her home, insisting that she would be better cared for at his house. So here she was, ensconced in his bedroom, waited on at every turn and with the two cats to keep her from getting lonely.

Not that she had been lacking for company. As well as Davenport's bevy of helpers, all of whom had eagerly declared themselves at her service, Redgrave had been in and out whenever he could get off from work, Mike Marshall had been deputed to deliver a splendid bouquet of flowers from the office, and even her parents were talking about coming down, once her father could free himself from a golf tournament at which he was officiating.

There had also been a rather more formal visit from Inspector Mallam. It was very clear that his relief at getting a positive result to such a perplexing case far outweighed any concern he might have felt at being upstaged by a mere amateur.

She felt a bit of a fraud now, having nothing much more than a very sore head, a perforated eardrum that was expected to heal itself given time, and a large sticking plaster covering most of her nose. From what anyone could tell, she had been hit by a hard piece of plastic ceiling tile which had been dislodged when Gary Dickson shot himself.

'I'll be off now,' shouted Lisbeth from downstairs. 'Bill said he would be home in a jiffy.'

He was. Scattering the cats with a more practised hand than Lisbeth's, he sat himself on the bed next to her.

'As your good friend Jack Daniels would say, "Read and enjoy".' Davenport had a twinkle in his eye. 'John Constance has given it the legal thumbs-up, Ellington loves it and – listen to this – even Mr Daniels said that he couldn't have done any better. How about that for praise?'

'Have they decided yet? Will it be on the front page?' she asked, preparing herself for disappointment.

'Where else?' he demanded. 'And . . . I don't suppose that you might have any other questions?'

'Well,' she began, 'I was just wondering, about a by-line . . .'

'Oh, I'm forgetting myself. You're sick and it's not fair to tease you. Here, read it – I think your name might just be on it somewhere.'

## Blackmail, Murder and Suicide
### A Sunday Herald *Crime Exclusive*
*By our Crime Reporter Alison Glasby*
*With additional reporting by our Special*
*Correspondent Bill Davenport*

It started with attempted blackmail, led to a brutal murder and ended with the suicide earlier this week of a Conservative Council leader and parliamentary candidate. An exclusive Oxfordshire public school was the connection between the blackmailer and the man who murdered him.

What follows below is the result of an exclusive investigation by the Herald's Crime Reporter and award-winning Special Correspondent.

Michael Fisher, 47, had lived alone for many years in his one-bedroom apartment in Amelia Street, in Camden, north London. His lifestyle was unorthodox. He was unmarried and jobless, but he enjoyed the company of glamorous escort girls and frequented so-called 'swingers' clubs and websites.

### Internet Fraudster

He seems to have found the funds to support these activities by engaging in an ingenious variety of fraud, deception and blackmail. Many of these activities were conducted online.

Fisher used a number of identities but invariably he adopted the persona of an attractive young woman from the former Soviet bloc who was in desperate need of cash. Vlada Romanova, Tania Kutuzova and Polina Gavrilova were some of the many names in which he set up email accounts, all with matching photographs and life histories.

Registering with dating or other social networking sites, 'Vlada' or 'Tania' would seek unwary Western men with whom they would engage in rapid long-distance love affairs, all the while preparing a hard-luck story for their unlucky victims. Once the object of their amours was foolish enough to oblige by sending money, Vlada or Tania would promptly disappear.

It is not clear whether Fisher had a female accomplice in these activities, but they seem to have netted him a reasonable income over the last few years.

### Blackmail

Michael Fisher was not content with these internet scams alone. He approached this newspaper and possibly others attempting to sell information (none of his stories could be substantiated and the Herald at no time paid him any money).

He also engaged in a darker form of criminality: blackmail. This is what led Fisher to Gary Dickson and ultimately to his death.

### Conservative Candidate

Gary Dickson, 48, of Burstone, Oxfordshire, had been selected in 2006 by the Conservative Party to fight the safe seat of Oxfordshire South-West at the next general election. He was a natural choice: a powerfully-built former rugby player for the county, a successful businessman and leader of the local Council. But Dickson had some secrets in his past which would bring all this crashing down.

The men had met more than three decades before as pupils of Burstone's exclusive King Edward VI school. Although they are not thought to have kept in touch, Fisher made a practice of following the careers of his former classmates and is thought to have engaged in blackmail attempts on others.

Fisher knew that as a younger man Gary Dickson had espoused openly racist and anti-Semitic views. He threatened Dickson with exposure and the end to his political ambitions, which would inevitably have resulted.

### Brutal

What followed was swift and brutal. Dickson visited Fisher at his flat late in the evening of — July. Some form of confrontation occurred, at the end of which Fisher was dead, brutally beaten around the head and body. No murder weapon was found. Given the scale of Fisher's criminal activities it was hard for the police to be sure of the murderer's motive or identity.

Gradually, however, the net closed in on Gary Dickson. Faced with the certainty of a life sentence he chose a quicker end. Around 3 p.m. on Wednesday, — October he shot himself with his own legally-held shotgun, in his office in picturesque Oxford Road, Burstone.

Not more than five hundred metres away stands King Edward VI school, where Michael Fisher and Gary Dickson met.

'Well?' asked Davenport, impatiently.

'It's not bad,' was the most that Glasby would say. 'I still think that we should have got some quotes in, from some of the neighbours, or Mia.'

'Funny you should say that. I've got Hetal round at Fisher's apartment block in Camden now. And even your mate Marshall has been busy, getting some character quotes on Dickson.

They'll give us space for another couple of hundred words or so, if we want them. Don't worry, we've got time.'

Glasby lay back and allowed herself a small moment of satisfaction.

'It worked, didn't it, Bill? The quality of the recording is amazing; you know I spent the whole time worrying about sitting up straight, to make sure that my clothes didn't rub against the microphone.'

'Our friend Mr Smith only deals in the best, you know. He was pretty anxious to get it back from me, actually. I think he was worried that an old pensioner like me might not be good for the money if we damaged it.'

'And when you shouted like that – "Armed Police!" – you were so quick, and convincing; even I believed it, for a moment. He would have shot me, if it wasn't for that. I could be dead. That *thing*, it would have blown my head off, instead of . . .' She tailed off.

Davenport looked down at Glasby a little anxiously, but she seemed calm enough.

'That would have been an awful waste, young lady. And I'd have been in the doghouse with a certain upstanding chap from Scotland Yard.'

They exchanged fond smiles, then Davenport looked more serious again.

'Of course two men *are* dead – neither of them particularly inspiring citizens, I know, but you have to feel for Dickson's wife, and they had a young child as well. And even Fisher must have had someone who cared about him, I suppose. If Richard Bedingfield hadn't have died on active service in Afghanistan, Fisher would still have had those payments rolling in and none of this might have happened at all.'

Glasby remembered something. 'Bill – talking of Fisher's friends . . . ?'

Davenport fished into the inside pocket of his tweed jacket, dislodging a tuft of fur from Lord Jim as he did so. 'I hadn't forgotten. Five thousand quid, for your young girlfriend Mia. Courtesy of our Mr Ellington. And by the way, he made it clear that the *Herald*'s chequebook will be opened wide if your girl can get hard information on Messrs Fish and Chips. This payment is just for the information on Fisher in your article. Mia can have the laptop back as well now if she wants it, by the way.'

'I have a feeling that she's planning to buy one of her own soon. I do hope she's OK, though. I was expecting to have heard from her by now.'

# British Patriot Magazine, October 1985

*Dear Sir,*

*I want to thank you for publishing the British Patriot magazine. The BBC and the other mainstream media are in the hands of foreigners and Zionists, pushing their race-mixing views on to the masses. We true English white patriots rely on you to tell the truth.*

*Too many people simply do not understand that our cities are being taken over by non-whites, criminals and foreigners with different religions to ours. The government pays for their huge families while the white man has to struggle to find a job to feed his loved ones. Even the most historic English cities like Oxford are being delivered into the hands of the non-white races.*

*All it will take for the battle to be lost is for the white man to continue in ignorance and apathy. Some of us are not afraid to stand up and fight for our rights. The blacks have shown us that whenever they are threatened they can fight – now it's our turn!*

*Yours, G. Dickson*

*From the notebook of Michael Fisher*

# Twenty-One

'How did you do it? Wasn't it dangerous?'

Now it was Mia who was perched at Glasby's bedside, competing for space with the two cats which had taken advantage of Davenport's absence to return to their favoured spot.

Mia quickly abandoned a half-hearted attempt to look modest.

'I am very clever girl,' she announced, lifting her head and looking around as if for acclamation.

'I send in one Russian man to this place, I tell him he must pretend that he is customer. He see Lithuanian girl there, she don't speak English, he tell her in Russian she must call me.'

'How did he persuade her to call you?'

Mia looked scornful. 'Oh, *he* not persuade her, he is only *man*. He tell her, call me, and she will have a lot money. This is what I teach him to say. So of course, she call me, when no one can listen to her.'

'And what did this girl say? When did you speak to her?' Glasby pulled herself upright.

'I see her this morning. I buy her cup of coffee. And we talk. We talk on many things.' She giggled.

'So this girl, she wasn't a prisoner, then? If she was able to meet up with you, I mean.'

Mia shook her head. 'No, she not prisoner. She just simple village girl. Man brings her here, Albanian man, she thinks he is boyfriend, at first he say her that he loves her, then he tells her that she must start to work for him. She don't speak English, he says that if she tell anyone, she will go to prison here long time, no see her family ever again. He gives her little money, for send to her country.'

'And the photos that I gave you. Did she recognize the men in the photographs, the two policemen?'

Glasby held her breath.

'This two men, they visit place where girls worked, two, three times in week. They take money. One time, one of these mans he hit her, say she must work better. She remember them, no problem.'

'That's fantastic, Mia! Thank God for that. And this girl, she'll confirm what she told you to me, will she? Did you explain that we'll need her to put everything in writing, to make it legal? Do you know what her name is?'

'You don't have to worry, Alison. You and me, we are professionals! I take care of everything, exactly how you ask me. When this girl hear that newspaper will pay her too much money, she very happy to write all that she told me, everything. And her name? Her name it is Laima. She say me, that in her country it means "good luck".'

'Henry!' Assistant Commissioner Horgan stood up from his desk and advanced across this office, his arm outstretched. 'Congratulations are in order. I can't tell you how delighted I am for you!'

'Thank you, sir. There's still a bit of work to do before we go to the prosecution service, but Shipp and Salmon have both put in an immediate request for early retirement, so they clearly know which way the wind is blowing. We'll have them behind bars soon now.'

'And the Met will be all the better for it. Henry, I know that you've been in a tough spot, but you always had my personal support, and so you will. Now tell me, do you think that Longhammer has still got work to do?'

Dunne nodded. 'I do, Alec, yes. The boys are putting together a list of names now. For your eyes only this time, as we agreed.'

'That's grand, Henry. So you and I will meet next week. We'll work out what your next steps will be, and—'

'Alec,' Dunne interrupted, speaking quietly, 'there's something else that I need to tell you. I'm afraid that you'll have to find someone else to run Longhammer. I've got to put my family first now, not the job. I only hope that I haven't left it too late. It's something that, I realize now, I should have done a long time ago.'

\* \* \*

'So what do you think now, about who killed the games teacher?' asked Redgrave. He and Glasby were back in their usual positions on her sofa.

'Honestly, I don't think that we'll ever know. There were three boys. All of them somewhere nearby, Bedingfield, Gold and Dunne. They all disliked the man – possibly they even hated him – and with everybody panicking and the weather as bad as it was, any of them might have had the opportunity to push him over the edge. But I'm not convinced that Fisher saw enough really to know. And even if he was still alive, you couldn't trust a word that he said, and his so-called evidence didn't really amount to all that much. You know that they found the famous notebook, hidden in Gary Dickson's office?'

'Yes, I heard. But it was mostly full of rubbish, wasn't it?'

'I think that Fisher just jotted down anything he was interested in, and in his case that was pretty random. There were a couple of references to Dickson – and there were some things about me, too . . .'

'Well, he's not the only one who's interested in you. Try to remember that. Next time you feel like confronting an armed man who's already killed once, ask for some help from your local policeman first. Promise?'

Redgrave had to be content with a kiss for an answer.

'I suppose that your job on the newspaper is safe now?' he asked Glasby. 'Now that Salmon and Shipp have got other things on their minds, rather than bringing legal claims against you?'

'Yes, Mark Ellington called me himself to say so. The doctor says that I can start back at work tomorrow. My story is going to be on the front page, and Mark has absolutely promised me this time that I can focus on doing investigative work. It looks like my career's back on track again after all. Isn't that just the most awesome thing, John?'

Redgrave did his very best to look as delighted as she wanted him to be.


'I think that they'll be ready for us in a moment,' Glasby told Mia, who was looking quite the young businesswoman in a grey suit, her hair tied into a neat bun. 'Look, they're just in that meeting room there; Bill Davenport and Mark Ellington, the *Herald*'s editor.'

Mia glanced across the corridor, then peered in again through the window opposite. She jumped back out of sight of Davenport's office.

'Alison,' she hissed, dramatically, 'I *know* that man.'

'Know him? Which man? What do you mean, Mia?'

'That man in there, old man, he was . . .' She tailed off. Glasby stared at her.

'What?'

'He . . . he was my customer!'

Glasby stared at her in surprise. 'Your *customer*? You mean . . . Which one? Which man do you mean?'

'I said, old man. I see him few times, maybe three, four.'

'Old man?' Glasby echoed. '*Bill*? I don't believe it! No!'

The women exchanged a look and then burst out laughing. Through the glass wall the two men turned their heads towards them. Glasby hastily tugged at Mia's sleeve and pulled her into the empty office next door.

A moment or two later Davenport walked in, smiling broadly at them.

'Alison, it's wonderful to see you here and looking so well again. Welcome back! And you must be Mia, here to collect your very well-earned fee from the *Herald*. It's a pleasure to meet you at last, an absolute pleasure!'

Glasby gave him a meaningful look. 'But Bill, I think that you and Mia have already made each other's acquaintance.'

Davenport looked at Mia, then at Glasby, then back again at Mia. He smiled uncertainly, as if expecting to be told what the joke was.

'I know that I'm not as young as I was, but I've always been good with faces. And I don't think I'd forget one as pretty as yours.'

Glasby persisted. 'Are you sure, Bill? I think that you know Mia very well indeed. Don't you?'

'Alison . . .' he began, at the same time as Mia burst out laughing.

'No, Alison, I did not mean Bill,' she told Glasby. 'I said, *old* man!'

'Ellington? Mark Ellington was your customer? But . . . but I'm sure that he's married!'

Now Davenport understood everything, although he wasn't sure whether to be indignant at Glasby's assumptions about his private life, or pleased that Mia thought him younger than Ellington, who was in fact some fifteen years his junior.

Meanwhile Glasby's face was changing rapidly from brightest pink to deepest red.

Davenport cleared his throat. 'You two young ladies deserve to celebrate, and I was going to suggest that we go into town for a glass or two of champagne. Under the circumstances, I think that we probably won't invite Mark. What do you think, Alison?'